HACKNEY LIBRAR

Please return this book to any
before the last date stamped. Fine
Avoid fees by renewing the book (subj

Uncommon Romance

Three Erotic Novellas

LONDON BOROUGH OF HACKNEY

9130000885164

What Reviewers Say About Jove Belle's Work

Edge of Darkness "wins points for its well-rounded and developed main character and its breezy, light writing style, making it a fun read...The plotline has its share of twists, turns and revelations...I look forward to reading more from Jove Belle."—*Our Chart*

"*Edge of Darkness* is a very well written book. It has sympathetic characters, an exciting story, hot sex, and a wonderful cliff-hanger ending. This is a book that makes the reader forget everything but turning the next page."—*Just About Write*

Indelible has "some pleasing plot twists and delicious sex scenes." —*Seattle Gay News*

"*Chaps* grips the reader in its first few pages and never lets go. ... There are heart-pounding scary scenes contrasted with plenty of quiet country roads, and enough action to keep the pages flying." —*Just About Write*

Visit us at www.boldstrokesbooks.com

By the Author

Edge of Darkness

Chaps

Split the Aces

Indelible

Love and Devotion

Uncommon Romance

UNCOMMON ROMANCE

THREE EROTIC NOVELLAS

LONDON BOROUGH OF HACKNEY LIBRARY SERVICES			
LOCAT		No. VOLS	
ACC No.			

by

Jove Belle

2014

UNCOMMON ROMANCE

© 2014 BY JOVE BELLE. ALL RIGHTS RESERVED.

ISBN 13: 978-1-62639-057-7

THIS TRADE PAPERBACK ORIGINAL IS PUBLISHED BY
BOLD STROKES BOOKS, INC.
P.O. BOX 249
VALLEY FALLS, NY 12185

FIRST EDITION: APRIL 2014

THIS IS A WORK OF FICTION. NAMES, CHARACTERS, PLACES, AND INCIDENTS ARE THE PRODUCT OF THE AUTHOR'S IMAGINATION OR ARE USED FICTITIOUSLY. ANY RESEMBLANCE TO ACTUAL PERSONS, LIVING OR DEAD, BUSINESS ESTABLISHMENTS, EVENTS, OR LOCALES IS ENTIRELY COINCIDENTAL.

THIS BOOK, OR PARTS THEREOF, MAY NOT BE REPRODUCED IN ANY FORM WITHOUT PERMISSION.

CREDITS
EDITOR: SHELLEY THRASHER
PRODUCTION DESIGN: SUSAN RAMUNDO
COVER DESIGN BY SHERI (GRAPHICARTIST2020@HOTMAIL.COM)

Acknowledgments

I have such a wonderful group of friends and family. They all help me find the inspiration and reason to write. Every new word is a creation belonging to many people. I'd especially be lost without the trusted advice and guidance provided by some of my fellow authors.

I'm thankful for Yvonne Heidt and her endless enthusiasm and cheerleading; for Ashley Bartlett for being painfully, sarcastically honest when something is absolutely broken; for Karis Walsh and her sincere, patient willingness to answer a never ending stream of questions; and for Larkin Rose for always encouraging me to write something just a little bit naughtier.

I'm thankful for my friend Andi Marquette who helped me find my way back to writing from a very unhappy time, for Gill McKnight who encouraged me and never let me forget that words are worth the breath of life, for Cate Culpepper who includes me in her tribe even though I can't get over my serious case of fan-girl squee whenever she's around, and for Cathy Rowlands who brings everyone into her sphere of love and kindness with open interest and encouragement.

I'm thankful for the solid guidance and patience from Radclyffe; for the warmth, humility, and generosity Georgia Beers has shown throughout my writing career; for the keen eye and wonderful working relationship I share with Shelley Thrasher; and for Lee Lynch for thinking she's just like the rest of us even though I know she's the coolest person around.

I'm thankful for the opportunity to write. That my words might be read by people all over the world is an awe-inspiring thought. It truly is a small planet. Thank you to everyone who ever downloaded an e-book, opened a fan fiction website, checked out a book from a library, borrowed a book from a friend, or bought a book at your local bookstore. I'm not sure that writers would stop being writers without an audience, but the validation sure is nice.

And, I'm thankful for my family. How lucky am I that my children understand that I really am working when I'm sitting at my computer? As for Tara, what else can I say? None of this would be possible without her love and support. I can't imagine a world without her. Thankfully, she's promised that I'll never have to find out.

Dedication

As always, this is dedicated to Tara. Without her, there would be no reason to write.

Contents

Raw Silk

Chapter One

The conference room was empty when June Phillips walked in. Her friend and colleague, Robert, entered as she settled into her chair. She selected a seat that was halfway down on the far side. It gave her a perfect view of others as they entered the room, without positioning her too close to either end. She wasn't sure where her boss would sit, so had no clear idea which end was the head of the table.

The last thing she wanted was to sit at his right hand as he worked through the presentation. She was thankful to have been included in the meeting but had no idea what it was actually about.

"What are you doing in here?" Robert asked the question with his usual eloquence.

"Simmons told me to come." June felt self conscious about the answer. Simmons was their boss's boss's boss. It was either a really good thing that he'd singled her out or a really bad thing. She had yet to decide which.

Robert nodded his appreciation. "Nice. Do you know what it's about?"

"No clue." She straightened her tablet and aligned it perfectly with her pen.

"We have a new client. Or a potential new client. This is a wooing meeting."

That didn't explain why June was there. She made a non-committal noise but didn't comment further. Robert sat across from her and two spaces to the left. Did he know which end would be the head of the table?

A woman June had never seen before walked past the conference room. Her custom tailored suit hugged her body and showed off her form. Rather than a skirt, she wore pants that draped dramatically over her heels. Her auburn hair was pulled back into a tight bun. She caught June's gaze and held it as she crossed the doorway.

"Damn, she's hot. Do you know her?" Robert watched the woman until she left their field of vision, no doubt staring at her perfect ass as she walked. June had no room to judge him since she did the exact same thing.

"No." June mentally refocused herself. The last thing she needed was to be distracted by thoughts of chasing tail when she needed to focus on the meeting about to take place. The invitation from Simmons could prove to be career changing. "But I'd like to."

She wouldn't say something so blatantly lustful in front of anyone else, but she'd gone to school with Robert. He'd proved more than once that he had her back.

"Don't let your wife hear you say something like that. She'll kick your ass."

June's wife, Ashlyn, was terribly jealous, but equally adventurous sexually. They'd participated in threesomes more than once and been just fine. It would only turn into a problem if June flat-out cheated on her. "Ash wouldn't care as long as I shared."

Of course Simmons chose that exact moment to enter the conference room from the side door. The woman they'd been staring at entered with him.

"Shared what?" Simmons asked.

June stumbled over herself trying to answer. That Simmons had asked her anything at all was flustering. The man issued orders. He did not initiate conversations. For him to do so now was doubly disconcerting.

"Ummm…"

"She was just saying how her wife appreciates it when June brings home that fabulous chocolate cake from the deli in the lobby." Robert came up with the impromptu story smoothly enough to make

June wonder how often he covered for other people's awkward social faux pas. She made a note on her tablet to pick him up a piece of the chocolate cake he referenced. It was heavenly, and he definitely deserved the treat for bailing her ass out.

The woman arched her brow and regarded June with a sultry smile that was better suited for the bedroom than a conference room. "Chocolate cake, hmm? That's what you share with your wife?"

"Right." June's face flushed red hot. "She loves chocolate cake. She can't get enough of it." June babbled like an idiot and internally chastised herself. Ash would kill her for making her sound like a four-hundred-pound, cake-snarfing troll. She couldn't even remember the last time she'd seen her eat dessert of any kind.

"Of course." The woman's smile deepened, but she still didn't look amused. Any time June had been on the receiving end of a smile like that while out in a club, the night always ended in orgasms.

"Well, you'll have to take a piece home to her tonight then. Hopefully they have one left by the time we finish up here." Simmons smiled and straightened his tie. "And now that the pressing matter of dessert has been addressed, let me make introductions. This is Katerina VanderVort. Katerina, meet Robert Bladen and June Phillips, two of our most promising junior associates."

At the conclusion of his introduction, he selected the end of the table closest to Robert, gesturing at the open seat to his left for Katerina. She smiled and circled the table, ignoring the seat he indicated in favor of the one next to June.

"It's very nice to meet you, June." Katerina rolled June's name around in her mouth in a way that made it sound far too sexy for the situation.

June sucked in a breath and tried not to pass out. She'd been married for a couple of years, and the ring kept most would-be suitors at bay. She'd forgotten what it felt like to be on the receiving end of such blatant flirting. When she trusted herself to speak, she said, "It's nice to meet you, too, Katerina." Instead of sexy and in control like Katerina, she sounded flustered and out of breath.

"Please, call me Kat."

The others shuffled through the door before June could do much more than swallow and nod. She opened her tablet to a fresh sheet of paper and tried to pay attention to the presentation. Kat's perfume, a light, breezy fragrance that reminded June of summertime, made it very difficult for her to concentrate.

At one point, Kat shifted in her seat until her foot bumped up against June's and their legs were touching. June held perfectly still and waited for Kat to move again. She didn't. June spent the rest of the meeting inhaling summertime and trying to ignore the current flowing through her body that originated from the press of Kat's leg against hers.

After the meeting concluded, June sat there for several moments after everyone else, including Kat, had stood. She collected her tablet, suspiciously blank for such a long meeting, and tried to exit without drawing attention to herself. Robert had several pages of scrawled notes on his, she noticed.

"June, please wait." Simmons called her over. He stood with a small group of executives. And Kat.

She turned her tablet toward her body and hoped no one noticed the empty pages. Kat repositioned herself in the group until she stood next to June. She smiled like she knew something. Everything about the woman was just unnerving.

"Yes, sir?" June tried to ignore the brush of Kat's arm against hers.

"Good news, June." Simmons clapped his hand on her shoulder. "Kat was impressed but would like to schedule a follow-up meeting to discuss further options. She'd like you to join us. I'll have my assistant loop you in on the details."

June squeaked and turned red. It was not the response Simmons was hoping for, she was sure, considering he had just publicly announced a massive professional coup. She could practically hear Robert turning green from across the room.

"That sounds fabulous, sir. Looking forward to it." She shifted her smile from Simmons to Kat, determined to not show how flustered she was. Kat smiled back at her in a way that confirmed she knew exactly how she was impacting June.

June smiled and nodded and shook hands, but the entire time she questioned the integrity of the situation. Yes, she'd worked hard and by all rights was ready for and deserved a promotion, but on the other hand, she'd done nothing special in this particular case. In fact, she'd done less than nothing. She hadn't even paid attention. It felt unfair. Thank God they'd handed out a prospectus at the beginning of the meeting. She could review it and be prepared for the next time.

"It was very nice meeting you, June." Kat held her hand a few seconds too long, and June let her. She was married, at work, and incredibly turned on nonetheless. "I look forward to our next meeting."

"Thank you. I promise I won't let you down." At that, June made her escape. She wasn't sure if it was a breach in etiquette for her to leave without seeing the client out, but she desperately needed to take a moment and collect herself.

She'd just cleared the conference room door when Kat called out, "June, wait." She caught up to June and placed her hand on her forearm. She held it there as she spoke. "Why don't you see me out? I don't want to take any more of Mr. Simmons's time."

June nodded slowly. There was no gracious way to decline. "Let me just collect my things."

While she collected her files and other belongings, Kat scanned her office. She picked up a picture of June and Ash embracing on the bow of her father-in-law's boat. Ash's hair was sun bleached and blew out slightly in the wind. She had her arms around June and a beautiful, carefree smile on her face. Her focus was on June, not the camera. It was one of June's favorite photos of the two of them.

"Is this your wife?"

"Yes." June took the picture from Kat and smiled as she placed it back on the shelf. "This is from last summer."

"She's very beautiful." Kat looked at her intensely.

"Yes, I'm very lucky." June had said those exact words more times than she could count. She genuinely had no idea how she'd managed to convince Ash to love her, let alone agree to spend the rest of their lives together. It was an absolute mystery to her and she readily admitted it.

She felt guilty looking at the picture of her wife with the tingle of Kat's attention still travelling through her body. She took a careful step back and repeated herself. "Very lucky."

Kat nodded but said nothing further about Ash's beauty or June's luck. June collected her things and led Kat out of the building.

As they passed the deli she laughed and asked, "Didn't you want to stop for cake?"

June's face flushed with heat. "No, not tonight."

"Perhaps another time then." Kat stared into her eyes like she was offering more than just dessert. June thought fleetingly about what would happen if she invited Kat home with her, then let the thought drift away. Kat lowered her gaze and the mood was broken.

June said good night and left Kat on the sidewalk. It was time to go home to her wife.

Chapter Two

Ash had dinner waiting by the time June made it home. Traffic was worse than usual, and the delay reflected in June's mood. She wished, not for the first time, that she had some discernable talent that would allow her to work from home like Ashlyn did. She didn't suppose, however, that their monthly expenses could take the hit of two erratic-artist paychecks.

She dropped her files on the coffee table, slipped out of her shoes, and joined Ash in the kitchen.

"Looks great." She kissed Ash on the cheek and snagged a piece of cubed chicken that was destined for the salad Ash had prepared. "You want a glass of wine?"

"Wait." Ash grabbed the waistband of her skirt and pulled her back. She looped her arms around June's neck and pressed her lips to June's leisurely, taking time to explore as though it'd been years since they had spent time together. In reality, it'd been that morning. In the shower. And Ash hadn't stopped at June's mouth. "I missed you."

"Mmm." June hummed against Ash's lips. She never got tired of kissing this woman. They fit together perfectly. "Missed you, too."

Ash spun out of June's embrace, her paint-speckled smock flaring out at the bottom with the movement. It appeared that she'd removed her pants, as she often did, when she left her studio.

June slapped her lightly on her ass. "Did you lose something?"

Ash laughed and flipped the tail end of her shirt up, showing June her bare bottom. June wondered if she'd spent all day without underwear. It wasn't an uncommon event, but it wasn't something June could dwell on either. If she did, she'd never leave for work in the morning.

"I hung them on the line," Ash said.

June glanced out the window. As expected, Ash's denim overalls were draped over the clothesline in the backyard. She didn't know anyone else their age that had a clothesline, but none of them had a wife like Ash either. She immersed herself in her work until her clothes were covered in the evidence. On her way in from her backyard studio, more often than not, she stripped them off and sprayed them with the hose to remove the bulk of whatever she'd gotten into that day. Today it looked like rust-colored paint. Or blood. June could never be sure.

"Productive day?"

"Mmm-hmm. I'm going back out after dinner."

June molded herself to Ash's backside and glided her hands up her bare thighs to rest on Ash's waist. She nuzzled the collar of her smock to the side and kissed her neck lightly. "Are you sure?"

Ash dropped her head to the side, opening the line of her neck to June. She obliged Ash by kissing it again and again until Ash's body went limp and languid against her.

Ash moaned. "I really should."

"Okay." June didn't stop kissing Ash. She tried to never come between Ash and her creations. She'd chosen to share her life with an artist, and that meant she had to make certain concessions, like accepting that Ash would disappear into her studio for days at a time. During those times, June was lucky if she came into their bedroom to sleep. That Ash had stopped working to fix dinner was a surprise, now that June knew she was mid-creative burst. "What are you working on?"

"I'll show you when it's done." Ash stepped out of June's embrace and turned to give her one last kiss, then gathered their plates and carried them to the table.

June followed with two glasses of water. She'd have preferred a glass of wine, but Ash wouldn't drink while working, and June wouldn't drink alone. Besides, this way she'd be clear-headed when she reviewed her files later. "Do we need anything else?"

Ash looked over the table. "I think we're good." She'd made a simple dinner—green salad with chicken on top. She held out a chair for June to sit. She was oddly chivalrous about some things. She also routinely opened doors, wrote poems, and woke June with kisses. For her part, June bought flowers, made romantic playlists, and booked weekend getaways.

June tried the salad. Ash had added a light raspberry vinaigrette that gave it an odd tang. She let it settle on her tongue before washing it down with a sip of water. She decided, on the second bite, that she liked it. "Delicious. Thanks for cooking."

"My pleasure." Ash was halfway through her salad. "I was starving. Forgot to eat lunch today."

That happened sometimes. Only when it did, she usually forgot dinner, too. June would arrive home to find Ash still in her studio, having completely lost track of time. On those nights, June would fix a quick dinner and deliver it. Ash barely registered her presence. She'd leave the plate with a stern reminder for Ash to eat, which she fully expected to be ignored.

"I'm glad you remembered to eat tonight."

Ash smiled and looked at June the way she sometimes did, with her head tilted to the side and her eyes thoughtful. She paused with her fork in the air for a moment as she regarded June like she was just now really seeing her for the first time. It was unnerving to be under that much scrutiny at random intervals from the woman who knew her better than anyone else in the world. She'd asked Ash once what she saw during those times. She said she was just overwhelmed with how much she loved June and had to take a moment to be thankful.

"Okay?" June asked.

Ash lifted her fork slightly in an impromptu toast, then slipped it between her lips. When she finished chewing, she asked, "How was your day? Anything interesting happen?"

June thought out the meeting she'd attended and her new client, Katerina VanderVort. "Mostly routine." She kept her answer vague.

She didn't want to distract Ash when she was working. They'd have plenty of time to discuss Kat's actions and June's reactions, all of which surprised her a little.

"Mostly?" Ash's mouth curved into a teasing smile. She'd picked up on June's attempt at diplomacy and wasn't falling for it. "Tell me about the part that doesn't fall under the heading of 'mostly.'"

"I was invited to a meeting to woo a potential new client."

"Oh yeah?" Ash moved to the kitchen and refilled her salad. She spoke loud enough for her voice to carry to the dining room. "That's a big deal, right?"

"Yeah, it is." June wasn't nearly as excited about the opportunity as she should be.

Ash rejoined her, her plate full of salad and two slices of homemade buttered bread. She slid one slice onto June's plate. June hadn't noticed the bread earlier. Ash liked to bake when she had time. "So did he sign on the dotted line, or whatever it is you have people do?"

"*She* asked for another meeting." June debated the best way to reveal Kat's forward behavior. She'd definitely tell Ash eventually, but was this the best time?

"She? Nice. Girl power." Ash raised her fist in salute. "Are you going to the next meeting?"

"Yeah, she requested me," June said.

"You sound like that's not a good thing."

"No, it is. I'm just not crazy about how it happened."

Ash looked at her and took a big bite of bread. She'd do that sometimes, fill her mouth so June had to keep talking. She was tired of dragging the information out of June.

"The client hit on me. A lot."

Ash swallowed hastily, her eyes narrowed and heated. "Bastard. I'll kill him." Jealousy made Ashlyn forget details.

"Her. The client is a her, remember? Katerina VanderVort."

"That's right." The flash of anger was replaced by a curious, if not a little devious, smile. "Katerina?"

"Yeah, she told me to call her Kat." June pushed her salad around with her fork. She wasn't nearly as hungry as Ash, but she'd remain at the table for as long as Ash did.

"Kat?" Ash laughed lightly. "Is she hot?"

June nodded reluctantly. Ash was laughing now, but she didn't want to give her wife any cause for genuine jealousy, either. "She is. She's dark, like Mediterranean. She doesn't match her Scandinavian last name at all."

"Did you ask her why?"

"No, I was too busy trying to get her to stop touching me."

"Wait, she touched you?" The jealousy June feared threatened to surface again.

"Sort of. She sat really close, like close enough for our legs to touch."

Ash smiled again, then slid her chair closer to June. She stopped about a foot away. "Like this?"

June shook her head. "Closer."

Ash shifted again but stopped before they touched. "Like this?" Ash leaned in intimately close and spoke directly into June's ear. Her hot breath puffed against June's skin, and she almost forgot what Ash was asking.

"Closer." Her answer came out hushed and secretive.

Ash moved until her chair touched June's and their legs touched from floor to knee. She slipped her bare foot over the top of June's and caressed it. "Like this?" Ash whispered the question with her lips pressed to June's ear.

June nodded, but she couldn't force herself to speak. The words were trapped in an emotional bunch in her chest.

"And you liked it." Ash worked the buttons on her blouse open in the middle until she was able to reach her fingers in and touch skin. June jumped at the contact. Ash rolled the backs of her fingers over June's abs, tickling and teasing. "Didn't you?"

June gasped and found her voice once again. It was shaky and uncertain, but it worked. "I did."

Ash pulled her shirt free from her skirt and smoothed her palm flat against her stomach. She draped her other hand over the back of

June's chair and played her fingers through the ends of June's hair. She pushed the hair out of the way and bent her mouth to June's neck. Her kiss was hot and open mouthed, and she sucked hard on the skin where neck met shoulder. "Did she do this?"

She moaned and reflexively clutched Ash's head to hold her close. She held her body tense and perfectly still. "No."

Ash worked her way up until her mouth was once again upon June's ear. She sucked the lobe into her mouth and breathed hot air over the wet skin. Excitement rushed to the surface and June groaned.

"You wanted her to." Ash massaged her hand through June's hair. The touch was rhythmic and lulling and robbed her of her ability to focus on anything but Ash's fingers against her skin and in her hair. Ash nipped the sensitive skin behind her ear. "Didn't you?"

"Yes." June answered in a desperate gasp. Ash drew her faster and higher than anyone else ever could.

Ash slipped her hand out of June's shirt and rested it on her thigh. She glided up June's leg, slipping beneath her skirt and not stopping until she brushed against her panties.

June held her breath and waited. She was turned on and so wet, she was sure Ash could feel it through her underwear. She wasn't sure how Ash would react, but hoped it would excite Ash the way it was affecting her.

Ash rolled her knuckles over the fabric over and over, drawing all the moisture in her body to her cunt. Ash breathed, steady, even, and hot in her ear, but she didn't progress further.

God help her, Ash was going to make her beg.

June held out until the wanting overwhelmed her. She couldn't imagine being more turned on than in that moment. She gulped air and forced herself to form words. "Ash…" The name was all she could manage. Nothing else would come out, no matter how hard she tried.

"Yes?" Ashlyn continued to roll her fingers over her panties without urgency or apparent agenda. She was going to drive June mad.

"Please."

"Please?" Ash's voice washed over her, seductive and full of promise. "Please what? Touch you the way you imagined that other woman would? Push my fingers into you and fuck you like you fantasized she would? What's her name?"

There were too many questions and June didn't know what to answer first. She didn't want Ash to fuck her like anyone except herself. She was the only one who really knew June, who knew how to take her through orgasm every time. Still, Ash didn't do what June wanted. She didn't slip her fingers into June's panties to feel firsthand how very turned on she was. By the time Ash finished with her, this pair of panties would be completely wrecked.

"What's her name, June? Tell me again."

June wanted to thrust against Ash's fingers but knew from experience, could tell by the tight pull of Ash's other hand in her hair, that would be a very bad idea. She held still even though every instinct in her body told her to move, to rut against Ash until she came in a heaping, sobbing mess on her wife's hand.

"Kat, her name is Kat." Kat's face flashed before her, dark and dangerous and inviting. A new flood of arousal hit her core. "God, Ash, please."

"What did you want her to do to you?" Ash stared into her eyes, her focus intense and heated. Her pupils were blown wide, and June knew if she dared to reach between Ash's legs, she'd find her just as desperately wet as she was. But first she needed to remain still and let Ash have her way.

She couldn't think beyond the brush of Ash's fingers and the tug of her hand in her hair.

"June, tell me what you want her to do."

"You, I want you." June shook her head, and Ash's grip on her hair caught when she moved too far in either direction. It snapped almost hard enough to be painful, but then Ash released her hold and stroked her hair over and over again.

"Yes." Ash licked a line from her shoulder to her ear, then spoke in her ear, her voice low and dangerous. "But you want her, too. Tell me what you want her to do."

"Jesus." June wanted Ash inside of her so badly she no longer held back. "Please, yes, I wanted her to fuck me."

"Good girl." Ash pushed her panties to the slide and thrust her fingers into June hard and fast. "So wet."

June sobbed with relief when Ash finally entered her. "Yes."

It didn't take long, just a few sharp thrusts and the combined bite of Ash's teeth at her throat and hand in her hair, before the knot of tension inside June's cunt built to the brink of exploding. Her body tightened to the point of painfully rigid, then crashed apart.

The entire time, Ash alternated nips on her skin with sweet, hot whispers in her ear telling her how hot she looked, how badly she needed to feel June come.

June slumped against the chair, and Ash released her hair and pulled her hand free of June's folds. Ash held her while she recovered, sprinkling her face and neck with light kisses. "You're so beautiful. I could watch you do that all day."

June gathered herself. She knew Ash wanted to work, but now that her own desire was slaked, the need to take care of Ash grew to the point where she couldn't ignore her body's plea. "Yeah? How about I watch you this time instead?"

She wasn't sure Ash would agree. She knew Ash had her creative muse tugging at her brain, pulling her back to her workshop, but she really, *really* hoped she'd say yes.

Ashlyn hesitated for a moment and glanced over June's shoulder to the backyard. She wore a smile when she returned her focus to June. "I think I can manage that."

June led Ash down the hall to their bedroom, ready to make sure her wife didn't regret her choice.

CHAPTER THREE

June waited until the last possible minute to enter the meeting. She reasoned that she'd been first last time, leaving plenty of room for Kat to sit next to her. This way she could settle quietly in the corner, where she could listen in peace without worrying about her body's reaction to Kat's obvious interest.

She opened the conference room door at three fifty-eight. If she could have made herself wait the extra two minutes, she would have entered at four on the nose, but her work ethic was too firmly engrained for her to push that far.

As she hoped, the chairs surrounding the table were full, and a few people had already selected seating around the perimeter of the room. All the chairs, except one. Kat sat in the same location as last time, and the seat next to her, June's seat, was empty.

Kat smiled and beckoned her over. "June, I saved you a seat." Kat stretched her name out into a long seductive purr that was better suited for the bedroom.

June clutched her folder to her chest and forced her legs to work. To select another place at this point would create a scene and possibly get her fired.

"Thanks." She eased into the chair, careful not to brush against Kat. She slid the chair a few inches away from Kat, far enough to give her a little room to breathe, but not so far as to crowd the other person.

Kat matched her movement seamlessly, aligning her chair with June's. "I was afraid you weren't going to make it." She spoke quietly, just to June rather than the room. She touched June's arm lightly and leaned in slightly.

"Sorry, didn't mean to make you worry." June searched for a believable reason for her late appearance, but couldn't think with Kat's fingers lingering on her skin. She considered it a win that she didn't blurt out, "I was avoiding you."

The statement would have been only partially true anyway. Since their last meeting, June hadn't been able to clear her mind. Images of Kat, the smell of her perfume, the smoky seduction in her voice, all of it, haunted her throughout the day. Yes, it'd resulted in some amazingly dirty sex with Ash. God, the words that came out of Ash's mouth. She'd been absolutely filthy as she talked June through orgasm after orgasm featuring Kat as inspiration.

But there was a thick, solid line between fantasy and reality, and June knew better than to step over it. As fascinated as she was with the temptation, there was no way she would act upon it. Arriving late was her effort to avoid a divorce. Kat just happened to play a key role in that.

Without anything better to offer, June left the apology for arriving last hanging in the air with no further explanation.

"No matter. You're here now." Kat removed her hand and turned her attention toward the rest of the room. "We can begin whenever you're ready."

June sagged with relieve and regret at the loss of Kat's touch. She wasn't young and idealistic enough to believe that her body shouldn't react when she was attracted to another woman. She knew the biology of sex just didn't work that way. But that didn't erase the vows she'd shared with her wife. As much as she enjoyed Kat's attention, and oh how she enjoyed it, she valued her life with Ash more. She would do anything to protect that, including deny her own libido, despite the fact that it went into overdrive when Kat so much as smiled in her direction.

Midway through Simmons's opening remarks, Kat angled her body slightly and pressed her leg against June's. She kept her attention focused on Simmons, her face calm and interested.

During the last meeting, June had worn a skirt, but Kat had on slacks. While the touch of her leg had been distracting, it hadn't been catastrophic. Today, they were both wearing skirts. June cursed the warm weather as she felt an electric impulse surge up her leg where Kat's bare skin touched hers, ankle to knee. Her brain fizzled out and stopped working completely. So much for making a better showing at this meeting.

Thankfully, she wasn't asked to contribute. She was left to suffer through her own private version of torment, to be tempted by a fruit she could never actually taste. She wondered if that was the appeal for Kat, if she got off on the power dynamics of hitting on the one woman in the room who was clearly off limits.

God knew she wasn't the only lesbian in the room. There were at least two others, and one self-designated straight girl who had a reputation for experimenting. And, to top it off, they were all single. Still, Kat had singled her out, and as much as June wanted to be left alone, she also didn't want to share. Kat was intoxicatingly sexy and June luxuriated in her presence.

The meeting ended with celebrations. Kat agreed to sign the contract but asked for some time for her legal team to review the language contained in it. Simmons brought in two bottles of chilled champagne, and before she could protest, Kat placed a glass in her hands. She cupped her hands around June's to hold them in place on the glass.

Kat smiled and said, "I insist."

June thought of cheesy lines about Kat trying to get her drunk, but all she said was, "Thank you." She had to remind herself to drink slowly three different times. When Simmons finished his first glass, she took that as a sign she could down the remaining swallows left in hers.

"Another?" Kat's eyes crinkled with encouragement that didn't quite muster a full smile. She reached for the bottle, but June placed her hand over the top of her glass.

"No, I have to drive home."

Kat eased her hand out of the way and filled the glass anyway. "I'll give you a ride. I have a driver."

"I don't think my wife would like that very much."

"Ah yes, your wife. Ashlyn." Kat sipped her champagne. Her first glass was still mostly full.

June tried to recall if she'd mentioned Ash by name the last time she met with Kat. She didn't think so but couldn't remember for certain. She pushed the full glass of champagne away, the physical distance to keep her from drinking any more. She was a slight woman. Another glass would affect her judgment, and Kat was doing a pretty good job of that without adding any more alcohol.

"It's time for me to excuse myself." June stood. "My wife is expecting me at home." She was uncertain if she kept using the term "my wife" for Kat's benefit or her own.

"I'll walk out with you." Kat rose gracefully and tucked her hand into the crook of June's arm. "Lead the way."

Stunned by the sudden, blatant public contact, June stood immobile. She stared at Kat's hand on her arm but couldn't bring herself to speak.

Kat gave her arm a playful squeeze. "You okay?"

June blinked and shook her head. When she opened her eyes, Kat was still there, hanging from her arm like she belonged. Rather than cause a scene, she nodded and led Kat out of the room. As before, she stopped at her office before heading to her car. This time, however, she closed the door behind them. She didn't want to be overheard. Simmons would frown upon the things she needed to say to Katerina.

As soon as the door clicked shut, she pulled Kat's hand from her arm and dropped it. "What are you doing?"

Kat smiled, slow and sexy. She traced a finger along the inside edge of June's open V-neck, barely brushing the skin there. "What do you mean?"

June took a step back. Kat took a step forward. They continued like that until June's backside hit the edge of her desk and she could go no farther. Kat stepped into the opening between June's legs and placed her hands on June's hips. The combination of Kat's perfume, the champagne, and her hands upon her hips made June's head spin. She stared at the picture of her and Ash over Kat's shoulder.

"I can't do this." Her voice came out weak and uncertain. If she were Kat, she wouldn't have believed her.

Kat flexed her grip, her fingers digging in slightly at June's waist. "Do what?" She angled her head as she spoke until their mouths lined up perfectly for a kiss. June could feel Kat's breath puff against her lips.

June closed her eyes and counted. She had seconds to get herself out of a potentially divorce-inspiring situation, and she couldn't clear her head enough to think. Everything she did, everywhere she looked, appeared layered in clouds. The only thing she could focus on was the desire in Kat's eyes and the temptation of her full, red lips.

Kat shifted closer, bringing her mouth close enough for June to feel the exchange of static pulse that happens the moment before two opposite forces connect. She thought of the moment when Ash first kissed her. They'd been kids, still in college, and they'd stayed suspended in that perfect moment seemingly forever before Ash finally pressed close enough to touch. It was the one moment of absolute pure perfection in June's life.

June snapped her eyes open and gasped. Kat was *so* close, ready to snatch away the only thing June ever truly valued, her love for Ash and the sanctity of their vows. She spun to the side, freeing herself from Kat's embrace just as Kat moved in to complete the kiss.

Kat stumbled forward with a curse. She hit the desk and opened her eyes. The desire was gone, replaced with a flash of anger. "What the hell?"

June wrapped her arms around her middle and took a deep breath. She focused on the rise and fall of her chest and refused to acknowledge Kat. The picture of Ash was just out of her line of sight, and she was strangely relieved to not have to look at it right then. She took one last deep breath and straightened to her full height.

"I'm going to ask again, what are you doing?" The question came out level, almost stern, and June was proud of herself.

Kat adjusted her clothes and brushed her hands over her skirt. "I thought that was rather obvious."

"I'm married."

"Yes."

"That means something to me."

"Good. A couple shouldn't enter into a marriage unless it means a great deal to both parties." She stepped close to June again and lightly rubbed her hand over June's arm.

June stared at Kat's lips and lost her train of thought. She licked her own as said, "I love Ashlyn."

"Good." Kat's touch on her arm became bolder, and her hand moved up to her shoulder. She played with the strands of June's hair. "That's very good." The sentence came out as a distracted whisper as she moved closer. She attempted to kiss June a second time.

June pressed her palm flat against Kat's chest and pushed. She held her hand there, feeling the heavy pounding of Kat's heart, to keep her from closing in on her again. "You can't do that." It would have sounded more convincing if she'd been able to stop staring at Kat's lips and imagining how they would feel if she could just give in. One kiss. Such a small thing. Her hold on Kat slackened and Kat moved closer again.

"So beautiful." Kat swept her hair out of the way and caressed her throat with the backs of her fingers. The touch was soft and sent tingles through her body.

"No." June pushed her away again. It was a small thing that could ruin everything.

"I can feel the way your body reacts when I'm near. I'm not imagining this."

June let Kat's hand linger for half a beat too long, then stepped away from her completely. "What do you want me to say? Of course I feel it. You're a beautiful, sexy woman. I'd have to be dead not to recognize that. But it doesn't change anything. I love my wife."

Kat blew a snort out her nostrils. It was the first unattractive thing June had seen her do. "Why do you keep telling me that? You obviously aren't thinking of her when I touch you."

That was close enough to the truth to make June's face flush with embarrassment. "I love her. Nothing you say will change that."

"And nothing you say will change the fact that you want me. And I want you." Kat reached out for her again. This time she cupped her hand around June's cheek and brushed her thumb over the skin.

"Stop it." She jerked her head away.

"Would it make you feel better if she was here? Based on her picture, I have to say I'm not opposed to that."

The invitation for Kat to come home with her, to spend the night with both of them, hovered in June's mind. Everything Kat said was right. She wanted Kat very badly, just not at the expense of her relationship with Ashlyn. She wouldn't sacrifice her marriage for a fuck, not even an incredibly seductive, rich fuck.

As much as she wanted to indulge the fantasy, to believe that Ash would respond favorably if she brought Kat to their home, she knew that wasn't the case. They'd explored June's attraction for Kat to exhaustion. Ash enjoyed the role play. She would not, however, enjoy having her sanctuary invaded by a predator. She might welcome an encounter with Kat, but she would not welcome being left out of the decision-making part of the fun.

"Excuse me." June scooped her keys from the desk. "You'll understand if I leave you to find your own way out."

For the first time since she'd started, June went home without a stack of files to review. All she cared about was getting home to Ash and tilting her world back to center.

CHAPTER FOUR

June found Ash still in her workshop. She stood in front of a canvas that was at least two feet taller than Ash and even wider across. For the moment, she stood back evaluating her progress, seemingly unaware of June's presence. She held a broad paintbrush in her hand, one better suited to house painting than fine art. At her feet stood an open gallon container of bright-red acrylic paint.

"Hi, baby." Before they graduated from college, June would spend hours watching Ash. She missed that time in their lives and could have stayed there, leaning against the doorframe, just watching. Eventually, though, Ash would realize she was there, and if that happened before she said hello, it would startle her. June didn't want that.

"Hey there." Ash set the brush on top of the paint can and crossed the room to stand before June. "I missed you today."

"Yeah?" The front of Ash's overalls was covered in red and yellow paint. There was a little bit of blue toward the bottom of one leg, but that looked more like an out-of-control splash had caught Ash than her usual practice of using her pants as a towel.

"Yeah." Ash kissed June, careful to keep their bodies from touching. June's workday clothes wouldn't survive being pressure-washed with a hose and draped over the line to dry.

When Ash pulled back, June studied her. She had her hair pulled up in a hasty bun that was half undone. She doubted Ash had done more than comb her fingers through it before putting it up that morning. She had brushstrokes of paint on her face—one on her cheek and the other just above her eyebrow. The knees of her overalls were worn to thread, and skin showed through in places.

"We should get you a new pair of these." June fingered the strap of fabric over Ash's shoulder that held the overalls on her body. She wondered if Ash had remembered underwear that morning. More often than not, she didn't.

Ash looked down at herself, registering for the first time, June guessed, how beat-up her clothes were. She shrugged. "They'll last awhile longer."

June nodded. "They will." She popped the button on one side free and the overalls drooped from one shoulder. She smiled, kissed Ash carefully, then popped the button on the other side. The overalls fell to the ground and pooled around Ash's feet. "I still like you better without them."

"Oh?"

Avoiding the few stray blotches of paint on the front of her smock, June deliberately opened button after button. She stared into Ash's eyes the entire time, and by the time it fell open in the front, Ash's pupils were dilated so much she could see only the slightest outline of blue around the rim.

"Definitely." June laid her palm flat against Ash's abdomen, her muscles rigid and hard beneath June's fingers. The skin twitched and flexed, and June smiled.

She eased her hand down and urged Ash to spread her legs. She shuffled her feet as wide as they would go with the material around them. It was far enough for her to slip her fingers between Ash's lips and feel the moisture pooling at the opening of her cunt.

Normally June would take her time. She'd kiss Ash's body and suck her nipples until Ash threatened to fall apart just from that stimulation alone. She'd tease her clit and drop to her knees to taste Ash on her tongue. Not tonight. This time she needed to feel Ash from the inside, to get lost inside her and remember the way she felt wrapped up in her wife. She needed to feel Ash as she tightened around her. She needed to immerse herself in Ash as she cried out in orgasm.

Most of all, she needed to forget the way her body had reacted to Katerina's touch, to her almost-kiss earlier that afternoon inside June's office. She'd closed the door, locked it, with the intention of talking without interruption, and it'd taken every bit of her strength to walk away when all she'd wanted to do was fall into Kat. She wanted to see if the fire Kat brought to the surface with even the slightest touch ran deeper than surface level.

June sank her fingers knuckle-deep into Ash and held them there. Ash stared into her eyes and gripped her forearm tight enough for her fingers to indent June's skin.

She let Ash grow accustomed to the feel of her, pulsing her fingers occasionally just to watch Ash gasp silently and grip her arm a little tighter before relaxing her hold.

"Ready?" June pulled out even as she asked the question. She wanted to fuck Ash and she'd never been denied before. She didn't expect her to start now.

Ash sucked her bottom lip into her mouth and worried it between her teeth, then nodded slowly. June thrust in hard and fast, then did it again without pausing. She wasn't interested in the slow build, the careful buildup. She wanted to feel Ash come now. Right now.

Ash whimpered, a sweet, needy noise that said she wanted more, that she could take more. June added another finger and kept thrusting as hard and as fast as her body would allow. Ash's cunt grew sloppy and wet, and she felt the familiar tug as Ash flexed and released deep inside. She was very close.

"Touch yourself." June rarely asked Ash to participate in the creation of her own orgasm. She wanted the thrill of doing it all on her own. But the position was awkward, and it was taking longer than June liked. She'd wanted Ash's orgasm before she ever even touched her. That it'd only been a few minutes was irrelevant. She wanted it all now.

Ash kept her grip on June's forearm, adding pressure and urgency to her thrusts, but she moved her other hand from June's shoulder to her clit. She groaned at first contact, then set a fast pace to match June thrusting inside her.

"Yes, baby, let me see you come. Let me feel it."

Ash's eyes squeezed shut and her head arched back. Her whole body drew tight and then shook as she came. She held June's hand immobile, her fingers buried deep inside, until her body finally went slack and June slipped free.

"Not done yet." June dropped to her knees like she'd wanted, but hadn't been allowed, and separated Ash's folds until her clit stood exposed, hard, and glistening with arousal.

She licked carefully around the tip, and Ash slipped her hands into her hair, twisting her fingers until the hair pulled tight at June's scalp. Her body hadn't had enough time to recover. June knew this from years spent learning the planes and contours of her body. Still, she felt her growing tight again, the muscles in her legs becoming rigid and hard. June smiled, then flicked her tongue over Ash's clit.

Ash cried out and held June tight against her. Already she was close to the edge of release again. June brought Ash into her mouth and worked her with the flat of her tongue, circling and flicking and just enjoying the taste and feel of this woman, this perfect woman who loved her.

"God, June…" Ash tensed, then orgasmed hot and wet onto June's tongue. June kept licking as Ash slumped over her body and didn't stop until Ash pulled her head away. "No more, God, I can't take any more."

June sat back on her heels and wiped her mouth on the back of her hand. This wasn't their most eloquent or romantic encounter, but it'd given her exactly what she needed.

Ash tugged on her until she stood. She looked into Ash's eyes and smiled at the satisfaction reflected back at her. She kissed Ash then, slow and sweet. She let her tongue explore, slipping it into Ash's mouth and simply feeling her.

When the kiss ended naturally, Ash pulled her into a hug. "I guess you missed me, too."

Ash pulled her close and inhaled deeply until she forgot everything except the scent of her wife's body after orgasm, mixed with the chemical tang of acrylic paint. "You have no idea," she whispered into Ash's hair.

"Does this mean your meeting went well?"

June sighed and pulled back. They had to talk about the events of that afternoon, but she wasn't at all happy about it. "I have no idea."

"What do you mean?" Ash cupped June's cheek, her palm burning an impression over the one Kat had left earlier. "You did have the meeting, right?"

June buttoned up Ash's smock. The bare expanse of skin distracted her, and she was tempted to work a third orgasm from Ash. There would be time for that later.

"We had the meeting. I just couldn't focus."

Ash led her over to a wicker couch in the corner. It was left over from a patio set long ago discarded. It was piled with soft pillows and a patchwork quilt that Ash had made during a crafty phase. June wanted to keep it in the house, but Ash insisted it belonged in her studio. She wrapped up in it on the nights when she was too tired, and too overcome with a project, to make it inside. It kept the wicker weave from leaving indentations on Ash's bare skin because she slept naked more often than not.

"Did she sit next to you again?" Ash released June's hair from the tight bun and smoothed her hand over it. The motion was comforting and arousing at the same time.

June nodded, then leaned into Ash's touch.

"I thought you had a plan."

"I did. I entered the meeting last, thinking I could slip into a perimeter chair unnoticed. But she saved a seat for me."

"And you had to take it. You can't be blatantly rude to a client in the middle of a meeting." Ash's voice was soothing. She spoke softly, carefully, and released her words like caresses over June's skin. June never knew if Ash did it on purpose, if she knew how deeply it affected June when she adopted that tone, or if that was just her natural response when someone was distressed. Thank God she'd never seen her do it with anyone else. She'd have been arrested for assault after she punched the person out. This time with Ash wasn't something she was willing to share.

"Right."

"Did she touch you again?" Ash's voice took on an edge, but was still low and melodious.

"She pressed her leg against mine again, yes. This time she was wearing a skirt."

Ash's breath hitched, but she kept stroking June's hair. "Bare skin?"

June's eyes slipped shut and she nodded. The sense memory was too much to ignore.

"What else?" Ash rested one hand on June's thigh and teased the edge of her skirt.

"I couldn't focus again. I have no idea what was said, but she agreed to sign the contract, so my boss is happy. They served champagne."

Ash pushed the fabric up and urged June to lift her hips. She inched it up until it bunched around June's waist.

"Champagne?"

"Mmm...It was good stuff, too. I should have paid attention to the brand. You would like it."

"You were a little distracted." Ash moved her hand restlessly over June's thighs, marking a random pattern with her fingers that occasionally dipped between her legs and pressed against the juncture of her thighs. She kissed June's throat, her lips delicate and hot against her skin. "How many glasses did you have?"

"Just one." June eased her legs apart slightly. She knew Ash would let her know when she wanted greater access, but she'd been so frustrated, for so long, she couldn't help but offer encouragement. "She poured me a second, but I didn't drink it."

"Why not?"

"I wanted to be able to drive, to come home to you."

"And two glasses would have prevented that?"

"Two glasses would have led to three and three would have led to four."

Ash pressed her lips close to June's but didn't kiss her. "And four would have led to?"

Ash slipped her fingers beneath the fabric of June's panties but didn't move. June moaned. "She offered to give me a ride home. She has a driver."

"So four glasses would have landed you in her backseat." Ash massaged a slow circle over June's clit one time, then stopped again.

"Yes." June barely kept herself from begging.

"Why didn't you?"

"You wouldn't have liked it."

Ash pulled her hand free and brought her fingers to June's lips. She pushed them into June's mouth and said, "I wouldn't? Why not?"

June licked and sucked Ash's fingers but couldn't track the conversation properly. Ash sounded disappointed that she hadn't brought Kat home with her that night. "You want me to bring her here? To our house?"

"Don't you want to?" Ash replaced her fingers with her tongue. She kissed June deeply, deep enough, June thought, to find the answer to her question.

They were off track. There was more she needed to tell Ash, and instead they were getting lost in the fantasy. She wrenched her mouth away. "She tried to kiss me."

Ash's hand stilled, the tips of her fingers barely inside the lace of her panties. "What?"

June looked into Ash's eyes. "She tried to kiss me."

"Tried? As in didn't succeed?"

"Right. I didn't let her."

"Good." Ash started moving again. Her fingers brushed against June's clit and slipped lower until they rested at the opening of her pussy. They glided easily through the moisture gathered there. "Did you want her to? Kiss you." She rolled her knuckles through June's desire, then over her clit.

June bucked against her. "God, yes."

"Yes, you wanted to kiss her?"

June gulped and nodded. "Yes."

Ash slipped her fingers inside June and curved them until she touched June's G-spot. "Is that what made you this wet?"

June shook her head and said, "No...yes...I don't know." She bucked her hips against Ash's hand.

Ash withdrew. "You don't know? You don't know if you want her? If she turns you on?"

"She does, yes."

Ash slipped back inside and pushed until she bottomed out. "Good girl."

June groaned. "But not as much as you do."

"No?" Ash slipped out again and teased the tip of her finger over June's clit. "Are you sure? You're really wet."

June held perfectly still and whimpered as Ash fingered her clit until she was hard and balancing on the edge of orgasm.

When Ash pressed her lips to her ear and whispered, "Next time bring her home with you," June came with a shout. Her body drew tight and flew apart as Ash's words traveled from her brain to her cunt with a visceral jolt.

"God." She curled up in Ash's arms. "The things you do to me."

"I'm serious, June." Ash pulled back until June was able to look into her eyes. "Bring her home."

"Are you sure?" They'd played in the past, but never quite like this. June stared hard into Ash's eyes for some sign that this wasn't what she really wanted. She found nothing but open, honest desire.

"Oh yeah, I'm sure."

June curled back up in Ash's embrace again. She nodded against her chest as she listened to her heart beat. Relief and excitement flooded her system. Thank God she wouldn't have to fight her body when Kat was around anymore.

CHAPTER FIVE

June stared at the coffee machine and willed it to brew faster. Yes, the single-cup machine was brilliantly quick and produced a fabulous-tasting cup of coffee, but it wasn't instantaneous. Ash had kept her up far too late last night, but her boss didn't care about how late she was up the night before, only that she made it to work on time and prepared to function. For that she needed coffee. Lots of it. This would be her first cup of many today.

"Hey, baby." Ash hugged her from behind.

"Hey." June turned and gave her a kiss. "What are you doing up?"

Ash rubbed sleep from her eyes. She wore a faded T-shirt that hadn't fit since middle school and a lacy pair of panties that June had picked up during her last trip to the mall. It was a pretty good way to say good morning.

"I wanted to talk before you left for work." Ash reached around June and pulled the cup of coffee from the Keurig. She smiled and took a drink. June got down another mug and a new canister for the machine. She would never be so tired that she couldn't share the first cup of coffee with Ashlyn.

"What about?" She pushed the button to start the next cup. Ash held the first cup up to her mouth and June took a careful sip. She wasn't awake enough to trust her lips to catch all the liquid while Ash was in control of the cup, and she didn't have enough time to change before work if she spilled on herself. Not to mention she needed to stop past the dry cleaners. She only had one work-appropriate shirt left.

"Your not-so-secret admirer, Kat."

"What about her?" For some reason, she felt dirtier talking about Kat over coffee than she did when Ash was pushing her fingers inside her.

"I thought we should discuss her when we're not filled with crazy sex hormones."

June palmed Ash's bare thigh, then slid her hand up until it rested on her waist. She slipped her fingers beneath the bottom edge of Ash's T-shirt and ran her thumb over the slope of Ash's breast. "Speak for yourself." She was pretty much filled with crazy sex hormones any time Ash even looked in her direction. She didn't require much encouragement from her wife.

Ash pecked her on the lips, then stepped out of reach. "I'm serious."

The second cup of coffee finished, so June took it to the table and sat. She pushed the other chair out and invited Ash to join her.

She waited for Ash to sit before she asked, "What about Kat?"

"I really do think you should invite her over." Ash said the words easily, like the concept of sharing June in their own home was something they did all the time. Yes, they'd played with other people, but never at home.

"Why here? We could go to a hotel or something."

"We could." Ash agreed. "But this is simpler. And I don't have the same hang-ups I used to."

"What do you mean?"

"In the past it was important to me that we keep our home... ours. We were still new to each other. There were some things I didn't want to share.

"And now you do?"

Ash laughed. "No, I still don't want to share those parts of you. But now I know very clearly what I want for myself, and it has nothing to do with our house." She slid closer to June and placed her palm flat against her chest. "Everything I want is right here. That's mine, no matter what."

June kissed her impulsively. When Ash said overwhelmingly sweet, romantic things like that, June had no choice but to show her how happy the sentiment made her. Normally, she liked to show her for hours and in several different positions. Right now, however, she needed to leave for work very soon.

"You say the nicest things."

"How do you feel about bringing someone else into our home?"

June thought about that. She'd been so worried about Ash's reaction she'd never really thought of how it would affect her. "I don't know."

"No?"

"Can I have some time to think about it?"

Ash raised her eyebrow and smirked. "You need to think about it some more?"

June laughed. She'd dedicated a lot of time, too much, really, to thinking about what they would all *do* together, but hadn't thought at all about how she would *feel* about it afterward. Ash obviously had spent some time on both. "I don't need to think about *that*." June flushed with heat, then stammered, "Not that I won't think about it. Obviously I will. I meant I need to think about the emotional impact. I don't want to do anything that will cause problems for us. You're more important to me than anything else. I don't want to fuck us up."

"Well, as far as I'm concerned, it won't. You could bring a hundred other women home to me, and it wouldn't change anything. I know you love me. And I know that if I asked you to be with me and only me, you would. But I don't need that. I just need your love. That's all I'll ever need. And I already have it."

"I know. I just…" If she brought Kat home, that meant she'd know what she looked like when she came. And she'd be in their bed, the bed she shared with Ash, when it happened. She wasn't sure that was a memory she wanted to have popping up randomly. When she went to bed with Ash at night, she didn't want the vision of Kat joining them on a regular basis.

"What are you worried about?"

"Are you sure the thought of another woman in our bed won't bother you? Like the actual memory of it."

Ash paused for a moment, a thoughtful look on her face. "No, I don't think it will. Like I said, I know what it means and what it doesn't mean."

June nodded. "Okay. You've obviously thought about this a lot more than I have. I need to think about it some more." She hated that her brain was so clogged with desire for Kat that she hadn't even considered the emotional side effects. It'd never been an issue in the past, but this was different. Not to mention that connection she shared at work. Kat had a great deal of influence over her career. She wasn't sure she wanted to add sex to that relationship. Kat clearly did, and June's body was definitely interested. But that didn't mean her brain shouldn't put the kibosh on the whole thing.

"Take as long as you want. I'm in no hurry."

June sipped her coffee and stared at the wall over Ash's shoulder. The thought of sharing Kat with Ash, of experiencing Kat with Ash there to guide her through the experience, was exciting to June, but what if Kat only wanted June? Alone. Blood pounded in her ears. The thought was a little too much to contemplate at six forty-five in the morning. She had to ask. "What if she doesn't want to?"

"Doesn't want to…what?" Ash wrinkled her nose. It was early and she'd gotten even less sleep than June.

"You know…come here…with us…" June was handling this poorly. There had to be a better way to say what she needed to say, but she couldn't think of it.

"She's clearly interested."

"In me. Yes."

"Oh." Ash spoke softly and held herself very still. "But she knows you're married."

June nodded vigorously. "Yes. Absolutely."

"Are you asking if you can fuck her without me?"

June swallowed hard. The words sounded much worse out loud than the idea did in her head. She nodded, the movement much tighter than before.

"Is that what you want?"

Once again June was forced to consider the differing desires within her. "My body does. But the thought of hurting you makes my heart ache. And my brain…"

"Your brain checks out of the conversation when the hot woman presses herself against you."

"Pretty much, yeah."

"Go with your heart, June, because I'm pretty sure that would hurt me."

"Yeah?" June felt a strange relief. She no longer had to think about the rules of engagement with Kat. Ash, as always, gave her a clear path to follow.

"I think so."

"Okay." She exhaled in what felt like the first time since the conversation started. "Okay, that's good. Good. I'm not okay if you want to sleep with someone else either."

"You can manage that with this woman?" Ash stared hard at June, her mouth curved into a small half-smile.

"Definitely. No problem at all. I promise."

Ash sat back in the chair, the tension gone from her for the moment. "So, when do you plan to see Kat again? When's the next meeting?"

"God, I have no idea. I'm not even sure I'll be included."

"But you think you'll see her again?"

"I don't think she'll let me off without it." After June had fled her office and left Kat hanging there, she was absolutely certain Kat would seek her out again. Probably to tell her off.

"Okay, call me if you decide to invite her home with you." Ash stood and pulled June up with her and led her to the front door. "Now, don't you need to get to work?"

June grabbed her bag, kissed Ash good-bye, and headed to work with her thoughts clearer than they had been since she'd met Katerina VanderVort.

❖

"Are you coming to the meeting later?" Robert stuck his head into June's office, his body positioned in a way that said he wasn't staying but had merely dropped in to ask the question.

"Yeah, at two, right?" June held up the contracts. She'd been reviewing them for the past hour. Sometimes, the lawyers of the group drowned otherwise simple negotiations in overly complex language. She'd contemplated law school but ultimately decided on finance. Times like this she was thankful for that decision. "I'll be there."

"I heard she's already in the building. Wonder if they're going to move it up."

"Who?" June didn't understand why they were having the meeting in the first place. Typically contracts were signed and sent via courier. They didn't have meetings with everyone in full attendance. It was weird.

"Ms. VanderVort."

Kat was already here? June's heart rate spiked. She'd gone two weeks without seeing her. She'd prepared herself for the group meeting that was scheduled for later that afternoon, but knowing she was in the building three hours early was not an eventuality she'd considered. "What? Why?"

"I have no idea. I—" Robert stepped back. "I gotta go."

Kat walked into her office and closed the door. "Just the person I wanted to see." She sat in the chair opposite June.

June closed the file on her desk. "Ms. VanderVort, how can I help you today?"

Kat raised an eyebrow. "Ms. Vandervort? Where did that come from?"

"Since you're not sitting in my lap, I can only conclude you're here for official business."

"Do you want me in your lap?" Kat moved to stand.

"No." June spoke hastily, bordering on a shout. "At least not right now."

Kat settled into her seat. "That implies you will at some point in the future."

"I think we should talk about it."

"What's to talk about? I find you very sexy. I know that attraction is mutual, and I'd really like to do something about it."

"And I'd really like to not get a divorce."

"Ah, yes, the good wife at home minding the hearth."

June laughed. The thought of Ash as a housewife was too shocking to be anything more than farce. "You know nothing about her."

"No."

"Do you want to?"

"Would it make you more inclined to say yes?" Kat leaned forward, sharp, keen interest on her face.

"Do you always do this?" June wasn't a prude. She and Ash were adventurous with their sex lives, but she'd never encountered someone like Kat. She was blatant with her desire and open to the point of vulgar when talking about it. Yet she was pointedly matter of fact, like she didn't know the passionate side of sex. June knew that to be untrue. Every encounter she'd had with her had been overwhelmingly, if inappropriately, sensual.

"Do what?"

"Approach sex like a contract negotiation."

"Are we negotiating? I'd resigned myself to your continued resistance. What changed?"

Ash had changed, but June wasn't ready to share that just yet.

"Nothing has for certain. Before we get to that, let's talk about my career. I like it. I don't like how much influence you wield over my ability to continue it."

"Is that what this is about? You're afraid I'll have you fired?" Kat held up two fingers in the Boy Scout salute. "I promise not to interfere with the trajectory of your employment, here or with any other firm. Who I fuck, or not, does not inform my business decisions, Ms. Phillips."

"Okay." June smiled. She had no reason to believe Kat, but the other woman hadn't lied to her about anything else. She didn't see why she would now.

"Okay? Does that mean I should move to your lap now?" Kat scooted to the edge of her seat but didn't stand.

June's phone rang at that exact moment and she exhaled fully. Facing Kat without Ash beside her was overwhelming. She wanted her to a degree that made it unsafe for them to be alone together. Being with Ash *and* Kat at the same time would be even more overwhelming, she was certain, but then she wouldn't have to censor her desire.

She wanted, very much, to tell Kat that, yes, in fact, she did want her to move to her lap. And that she'd prefer for her to remove her clothing first. Instead she held up her hand and said, "Hold that thought."

And then she answered the phone.

Chapter Six

"Tell me what you're wearing." It wasn't a request. It was a command, given with such casual authority, it took a moment for June to register what Ash said. Then it took another moment for her body to spring into action. She scrambled to grab the receiver, almost disconnecting the call completely as she silently cursed her habitual use of speakerphone while at the office. When she picked it up, the speaker disengaged.

She cradled the phone to her ear and turned slightly toward the window. "Uh, Ash, now is not the best time." She tried to keep her voice low, but it sort of squeaked its way out. Ash had never made a call like this before, let alone to June while she was at work. It was like she'd been sucked into a surreal vortex with her wife and her would-be lover tormenting her from all sides.

Ash's voice was melted butter and syrup. "Really? I think it's the perfect time." June could hear the challenge in Ash's tone. It was fair, she supposed, given how many times she'd brought her office into their bedroom recently. Ash was entitled on some level to reverse that.

Kat cleared her throat and June turned in her chair to face the other woman. She raised one eyebrow and almost smirked at June. She'd heard enough to be interested in the outcome of the phone call. Without a word, she rose and crossed to the office door. She twisted the lock, then went back to her seat.

As June watched Kat, her temperature spiked and her heart pounded into her throat. This was her office, and the situation was damn close to being out of control.

"Can I call you back?" June wanted to tell Ash what she was wearing. She pictured Ash sprawled naked over their bed with her phone to her ear, a teasing, seductive smile on her face. Or maybe she was in her workshop, her hand already easing into the gap between her side and her oversized overalls that she wore while working.

"You could," Ash said, "but I'm unbuttoning the top button now, and I'd hate to finish without you." She spoke slowly and deliberately, dropping each word with precision into June's imagination. June let the offer settle and marinate for a moment, then thought of the sizzle yet to come.

She stared at Kat. She'd started to finger the top button of her blouse, synchronous with Ash's announcement.

"I'm with a client." That was the understatement of the year. She was with a client who'd repeatedly asserted her attraction to June and her desire to act upon that attraction. A client who had guest-starred in her sex life with Ash several times over the past few weeks. A client who wielded a tremendous amount of power over her future career. They were all balanced together on a dangerous precipice, tipping over the point of no return.

And still, she wanted to tell Ash exactly what she was wearing.

"Who is it?" Ash asked, her interest rich and apparent. "Is it Kat?"

June stared at Kat as she opened the first button on her shirt. She nodded. "Yes." It sounded much more like a plea than she would have liked.

Kat's smile was slow and seductive. "I think you should take the call." She traced the exposed line of her throat with her fingers.

Sweet Jesus! June's vision swam with the implication.

Ash spoke again, her voice grounding June in the moment. "Tell me what *she's wearing.*"

June didn't think about the consequences before she spoke. "A cream-colored suit with navy flats and a matching bag."

Kat raised both eyebrows, a first in June's presence, and her smile grew.

"Cream?" Ash purred. "What kind of fabric?"

June stumbled. Ash's job, since their first months of dating, had always been to dress her. She picked out June's suits, all of her clothes. She paired her outfits before they went out for the night. She said June couldn't be trusted to pick out her own. According to Ash, she would end up with some horrid off-the-rack number with shoulder pads and a stitched-in belt.

"June, what kind of fabric?" Ash asked a second time.

Ash was pushing her to talk to Kat, to invite her into their game. Her tongue swelled to three times its normal size and her mouth filled with sand. "I don't know."

Kat stretched, slow and careful, every movement an orchestrated seduction. It worked. June felt completely, overwhelming, seduced by both women. All she could do is watch as Kat extended her body over the desk and hit the speakerphone button. She took the receiver from June and dropped it back into the cradle.

June forgot how to breathe.

Ash pushed forward, determined to carry this on. "Ask her."

"Ask me what?" Kat's voice was lower than it had been a few moments ago, more intimate.

Ash's breath caught, then she said, "Ask her, June."

June's heart pounded against the back of her throat and she swallowed hard. Her eyes were locked on Kat's. They were smoky brown, the kind that were sexy no matter the situation. In that moment, they were smoldering.

"What kind..." June cleared her throat to rid it of the rough, squeaky edges. "What kind of fabric is it?" And with one little sentence, June felt her career go up in smoke and wasn't sure she cared.

Kat relaxed back into her chair. Her elbows sat on the armrests, but her hands met in the middle, fingers laced together. She crossed her right leg over her left and openly studied June. For all her active pursuit, Kat paused inexplicably when Ash switched the light to green.

She didn't think Kat was going to answer and wasn't sure how far Ash would push it. She dug her fingers into the padded curve of her armrests and waited. The straining whiteness of her knuckles stood out in stark relief against her tanning-bed-cultivated skin.

Ash coughed. Not a real cough, but one of those polite "answer my question" coughs. And it worked.

Kat glanced at the phone, then back to June. She'd heard that the eyes were the window to the soul, but hers appeared to be a window to her clit because Kat's gaze went straight through her and landed square in the middle of her cunt with a heavy thud.

"Raw silk," Kat eventually answered, placing a guttural inflection on the word *raw*, and it tore through June to bounce on her clit a few more times.

Ash's breath hitched and then started up again, a little faster than before. "Is it soft?" Victory filled her voice. Not only was June on the hook, but Kat nibbled at the bait as well.

It took a minute for Ash's question to register. June felt like she was in a vacuum where she could hear the words, but they refused to translate into meaning in her head. It reminded her of the one time in college when Ash had convinced her she'd like the feeling of getting stoned. They'd shared a joint, with June taking two or three puffs at the most. She'd lost all track of her limbs, couldn't follow the conversation around her, yet knew it was all hysterically funny. The next time Ash asked June to join her, June declined. It wasn't a feeling she particularly enjoyed, yet in this context the haze was infused with sex, and she couldn't clear her head long enough to decide if she liked it this way or not.

She heard Ash's voice, demanding and familiar, but stared at Kat. It was a disconcerting combination.

"June?" Ash sounded impatient. June didn't blame her. Their respective roles in the scene had been cast, and she was taking far too long to fill hers.

"Hmmm?" She couldn't focus on Ash's question long enough to answer it, but it didn't matter. Ash was a clotheshorse. She knew exactly what the fabric felt like. What she really wanted was for June to touch it and tell her how *that* felt. And June was going to do it, just as soon as she regained control of her motor functions.

Kat rose from her chair and rounded the desk, her movement fluid and graceful. She spun June's chair until they were face to face and then placed her hands next to June's on the armrests. Kat's lips parted slightly and her tongue slipped out to lick along the edge. The red of her lipstick shone even brighter as she bent her head close to June's. She pressed her lips to June's ear and said, "I think she wants you to touch it." She drew the words out, low and sexy, just loud enough for the speakerphone to pick up the intention in her voice, if not the words themselves.

Kat wore a tailored cotton button-down. Only it wasn't the traditional style where the buttons go all the way to the top. Rather, they stopped three-quarters of the way and gave June a great view of her cleavage. The top button was open, revealing even more. It had an oversized collar and French cuffs with actual studs through the buttonholes. And all June could think about was how much better it would look off than on.

The front fell open as Kat leaned down, giving her a perfect view of the tops of her breasts. She couldn't move. All she could do was stare down Kat's shirt at the black-lace bra. And the expanse of exposed flesh. She wanted to trace the line where skin transitioned to lace.

Her hands almost touched Kat's, with just the slightest space between them on the armrest. She slid them carefully away, knowing that if their skin touched, she'd never stop. For now, she needed to let Ash dictate the pace of her actions.

She lifted her hands and curled them around the edges of Kat's jacket lapel. It wasn't soft, but it wasn't rough either.

Kat pulled back after a moment and looked into June's eyes. "Well?"

In order for Ash to know what was happening, June needed to speak. She swallowed, just to make sure her throat would respond to a basic command. "Not really."

Ash's voice rushed out of the phone. "Where are you touching her?" This wasn't a question June ever expected to hear Ash ask, but could tell she was excited to ask it.

She slid her hands up to Kat's shoulders, then down her arms. "Her jacket...the lapels."

Kat lifted her hands off the chair but remained bent close to June. She took June's hands in hers and asked, "Do you want to know what my shirt feels like?"

Kat stared into June's eyes as she said the words, but she had no doubt the question was intended for Ash. She was desperate to touch the shirt, and the flesh beneath, but she waited for Ash to respond. Her fingers twitched with anticipation and she hoped the answer would be yes.

She didn't hesitate. "Definitely. And June..." Ash paused and her voice dropped to that intimate level she used whenever they were all alone and the lights were off. For June the sound was as tactile as the caress that came in the moment between Ash saying "You're beautiful" and the next when she pressed her tongue to June's clit. "Describe it for me."

Reality swirled and dipped, then slammed into clear focus when Kat placed June's hands flat against her abdomen. June spread her fingers and curled them around the curve of Kat's waist. In contrast to the fabric of her jacket, the cotton of her shirt was soft beneath June's touch. The muscles underneath weren't.

"Ashlyn?" June's voice wasn't as strong as normal. She was on serious sensory overload and was amazed to find that it worked at all. "It's white, with tiny pearl buttons down the front. The one at the top is already open." She tried to think of everything Ash might want to know about it. "And it's soft."

She traced a winding pattern with her thumbs and Kat caught her breath hard and straightened. She looked down at June with hazy, lust-filled eyes, and June wanted to go a lot faster than Ash dictated.

"Where are your hands now?"

Before she could answer, Kat stepped in. "They're on my waist, just above the swell of my hips—" Her breath caught as June squeezed gently, asserting her position. Then Kat continued. "I want her to touch me...my skin." She hesitated slightly. "Is that okay?"

The question had a waver at the end, caught between a whisper and a whimper.

June knew Kat was unaccustomed to asking. She was the kind of woman who simply reached out and took. They stared at each other, scarcely breathing, as they waited for Ash's answer.

"Yes."

One word and June received a key she'd been silently pleading for. She closed her eyes and tried to focus her breathing. It was erratic and her head swam. She watched silently as Kat opened the buttons on her shirt. She wanted to help, but Ash hadn't said she could do that, so she licked her lips and stared fixatedly until finally, it hung open.

"June, what are you doing?"

June shifted her gaze to the phone and spotted her cell lying next to it on the desk. She picked it up and activated an iChat session with Ash. When her wife's picture filled the screen, she pushed the disconnect button on her office phone.

"Hi." June smiled, small and secret. She forgot all about Kat, who was well on her way to naked, when she saw her wife.

Ash's hair was down and mussed, the telltale swipe of paint covered her cheek, and June could see the studio in the background. She'd been working when she stopped to call. Her eyes were dark and hooded.

"Hey." Ash returned her smile, the one that said it would be the two of them forever. Seeing it, seeing Ash, made June feel so much better about what they were doing. It would all be okay if she could just look at her wife for a moment. "You didn't answer my question."

"Oh." June turned the screen until it focused on Kat's bared front, the black lace of her bra, the generous swell of her breasts, down to the hard lines of her abdomen. "She unbuttoned her shirt."

"Have you touched her?" The image on the phone only showed Ash's face. June closed her eyes and imagined the rest, Ash with her own shirt open, no bra, her fingers squeezing first one nipple, then the other. June wanted to hear that little gasp Ash gave every time she would suck one between her teeth.

"No, not yet."

"Do it."

She opened her eyes and looked up at Kat, who toyed with her belt, a sexy, inviting smile on her face. When June didn't move, Kat released her belt and took June's phone and rested it on the desk where Ash could still see, then took June's hands in her own. Once again, she placed them on her waist, this time against bare skin rather than with the barrier of thin fabric between them. Her body tensed beneath June's hands, the muscles twitching and flexing. She was soft and smooth and perfect.

June pushed her chair back and stood. Her hands gravitated lower until they rested on Kat's hips. They were the same height, Kat and June, and June's new position brought her kissing close to Kat. It wasn't a new situation for them. Kat had crowded in close to her more than once, but for the first time, June wasn't fighting the urge.

Kat's hands trembled between us as she returned to her belt, too uncertain to free the buckle. June moved her hands up to cover Kat's. She held them there for a moment, stilling Kat and giving herself a chance to breathe. Everything was happening too fast and yet far too slow. Kat, as far as she was concerned, still wore far too many clothes.

June shifted her grip and worked the buckle loose, then popped the button on Kat's pants. Then she pulled back slightly and let herself look at Kat. She pushed the shirt open farther and it slid, along with the jacket, off her shoulders and caught at the bend of her elbows. Kat's skin was golden and perfect, except it was natural, as opposed to the tan June worked hard to maintain. A shiver ran across her abdomen and June traced it with her index finger. Then she laid her palm flat against Kat's stomach as if to stop it from happening again.

Kat and Ash both moaned at the simple contact, and June smiled. Kat sucked her bottom lip between her teeth and held it there.

"Can you see, Ash? I'm touching her stomach. Her skin is soft, but the muscles are hard…tense."

Ash groaned and said, "God, yes, I see. Jesus."

June knew then that this technology-assisted threesome wasn't going to be enough. Kat in front of her and Ash on the phone. She wanted to end the call and take Kat home with her. She wanted Ash on her back with her legs looped over her shoulders. She wanted Ash. Kat was a nice distraction, but she would never be a suitable replacement.

But Ash wasn't there. Kat was, and she was trembling beneath June's touch.

"What do you want me to do now?" When she asked the question, June looked away from Kat, away from the heat in her gaze and the quivering want shimmering on her skin. She turned her focus to Ash—devastating, beautiful Ash. She wanted to beg Ash, she wanted to push Kat down on the desk and feel her from the inside. As much as she wanted Ash, the need to take Kat burned in her chest, tingled in her fingers. She didn't beg. She simply stared into Ash's eyes and hoped that was enough, that her wife would see how badly she needed her in that moment.

And she did. "Pretend she's me."

CHAPTER SEVEN

O h, God." Kat found her voice, but it was rough and uncertain. She sucked in a ragged breath.

That's what June wanted, permission to dictate the pace rather than waiting carefully for permission. "Yes."

June pushed the shirt and jacket to the floor. Kat looked fleetingly like she was thinking of catching it before it hit the ground, but June pushed her bra up and sucked one nipple between her lips—hard. The blazer and shirt rippled to the ground, and Kat gasped. She wound her fingers into June's hair and pulled her closer.

She abandoned the slow maneuvering of earlier and pushed Kat back until she lay flat against the desk. She released Kat's nipple with a pop, then grazed her teeth over the tip as she tugged on the edge of the bra. "This has to go."

June followed the fabric of Kat's bra around to the clasp and released it easily. The black lace sagged forward, and she hooked one finger under the thin straps on either shoulder. A trail of goose bumps rose in the wake as she slid it down Kat's arms and let it drop to the floor. She thought about kissing Kat but decided against it. She wasn't sure how Ash would feel about that. Kissing was a very intimate act. She would save her kisses for Ash, for when she got home later that night.

She returned her hands to their previous home on Kat's hips, curved around her waist to where her fingers could play with the bare skin of her low back. Kat trembled as she inhaled shakily, closed her eyes, and threw her head back. Kat slipped her hand around June's neck, her fingers laced in her hair. She drew June in, urging her mouth to her breasts again.

June kissed her fleetingly, then moved up to the pulse point at the base of Kat's neck. It called to her, the rapid flutter that betrayed the pounding of Kat's heart, and she pressed a kiss into her flesh. She inhaled deeply, taking Kat in. She smelled nothing like Ash. June looked to the side, to where Ash watched. Kat smelled of citrus and lavender. Ash was sage and sandalwood.

Ash's breath was harsh and uneven, amplified by the phone. There was no way she hadn't heard June and Kat, the noises they were making together—Kat's light whimpers and June's desperate fumbling. She wanted to give Ash more, to share more of the experience with her.

"Ash…" Her voice came out as a hoarse whisper, but no matter how hard she tried, she couldn't manage more. "She smells so good…" June ran her tongue along the curve of Kat's neck. "Tastes so good."

Ash moaned and Kat pushed her head lower. June left a trail of wet kisses down Kat's shoulder, then kissed the inside of her arm, that soft, sensitive spot that should never be neglected during lovemaking but usually was. She worked her way down Kat's arm, dropping to her knees as she went, and then sucked her index finger into her mouth. She bit down slightly before pulling back and pressing a light kiss to Kat's palm.

"Now these." She tapped the open belt at the top of Kat's slacks and pulled away to watch. She was talking more than normal, but not nearly as much as she wanted. It was all for Ash. She wanted to hear Ash come, and for that to happen, she needed to involve her as much as possible. She wanted Ash to feel it when she made Kat scream.

Kat's fingers trembled as she opened her pants, the manicured nails glinting in the light. June pushed her hands out of the way. Kat was moving too slow and she wanted her pants off now. She eased the zipper down, then moved to push the pants off her hips, but Kat stopped her.

"Wait."

Wait! The single most frustrating word a woman could say. But she did because it was never a good idea to push harder than was welcomed.

This time, June and Ash groaned in protest.

"Please," Ash whispered, apparently as frustrated by Kat's request to slow down as June was.

Kat wove one hand into the hair atop June's head, then tilted her head back until she could look into her eyes. Kat's were heavy and dark, and June knew Kat didn't want to stop. That's not what her "wait" was about.

Kat winked and gave June a slow, sexy smile. Then she moved her hips in a heated, undulating sway. Small circles, like she was dancing with June inside her, coaxing her to just the right spot.

June's jaw went slack and her mouth went dry, instant Sahara. She watched as the pants eased down her hips to pool at Kat's feet. She stepped out of her shoes and kicked the slacks aside.

Ash gasped into the phone. June knew by the sound of her stilted breaths that she'd progressed beyond them. She wanted Ash to stop, to wait for her.

Kat pushed against June's chest, a role reversal from earlier, until she plopped down in her seat. Then Kat leaned back against the desk and looped one leg around June's shoulder. Her panties were small and lacey. If June wasn't careful, she would destroy them. She didn't care. She should take the time to remove them gently, but she was done waiting.

"Jesus, June, take them off. You need to fuck her. Now."

June glanced at Ash. She was staring hard at the lace covering Kat's cunt, at the wet spot forming there.

June moved the lace to the side and held it out of the way, then pushed two fingers into her as deep as she could go. She didn't go slow or easy. That wasn't what this was about and not what she wanted. It wasn't what any of them wanted. No one was looking for love or romance. This was about fucking and orgasms and just feeling good. And by the sound of Ash's breathing, she was feeling pretty damn good.

Kat was slick with arousal and June curled her fingers forward just to hear her moan. She pulled out and pushed in again, harder than before. Kat was soft and velvety, and June wanted to crawl inside her. Or at the very least, push her tongue in and gather all the desire gathered there.

June wanted to make Kat wait, just a little bit, to make her work just a little harder for it, but Ash's breath was coming hard and fast through the phone, and the sound pushed June to go faster.

Kat fell back against the desk and pulled June's head closer with her leg. Her goal was obvious, but June wanted her to ask for it. Better yet, she wanted Ash to command it. She stopped moving her hand, just for a moment. Her face was close to Kat's cunt, close enough for Kat to feel her breath and for her to smell Kat's need.

"Please..." Kat moaned, louder than was safe in an office building in the middle of the day. The door only blocked out so much. Still, June wanted more.

"Please, what?" June asked in a long, drawn-out whisper and forced her breath out in slow little puffs against Kat's clit.

Kat's legs twitched and she wiggled closer to June's face. "Please...fuck me."

June held her fingers deep inside Kat and curled them up and back until she found just the right spot—the one that made her jerk and beg and cry all at once. Kat cried out and June pressed her tongue flat against her clit, just to say hello.

When she was with Ash, she liked to take her time. She drew this part out, the part between building and shattering. She wanted Ash to come harder, always harder. Harder than last time, harder than ever before. But Kat wasn't Ash. Ash couldn't feel her tongue flicking across Kat's clit. She couldn't feel the push and pulse of June's fingers as she slammed into her again.

Kat was close, gasping, and June fucked her hard enough to make her cry out. Hard enough for Ash to hear.

"God," Ash moaned into the phone. "I want to touch you so bad, June. To feel you, how wet you are."

June tried to pull away, to respond to Ash, but Kat clamped her hand down tight on June's head. "Don't stop," she gasped. "Don't you fucking stop."

She groaned into Kat's cunt. She needed to answer Ash, but she couldn't stop fucking Kat. She didn't want to stop fucking her. She sucked hard on Kat's clit and added a third finger as she stroked into her again.

"Please," Ash begged. "June..." She was so close, and June wanted to do whatever she needed to tip her over the edge.

Kat clutched her even tighter, not giving her room to do anything but suck and lick and drive Kat's body tighter and higher. Kat answered for her, her voice shaky and uneven, "She's...God... fucking...me..." Kat forced the words out through clenched teeth. "And...su...sucking me...off at the same time." The last part came out in a forced jumble.

"Oh God, June." And Ash was there, right on the edge, balancing a moment before she fell over.

Kat tightened around June's fingers, her clit hard and throbbing as June pushed just a little harder. She felt Kat's body tense, one fist balled in her hair and the other gripping the edge of June's desk.

"Yes!" Kat came with a shout. The word was loud and drawn out and not the kind of yes that goes with good investment returns. Kat's body slackened and she released June's head.

June extracted herself from Kat. This was the time when she would normally crawl up Ash's body and hold her as she fell asleep. But she wasn't at home and Kat wasn't Ash.

June pulled a sleeve of sanitizing wipes from her drawer and cleaned her hands, wiping away the evidence of their encounter. She cleaned her face as well and wished for a toothbrush. She still had a meeting to get through, and it was going to be harder than ever with the taste of Kat so fresh in her memory. She didn't need the distraction of it on her tongue as well.

Kat pulled her clothes back on and straightened her hair. Ash was surprisingly quiet through it all. Finally, Kat stood and headed toward the door. "Meeting starts in a few minutes. I'll see you there."

All signs that she'd just been fucked on June's desk were completely gone. She looked gathered and composed, ready to make a deal worth millions. June felt as though she was coming apart at the seams and didn't know how Kat pulled that off.

"See you then."

Kat smoothed her jacket one last time and exited the office, pausing only long enough to twist the lock and open the door.

June pressed her fingers to her lips. They were swollen and tender. Ash was still on the phone, waiting.

"June?" Her voice was back to normal, full of love and hope. "When are you coming home?"

"Soon. I have one more meeting and then I'll head out of here." They were talking like they did this every day.

"Good. Bring Kat with you." Ash smirked, then hit the disconnect button. The screen went black.

June gathered her things and headed toward the door, uncertain how she would sit through another meeting with Katerina VanderVort.

CHAPTER EIGHT

For the first time since Kat had walked into the conference room a few weeks ago, June was able to sit through the entire meeting without worrying if Kat was going to feel her up under the table. In fact, she was seated on the opposite side of the table. As relieved as she was by the distance, June didn't know what to make of it.

The extra space didn't allow her to follow the content of the meeting any more closely. Instead she dwelled on the fact that Kat had made it a point to sit away from her. Granted, she wasn't sitting suspiciously close to Simmons or Robert, the two men she was seated between, but that didn't calm June's mind at all.

Their encounter in her office was too fresh in her memory. Her lips were still tender and, she was certain, red. She could still feel the way Kat had pulsed around her as she rode her fingers. And, most distracting of all, if she moved her hand just right, she'd catch the lingering scent of Kat's arousal clinging to her skin.

June fidgeted, trying to find a comfortable position that wouldn't give away how turned on she still was. Every time she thought she'd found the right spot, placed her legs just so or angled her weight just slightly to the left, she'd remember the sound of Ash through the phone, her quiet panting as she listened and watched but couldn't participate. That was June's undoing every time. She'd almost find her focus, almost tune in to the meeting, and then she'd glance at Kat or think of Ash. She was lost over and over again.

She couldn't wait for the meeting to end so she could extend Ash's invitation for Kat to join them at home.

She was so distracted, she didn't realize the meeting had concluded until the people around her started to stand. She gathered her things as slowly as possible, giving Kat the opportunity to call out to her like she had at the conclusion of the previous two meetings. She didn't.

Finally, June had no choice but to leave or to appear like she was eavesdropping on Kat and Simmons as they chatted quietly in the corner, their heads bent close to one another. Kat's face was drawn tight in concentration, a deep crease bisecting her brow. She didn't look happy. June gave her one last glance, then left the room.

She walked to her office in a daze, uncertain what had just happened. When she got there, she closed the door behind her, then sagged into the chair behind her desk. This day had left her completely off her axis.

A light knock sounded on the door, and before she responded, the door opened and Kat entered. She gave June a soft, thoughtful smile, and June mirrored it without thinking. That it was completely out of place on Kat's face didn't occur to her until after Kat closed the door behind her and sat opposite June. She was accustomed to Kat's smiles being a declaration, sometimes a sexy challenge, sometimes a knowing judgment, but this was new.

"Hi." She didn't know what else to say.

"I'm kind of mad at you, you know." Kat's smile didn't fade, and she didn't look the least bit mad.

"Why?" This should be good. As far as scorecards went, Kat was far ahead. She'd had a killer orgasm, if the noise she made could be trusted as an indicator. June was still aching for completion.

"We could have done that much sooner, if only you'd told me the rules."

"What do you mean?"

"If I'd known all I needed to do was ask Ashlyn, I'd have done that when we first met."

"Really?" June was amused. People always made the mistake of assuming she was in charge in her marriage. After all, she worked in finance; she had an impressive title and wore expensive suits. Ash, on a good day, remembered to put on socks before she ventured to the market. On a really good day, she remembered to wash the paint off her face first, too. More often than not, however, she rode to the store on an old courier bike that she'd restored herself, wearing untied Chucks, her hair hastily thrown into a bun, and wet paint clinging to her overalls. Though she loved clothes, she rarely wore anything from her extensive wardrobe. She was attracted to the beauty of certain fabrics, certain outfits, but that beauty rarely found a place in her day-to-day life.

Despite all that, she was very much the one in charge. June would do anything, go anywhere, live however Ash wanted. She loved her too much for anything less to be acceptable. Fortunately, for all her flighty tendencies, Ash recognized how much easier their lives were with June's steady stream of income funding her fancies.

"Absolutely. I'd have called her in the middle of that very first meeting."

"The middle of it?"

"Yes. I'd have stopped Simmons from droning on and on and demanded that you phone. Then I'd have thrown you up on that table and had my way with you." Kat's eyes grew darker, heavier, as she spoke.

"Right there, huh?"

Kat nodded, her mouth dropped open slightly, and she licked along her bottom lip.

"So why did you sit so far away today?" It didn't really matter. It's not like they were going steady. They'd fucked. And June wanted to do it again, only this time with Ash in the room.

"It was my only hope of maintaining control. Now that I know the secret, I would have done any number of inappropriate things during that meeting if I'd sat close enough to touch you."

June shifted in her seat again. Kat's words awakened the passion she'd managed to calm. She needed to get home as soon as possible.

"You're in pretty bad shape, huh?" Kat leaned forward as she spoke, staring at June intently.

June closed her eyes for a moment. As much as her body might want it, she still couldn't do anything about her desire for Kat here. "You have no idea."

Kat leaned forward even farther, her fingers wrapped tight around the armrests. "I could help with that."

June nodded slightly, then opened her eyes. "Not here."

Kat drew back. She looked annoyed. "Why not? Here was just fine an hour ago."

"Ash wants me to bring you home with me."

Kat's smile returned, and her eyes grew so dark they were almost black. "Perfect." She stood smoothly and moved toward the door. She paused with her hand on the doorknob and turned back to June. "Coming?"

June nodded and swallowed hard. She definitely wanted to be coming and would be able to as soon as they made it to her house. She rushed to gather her things. As she followed Kat down the hall and out the main entrance, it took all of her control to keep from grabbing Kat's hand and running.

CHAPTER NINE

When she pulled into her driveway, June tried not to focus on how someone like Kat, someone with that much money, would view her home and instead focus on how little that would matter once they made their way inside to Ash.

"Here we are." June shut off the engine and gestured toward the walkway that led to the side entrance.

Their priorities when they'd bought the house had focused on what Ash needed to complete her work. She wanted an out building or garage that could be converted to a workspace, and few neighbors, as random external noise could negatively impact her creativity. Ash had wanted a garden full of flowers, room to grow veggies, fruit trees, and eventually animals. They hadn't made it to the animal stage, but Ash had her flower and vegetable garden, along with a variety of fruit trees. And she had an acre of privacy with a converted shed cum studio.

Those things were all Ash ever saw. Their home was her personal version of heaven, and June had worked her ass off to give it to her. For the most part, June saw all the plusses and forgot about the negatives, but with Kat walking beside her to the side door, the negatives were all she could see.

In addition to the well-tended vegetables, the back part of the property with the trees was overgrown. The house needed a new coat of paint, and the string lights that Ash used to light the path between the back door and her studio looked more tacky than charming when viewed with a critical eye.

June paused at the top of the steps and said, "Welcome to our home."

Kat might have been harboring any number of criticisms, but none of them surfaced. "It's lovely. Thank you for the invitation."

Kat responded like she'd been invited to a dinner party instead of a threesome, and her formality threw June for a loop. She stared at Kat, searching for the right answer. She still hadn't thought of an appropriate response when Ash opened the door and pulled June into a deep kiss.

It might have been rude to kiss Ash with such abandon with Kat shuffling from foot to foot next to them, but she didn't care. What they were about to do, what they'd already done, put June off-kilter. Kissing Ash righted everything in her world; it grounded her and reminded her of who she was, who *they* were. She desperately needed that right then. Rude or not, introductions could wait for a few moments.

Ash ended the kiss and followed up with a short, quick peck. Then she rested her forehead against June's. "Hi. Welcome home."

"Hi back. Thanks for the welcoming."

Ash kissed her one last time, then released her and turned to Kat. "And you must be Kat." She stepped close and pulled Kat into a kiss. It wasn't nearly as long or thorough as the one she gave June, but it swallowed up any response Kat was on the verge of issuing.

It also relieved the pressure in June's chest. The fleeting thought that maybe this had been a bad idea slipped away as she watched Ash kiss Kat. Any worry she had about things being awkward changed to much simpler thoughts about how quickly she could get them both into the house and out of their clothes.

She decided to follow Ash's lead of "do it instead of talk about it." She slipped around Ash and through the door, unbuttoning her shirt as she went. When she undid the last button, she slipped the shirt off and dropped it on the floor. She didn't pause, didn't look back to see if they were watching, but when she popped the clasp on her bra, she heard Kat gasp and Ash say, "God, June."

She dropped the bra in the dining room and stepped out of her shoes as she rounded the corner into the living room. She heard the side door close and hurried footsteps catching up to her. Ash giggled right before she grabbed June's shoulder and spun her around to face them.

"In a hurry?" Ash laughed and kissed her, pulling Kat into their embrace.

"Yes." June did her best to keep her voice even, but the need still worked its way into the tone. She didn't elaborate to explain that while Ash and Kat had both gotten off earlier, she hadn't and was about to pop the seams on her stockings if something didn't happen soon. Instead, she stared at Ash levelly, daring her to delay her longer.

"Really?" Ash's eyes darkened as she looked at June. She maneuvered them until June's back was pressed to the wall with Ash in front of her. "Maybe you should let us help you with that."

She gulped and nodded. Ash could do anything she wanted to her because it always ended with happy orgasms. By extension, she'd let Kat have her way as long as Ash was there to guide the encounter.

Ash stared into her eyes, then stepped to the side and tugged Kat into position until she was standing in front of Ash. June held Ash's gaze. She wouldn't look at Kat, or anywhere else, until Ash allowed her to.

"Her zipper's on the right side of this skirt." Ash spoke to Kat but continued to stare at June, her eyes focused and intense.

June felt Kat's hands on her waist, her response immediate once permission was granted to touch. Then one hand lowered the zipper until the only thing keeping her skirt up was the pressure of her body against the wall. Kat tugged on her hips, pulling her forward. The skirt fell to the floor and pooled around her feet.

Kat gasped and Ash smiled at her. "She's beautiful, isn't she?"

Kat traced the lace edge of her panties from her thigh to the juncture of her legs, but she stopped short of pressing her fingers against June's cunt completely. Next she played with the top edge of her stocking, following the line up to the garter. "Do you always wear this to work?"

Ash's hand curled around her body to cup her ass. She rubbed the bare skin, playing with the thin line of the thong as it dipped in between her cheeks, then tracing it up to the top. Her touch excited June, sending a surge of excitement to her already over-stimulated cunt. Ash squeezed lightly and said, "Not always, but often enough."

In reality, June typically chose function over form. Underwear served a vital function. It kept her business hers. She preferred as much protection from exposure as possible, but when Ash had insisted on dressing her that morning, on the lacey thong to match her bra, and even lacier garters to hold up her stockings, she'd been easy to convince. She liked to think she'd have defended her position better if Ash hadn't been stroking her clit and whispering naughty words in her ear at the time.

June looked at Kat through her lashes. "Do you like it?" Demure wasn't something she could normally pull off with any real success, but based on Ash's soft growl and the way Kat's gaze burned on her skin and her fingers dug into the flesh of her thigh, she thought it'd worked okay in that instance.

"Very much." Kat adjusted her hold, one hand on June's waist and the other cupped around the side of her neck, then eased closer. She slanted her mouth on June's and kissed her slowly. She eased her tongue between June's lips and caressed the inside of her mouth, her tongue, with easy, languid swipes of her tongue.

When Kat pulled away, she left June breathless and disoriented. June fisted her fingers around the lapel of Kat's jacket so tight the wrinkles might never come out.

"I can't wait," Kat murmured, then pressed her lips to June's again, this time with obvious need. Half a second later, she slipped her hand between June's legs, her fingers beneath the scant fabric of her panties.

Rather than thrust inside, which is what June's fantasy Kat had done in her mind time and time again, Kat slipped her fingers through her folds, sliding through the moisture and moving up to finally tease across her clit.

June gasped when Kat's fingers brushed over her clit for the first time, sucking in even more of Kat's tongue with the movement. Ash squeezed her ass rhythmically and whispered in her ear, her breath hot and hypnotic. "That's it. God, you look so hot."

The smooth circles against her clit didn't escalate. Kat kept the pressure, the rhythm, the motion, the same. June whimpered. She was so close, her insides clenching and releasing in time with Kat's touch. She thrust her hips, needing just a little more.

"I want you to come, June. You can do it. Then we'll take you to the bedroom and fuck you so hard your legs won't work after."

Kat growled and kissed her harder, but the fingers against her clit continued the same maddening pace.

"Do it now, baby." Ash whispered in her ear, and that was it. June clenched, receding like the tide, then flowing forward and crashing.

She sagged against the wall, relieved and happy and yet not at all satisfied. One orgasm against the wall while Ash and Kat were both fully clothed would never be enough for her. June broke away from Kat and gasped for breath. Her body twitched as she came down. She kissed Kat one last time, then turned and pulled Ash in for a kiss.

She kissed her hard and deep and with as much urgency as she could muster in the moment. She wasn't done and she wanted Ash to know that. When she felt like she could finally move again, she broke away.

"Let's go." She eased herself between their bodies and the wall to resume her trip down the hall.

"Is she always like this?" Kat asked.

"When I'm lucky," Ash responded.

"You both better be naked when you get to the bedroom, or I'm not letting you in." June worked her panties and garters off, not the easiest maneuver while walking, but she didn't want them in the way for the rest of the evening. The stockings slid down easily after she unhooked the garters. They were expensive and delicate enough that she didn't leave them crumpled on the floor with the rest of her clothes. She folded them neatly and left them on her dresser.

They'd never done anything exactly like this before, so June was a little at a loss. Should she stand at the door to greet them as they entered? No, it wasn't a goddamned dinner party. Still, she wanted to see Ash walk through the door naked. And the thought of Kat joining her made June clench low in her belly, as though she hadn't just had a pretty damn good orgasm moments before.

Finally she decided on the bed. She draped herself across it sideways, positioned with a perfect view of the door. She heard the rustle of fabric and Ash swearing softly, so she knew they were getting undressed in the hall. It wouldn't be long at all.

She braced her head on her hand, then took a moment to assess herself. As much as the position she'd chosen gave her the perfect view of them entering the room, it also gave them a perfect view of her. She adjusted her breasts, making sure they were behaving and pointed in the same direction. Not the sexiest thing she'd done, but the effect was worth it. Then she ran her hand through her hair, pulling it free and fluffing it until it flowed out behind her. She was halfway through tracing the edges of her mouth, checking for errant lipstick, when Ash cleared the threshold. Kat entered a step behind her.

They paused there together and simply stared at her. The raw desire on their faces made her nipples tighten.

She swallowed, then asked, "What are you waiting for?"

Ash gestured for Kat to go first, but Kat hesitated. "How do you want to do this?"

Ash smirked. "How about you just go for it? Do whatever you want, and I'll join in when I'm ready."

"Really?"

Ash looked from Kat to June, then back again. "Oh, yeah."

Kat returned her gaze to June and took a step closer. She kissed June, light and quick, then leaned close to whisper in her ear. "I have this fantasy of you on your hands and knees with me fucking you from behind. I haven't been able to shake the image since I met you." As she spoke, Kat rested her hand on her waist, then moved it up until it cupped the swell of June's breast. She swiped her thumb over the skin over and over.

A shiver ran through June and she swallowed hard. She liked Kat's fantasy a lot. Without saying a word, she climbed onto their bed and positioned herself on her hands and knees. She looked back over her shoulder at Kat and tried to smile provocatively. She felt exposed, like she was on display. Kat held her gaze for a moment, her eyes dark and unreadable, and then she pointedly looked at June's body.

"Perfect," she growled as she moved onto the bed behind June. She gripped June's hip, her fingers digging into the flesh in a way that shocked June. Ash was always so careful with her. Kat's hold on her would leave a mark, a bruise that she could look at the next day as a reminder of Kat fucking her. Kat tightened her grip incrementally, holding June firmly in place. "Stay there."

Kat issued the command through gritted teeth, and before she finished speaking, she sank her fingers into June. The sudden intrusion rushed through June. She bucked against Kat's fingers and rode out the entry. Everything about this, about the way Kat touched her, was foreign to her. Kat was rough, and she thrust like she was trying to fuck all the way through June.

God help her, it turned her on. With every thrust, every deep-reaching intrusion, she grew more aroused, more excited. All she could hear above the blood rushing through her body was Kat's rough panting and the wet slurping of her arousal as Kat fucked her fingers into her over and over.

She dropped to her elbows and finally released the groan she'd been holding back.

The bed dipped and she felt, rather than saw, Ash drawing closer. "So beautiful." She breathed the words into June's ear and her hot exhale washed over June's skin and seeped into her pores. Ash nuzzled her ear, her neck, kissed along her shoulder. Every touch of her lips was gentle and sweet and loving.

Kat added another finger and thrust in particularly hard, forcing her face into the comforter. June gasped for breath and pushed back to meet Kat. It felt so good, so dirty and wrong, and overwhelmingly sexy. She felt used, like she could be anyone beneath Kat.

Ash whispered sweet things in her ear. She kept her voice soft, gentle, as she begged June to turn her head, to let Ash kiss her. The building pressure in her cunt, the almost violent awareness of her body, of the rising need to orgasm, clouded June's brain. All she could focus on was the growing need inside her, spiraling and retreating with Kat's thrusts.

"Baby, please, kiss me," Ash pleaded, her fingers working gently along June's body, teasing her nipples, then dipping lower.

"I want more." Kat grunted as she thrust into her, adding a fourth finger and pushing hard enough to flatten June against the bed, trapping June's hand with her fingers barely touching her clit.

June yelped in surprise and turned quickly to let Ash swallow down any further noise. Her body was on fire, stretched and painful, yet so very good. She needed Ash, needed her kiss, the caress of her tongue to ground her here. She wasn't ready to shatter, but Kat was relentless. Her thrusts, her greedy pace were pushing June through a threshold she'd previously been unaware existed. This wasn't gentle or fun or loving. It was the rawest, purest form of fucking, and her body loved it. Her mind and heart, however, were terribly, overwhelmingly confused. She shouldn't have liked it, to be taken so forcefully, so roughly, but she did.

June poured all her confusion, her resistance, every ounce of passion into the kiss with Ash. She drew from Ash's love, her careful tenderness, and used the strength to push herself back up. She spread her legs and dropped her head to open her body to Kat, to give her what she was clearly going to take regardless.

Ash skimmed her fingers over June's clit, and her body trembled and skipped even higher.

"That's it. Just let yourself feel it, let yourself go." Ash kissed her cheek, sliding through the moisture there. June didn't know when she started crying, but she could feel the tears sliding down her face, highlighted by Ash's gentle brush of her lips over the hot skin.

With Ash's words fresh in her ears, June orgasmed hard and long, thrusting back to meet Kat and crying out in gratitude that Ash's fingers stayed with her and worked her clit throughout.

She collapsed against the bed, worn and cringing as Kat pulled out. Sleep pulled heavily at her and she wanted nothing more than to curl up in Ash's arms and give in to the need to rest.

Strong hands—Kat's? Ash's?—rolled her onto her back. She heard a deep, guttural growl, and then a tongue swiped over her cunt, dipping inside with a swirl, then flicking over the tip of her clit.

"Jesus!" She gripped the head, her fingers twining into hair that definitely didn't belong to Ash. Kat then. She'd thought she was done, but Kat was driving her rapidly into a second orgasm.

She turned her head to the side and saw Ash smiling at her. "Hi, baby," Ash said sweetly. June kissed her because she had no choice. She loved her wife—God, did she—but the things Kat was doing with her mouth amazed her. She ground her hips up into Kat's face, and Kat gripped her hard and pushed her back down. She groaned and nipped at June's inner thighs. Her teeth dug in, sharp enough to sting and bruise and definitely leave a mark. Then Kat smoothed her tongue flat against the aching flesh and licked and kissed, like an unspoken apology.

"Oh, God." June fought to keep her eyes open, to stay focused on Ash, but it was so hard. Ash's eyes were dark and heavy and she stared at June as she slipped her hand down between her own legs. June's eyes slid shut, then flew open when she realized what Ash was doing. It was her job, always hers, to take care of Ash. She wanted to make her come, not watch her do it for herself. "No." She moaned, unable to articulate anything else.

Kat, if she heard June, didn't acknowledge her. She kept teasing through her folds, thrusting her tongue inside, then moving up to flick it over June's clit as she lightly sucked it between her teeth. The pressure rose inside her hard and fast. She was dangerously close to coming again, and she couldn't do that while Ash needed her.

"Baby, no." She grabbed Ash's hand, stopped her from touching herself. "Come here, come up here." She rolled her hips in time with Kat's tongue, but managed to keep her eyes focused on Ash.

"Are you sure?" Ash moved into position even as she asked the question. She kneeled over June's open mouth but held her body too far away for June to reach. "Like really sure?"

"God, yes." June gripped Ash's hips and pulled her down until she was able to swipe her tongue through Ash's folds, gathering moisture and simply *tasting*. Ash was so wet it ran down her thighs and coated her cunt. Her clit poked out, big and hard and quivering pink.

June didn't waste time. She held Ash, guiding her to just the right position, and then she focused everything she had on making Ash come. She circled her clit, easily bringing Ash up as gently as she could. She was so close herself and really, *really* wanted them to come at the same time.

Ash braced one hand on the wall and gripped June's hair with the other. She held her in place as she bucked her hips, grinding as June sucked and licked her clit.

Kat's hand pushed her thighs open wider, her fingers pressing hard into the tender flesh of June's inner thighs. She was going to be so bruised and sore the next morning. Kat clearly wanted to leave her mark on June, and she was succeeding.

She sucked June's clit between her teeth, rubbing over it in a way that caused a shiver to run through June. The cold, hard surface of enamel scraped over her, then was replaced with warm, wet tongue, lapping and sucking until all June could do was let he dam inside overflow. She tightened and clenched and throbbed, and it all felt so good, made even better by Ash thrashing against her face.

June came harder than she expected, and all she could do was lie there with her mouth open. She held her tongue stiff against Ash, helpless to do anything but let her ride into her own orgasm.

Ash stiffened, her legs clamping down tight on June's head, and she came with a rush of wet heat. She collapsed against the wall and June gasped for breath, trying to both come down from her own orgasm and recover from Ash's. The position was awkward, and Ash damn near smothered her when she came.

"Sorry." Ash released the hold on her head, then rolled off her. June pulled Ash into an embrace and held her for a moment.

When June looked up, she saw Kat dressing and dialing her phone. "Are you leaving?"

June wasn't sure how she felt about that. She very much needed sleep, but she also wanted to play with Kat more. She'd barely gotten a taste earlier.

Kat spoke quietly into her phone, then disconnected the call. "I just called for a car. They'll be here soon."

"Oh."

Kat pulled on her shirt.

"Wait." Ash crawled off the bed and stopped Kat from putting on her pants. She pushed her hand between Kat's legs. It came out coated with moisture. "Let us take care of you."

Kat smiled and shifted her legs open slightly. "I really need to go. And your wife looks down for the count."

"Okay." Ash slipped her hand between Kat's legs again.

Kat stared into June's eyes, her gaze dark and intense, and Ash teased her easily into an orgasm. She built quickly and came with her mouth curved into a silent "O" as her body trembled with tension, then relaxed.

When she was done Ash removed her hand and licked her fingers. "Now you can go." June could hear the smirk in her voice.

Ash sat on the end of the bed and watched as Kat pulled her clothes on. A car pulled into the driveway as Kat was stepping into her last shoe.

"Do you want to wash up first?"

Kat laughed. "I did that while you two were snuggling, when I gathered my clothes."

Had they really been curled up together for that long? June felt almost bad for excluding Kat, except for the part where Ash was her wife and Kat had just fucked her hard enough that she probably wouldn't be able to walk properly for a couple of days.

"I'll walk you out." Ash rose smoothly and followed Kat out of the room.

The last thing June heard as she gave in to the pull of sleep was Kat saying she had a lovely time, followed by Ash saying this wouldn't become a regular thing. She loved June too much to share her on an ongoing basis.

June curled into herself and let sleep claim her. Maybe she should be worried about what would happen next time she saw Kat at the office, but she wasn't. Maybe she should be worried about how to separate the memory of Kat's hands on her body and keep it from becoming part of their home together, but she wasn't.

As much as she'd enjoyed Kat, she loved Ash just that much more. Her wife would guide her through the tricky parts; she always did. Kat's car left, and then Ash curled around her. With her limbs heavy with sleep, she kissed Ash and said, "I love you."

"I love you, too, baby. Now go to sleep."

And in her wife's arms, she did.

On Her Knees

CHAPTER ONE

How do I look?" Gavin fidgeted with the knot on his tie, and Abby Nelson shooed his hands out of the way.

"Don't fuss with it." She centered the tie and then smoothed her hands down his chest to clear the wrinkles in his vest. "You look very handsome."

Their relationship was completely upside down. Gavin worried about how he looked and primped like a *Glamour*-reading teenage girl. Abby, on the other hand, was content with her appearance. She'd learned long ago what look worked for her, and when the circumstances arose—for example, a celebration at a senior partner's house to celebrate Gavin's promotion—she fell back on a time-proven winner. Tonight she'd opted for a black sheath with long lines that accentuated her body and teased with more than a hint of leg via a slit up the side. It slid open and closed in the most tantalizing way, and Abby very much approved. She pulled her hair back in a twist and called it good. Wisps fell around her neck and curled around her dangling earrings. Gavin wore enough product in his hair for both of them. And still he thought his bosses considered him straight.

He kissed her lightly on the lips, a chaste expression of brotherly love. "You sure you don't mind?"

Abby threw up her hands. If reassuring him the fifteen other times he asked hadn't been enough to convince him, nothing would. "I give up."

"Don't be like that, Abs." He caught her around the waist and hugged her close. Side by side in the full-length mirror, they looked good together.

"I don't mind." Abby returned his hug, then slipped out of his embrace. She pushed her feet into the short heels that the dress demanded. She'd rather wear her cross trainers, but they weren't really high fashion. "But I think you'd be happier with a real date."

"Before or after I had a heart attack?" Gavin was so deep in the closet it would take a lot more than a few platitudes from Abby to chase him out of it.

"Fair enough." Hair up, shoes on, tiny purse in her hand, Abby was ready to dazzle the partners of Dmitri, Holt, and Stevens.

"What about you?" Gavin held her hand lightly as they walked to his car.

"What about me?" Abby asked as she slid into the passenger seat. She knew what Gavin was asking, but sometimes it was just easier to feign ignorance. She didn't want to think about what her life would be like if she allowed herself to enjoy a real date. The non-romantic relationship with Gavin was enough to satisfy her need for companionship. Sex was nice, but she could have orgasms all by herself, no partner required.

Gavin didn't respond until he was securely fastened into the driver's seat. "You should date."

"Hmmm." It wasn't a yes, but hopefully it was enough to get Gavin off her back. He was a little pushy about her love life. Her issues were completely different than his. Abby wasn't in the closet. She just really, really didn't like the vulnerability and possibility of pain that went along with a relationship. She was still recovering from the last one. When it was time to venture out again, she would.

Gavin maintained that his closet was so much more practical than the barriers that Abby set up around herself. He was reserved due to career pressures. First he'd needed the secrecy to please his parents, then to get the job at the schmancy law firm, then he had to make full associate, then it was junior partner. Abby believed he would always have some excuse to keep himself hidden, and that made her sad.

Abby, on the other hand, wasn't trying to get ahead; she was just trying to get by without falling apart. If she could figure out how to fall in love without getting hurt in the process, she'd be on board. So far, however, that hadn't been her experience.

"*Hmmm* isn't an answer, sweetie." Gavin was apparently in a matchmaker mood as he navigated through traffic. "Listen, there's a new woman at work…" He glanced at her.

"No. Keep your eyes on the road." Abby took Gavin's hand, laced their fingers together, and rested them together over the center console. "I'm okay. Don't worry."

"I'm just saying that when you're ready to stop being my beard, it's okay. I understand."

"I'm not ready yet. But when I am, you'll be the first to know." Abby didn't understand why Gavin was pushing so hard about this tonight. She only had to pose as his girlfriend a handful of times a year. It wouldn't matter if she started seeing someone. She'd still make time to help him out when the situation arose. She squeezed Gavin's hand. He was her best friend, and that wouldn't change regardless of her relationship status.

❖

When they arrived, the party was in full swing. The house was crowded to the point that Holt's four-thousand square feet of overindulgence seemed small. "What's up with all the people?"

"We hired a new round of associates. Business is expanding." Gavin helped Abby out of her overcoat and turned it, along with his own, over to the coat-check girl stationed at the door. When Holt threw a party, he didn't skimp on service. A caterer walked by with a tray of champagne, and Gavin snagged one for each of them. "Come on." He handed a glass to Abby. "Let's go be seen."

Abby saw Simone Davies before Gavin pointed her out. Her chest tightened and she took a quick gulp of champagne. Clearly she was imagining things. She'd recently received the invitation for their ten-year high-school reunion, and now her brain was conjuring up an old classmate in a place she clearly didn't belong. Abby was certain that when they got closer, she'd see that it was someone else entirely. Surely the distance and the lighting were conspiring against her.

They worked their way across the room and Abby met a host of people she wouldn't remember. She knew Gavin's bosses on sight, and that was the important part. Nobody else could promote—or fire—him. She kept tabs on the Simone doppelganger. The more she studied, the more convinced she became it wasn't really her. This woman smiled and laughed, and she held herself with open confidence. She was inviting and enticingly in control, not cocky and closed. She was a study in opposites from the Simone Abby had known in high school.

When they were halfway through the meet-and-greet, the woman met Abby's gaze and her eyes widened. "Abby?" Abby couldn't hear the word, but recognition and subsequent question were undeniable. It was definitely Simone Davies.

Simone started making her way toward Abby.

"Gavin?" Abby kept her eyes focused on Simone's progress across the room. It was slow going. "How long has Simone worked with you?"

"Who's Simone?" Gavin leaned in close, his hand on her waist with the familiarity of lovers.

Simone halted. Her eyes narrowed and she tilted her head to the side, evaluating. Abby stepped out of Gavin's embrace and pointed at Simone. Abby said, "She's over there."

"Oh, she's the new woman I mentioned earlier. I don't know her name, but I think she must be family." He moved in again as he spoke, his fingers toying with the ends of her hair.

"She is." The news that Simone Davies was a lesbian was decades old for Abby, but it still filled her with a forbidden, sudden thrill.

Normally Abby didn't even notice the little gestures like Gavin touching her hair. She and Gavin had been together, played the charade for so long, the trappings of false intimacy were ingrained. With Simone staring at her, judging every gesture, she was suddenly hyperaware of Gavin's touch. The room grew hot and stuffy, and she stepped away from Gavin a second time. She smiled and waved at Simone.

Simone nodded, the overly casual and totally indifferent move practiced by bitchy girls the world over. With that, Simone's body tightened and she turned away. Abby was dismissed.

"Her name is Simone Davies." Abby stared at Simone's retreating back. Every terrible thing she'd done in the name of status during her four years of high school threatened to dismantle the person she'd worked hard to become. It had taken a lot of hours in the company of her therapist to break down that façade and build real confidence in its place. One glance from Simone Davies and she was ready to fall apart all over again. "I had a huge crush on her in high school."

"Oh?" Gavin asked. "Small world."

Before Abby could explain, Gavin was greeted by another round of congratulations on his new promotion. Abby paid polite attention but otherwise focused on Simone.

Abby had been wholeheartedly envious of Simone when they were younger. Simone had been afraid of nothing and ready to take on the world. Abby, on the other hand, had been afraid of everything. She was afraid her family and friends would find out she was gay. More than that, she was afraid Simone would find out how Abby felt about her and that would have made it all real. She wasn't supposed to fall in love with a girl. She could pretend it wasn't happening as long as she didn't have to *think* about it. But when she'd heard the rumors about Simone with another girl doing all the things Abby wanted for herself, all she could do was think about it. When Simone didn't deny the rumors, Abby fell apart completely. She was angry and hurt and so very jealous. She'd lashed out and made Simone pay in every way she could.

Simone worked the room, maintaining a safe distance. When she stepped out onto the back deck, Abby excused herself and followed. Simone's body language had made it clear she didn't want to talk to Abby, but that wasn't good enough. After ten years, Abby wanted more than a dismissive shrug.

Abby slid the door shut, blocking out the sounds of the party. If there had been a way to lock it from the outside, Abby would have engaged it. She wanted to be alone with Simone, without interruption. The November air gifted them with a nearly vacant deck. Abby liked the crisp solitude. It was fitting for the conversation awaiting her.

She joined Simone at the rail and looked out at the city lights below. It was a nice view, but Abby preferred the stars above. It was rare for them to not be obscured by a layer of clouds. Living in Portland had many benefits, including lush greenery, but Abby didn't count the generous rainfall on the list of things she loved about the city.

"Planning to ignore me all night?"

"I wasn't sure it was you at first." Simone didn't spare a glance for Abby. She could have just as easily been speaking to the night itself.

"It is."

"I see that." Simone still didn't look at her.

"Why did you turn away?"

At that, Simone reversed her stance and rested her back against the rail. She gave Abby a half smile. "What do you mean?"

"You were almost to me."

Simone shook her head and issued a short laugh. There was no humor in it. She stared at the glass door, still refusing to meet Abby's gaze. "I didn't want to interrupt your date."

"Huh?" Abby hadn't dated in months.

Simone blew out a long stream of gray smoke, and Abby pictured her at seventeen at a party with a pack of her dad's cigarettes. She'd isolated herself from the rest of the group, leaning out an open window as she chain-smoked her way through the pack and growled at anyone who dared to step within a two-foot radius of her. "How long have you known Gavin?"

Abby could hear the trap in the question but couldn't figure out where to step. "Forever, it seems."

Simone tapped her ash and gave Abby half a smile. "Not quite forever or I'd know him too."

"Good point." Abby joined Simone at the rail. She felt emboldened when Simone didn't step away. Maybe they could have a conversation after all. "He was my professor for Intro to Sociology freshman year. He'd just finished law school and was waiting to take the bar."

"Eight years older?" Simone said it as a question, but Abby could tell she already knew the answer. They worked together, and Simone was the sort to educate herself about the people around her.

Abby nodded. "He's a good friend."

"Looks like he's a little more than just a friend." Simone's eyes were unreadable.

"That?" Abby gestured toward the house, intending to encompass what Simone was referring to. "That's just an act. He's not really my type." She slid a little closer to Simone.

"An act?" Simone spoke more to herself than Abby. "Of course."

What did Simone mean by that? Memories of Simone's viper-quick assessment, her ability to shred a person to bare bones with a few well-placed words, kept Abby from asking. She'd been on the receiving end of Simone's anger—rightfully so—too many times to want to go there again. And the deceptively calm look Simone had in her eyes right now always preceded those outbursts.

Instead she offered further explanation. Perhaps more information would help. "He likes for his colleagues to see us together, to think we're a couple."

Simone nodded but didn't ask another question. Her eyes remained the same enigmatic barrier as always. Abby bet she was a hell of a negotiator.

They stood together in the cool night air, the ease and beauty of the night corrupted by the layer of tension building between them. It was just like old times.

"I should go back inside." Simone finished her cigarette, and their reason for staying on the deck ended when she snuffed out the butt in the ashtray.

"Wait, Simone, please." Abby stepped in front of Simone, blocking her path toward the door. They were far too close and Abby couldn't remember how to breathe.

Simone stood still, her hands in front of her braced for an impact that never came. If Abby took half a step forward, those hands would finally, after years of wanting, be on her. She took a shallow breath, and her head swam with the smell of Simone, a hot mixture of Marlboro and perfume. It was far more intoxicating than the glass of wine she'd been sipping.

"Simone." Abby pressed in a fraction closer. "Please don't run away."

"Shit." Simone's eyes filled with thunder.

Simone took Abby in a rough kiss. It was fast and hard and completely consuming. For a brief moment, Abby felt blissfully owned. Then as quickly as it started, it was over and Abby felt abandoned. Simone pushed her away.

"Shit." Simone swore for the second time, and Abby still didn't understand the reason.

The taste of tobacco lingered from Simone's cigarette, and Abby wanted to taste it again, to suck the flavor from her tongue. She reached for Simone. As her fingers touched the fabric of Simone's dress, light flooded the patio.

"There you are, Abby." Gavin's voice boomed, too loud for the fragile intimacy woven into the night air.

The blood drained from Simone's face and she swore again. She tried to sidestep Abby, but Abby put a hand on Simone's chest and held her in place. "Stop, please." The words were a near whisper, completely desperate and needy.

Simone halted abruptly at Abby's touch. Her eyes were wide open and stormy.

"Abby?" Gavin spoke quieter this time. He sounded confused.

"Gavin." Abby kept her focus on Simone. One wrong move and she'd bolt. "This is my friend Simone. We haven't seen each other since high school."

The door slid shut behind Gavin, and the curtain fell back into place, shutting out the light. She felt him move closer. "It's nice to meet you, Simone." He extended his hand.

Simone's body tightened even more beneath Abby's touch, and then she made her move. "I have to go." She ignored Gavin's greeting and made her way to the door.

"Simone…" Abby might as well have been talking to the night air. Simone was gone.

"That was awkward." Gavin dropped his hand with an uncomfortable laugh.

Abby spun around, intent on following Simone. "Damnit, Gavin. I have to catch her."

Chapter Two

Simone didn't say good-bye, didn't excuse herself to her bosses. She ran. She made it all the way to her car before she realized she'd left her purse, and her keys, behind. She *hated* feeling so out of control. It went against everything she worked so hard to achieve.

"Fuck! Fuck! Fuck!" She punctuated each swear word with a kick to the door of her car. "Fuck!" The last time she kicked it hard enough to dent the metal and strain her toe. Her slingbacks weren't steel-toed.

She leaned against the rear fender and dropped her head into her hands. This couldn't be happening. She sucked in a breath and raised her head.

Tonight was supposed to be about finally, *finally*, proving her worth. Law school had been one long bitch of a struggle. Securing a position at Dmitri, Holt, and Stevens was her dream. And like the ghost of Christmas past, out pops Abigail Nelson. After all these years, Simone deserved a fucking break.

"Simone?" Abby skimmed her fingers over Simone's shoulder, her touch timid.

"Abby, why are you here?" Simone stared her down. She stood tall and proud, ready to defend. "Go back to your boyfriend."

Abby withdrew her hand. "I don't have a boyfriend."

"Really? I saw you together." Simone shook her head, filled with disbelief. Simone turned away, disgusted by how much Abby still affected her.

"Gavin is just a friend."

"My friends are…not that friendly." Simone refused to let her guard down. Abby had a history of lying to and about her.

"Please, we need to talk."

"Talk?" That ship had long ago sailed. They could have talked when Abby found out she was a lesbian freshman year. They could have talked when Abby held the power to destroy Simone's life in her hands. They could have talked every single time Abby chose to torment her in front of their friends, the threat ever present. Every word Abby said was a reminder, a challenge.

"You're wrong." Abby reached for her again, her hand stretched between them, but not quite far enough to bridge the divide. "We have everything in the world to talk about."

Simone stared at Abby's hand, her fingers, long and tapered and capable of such unrepentant cruelty. She'd dreamed about how much pleasure they must hold but had never been allowed to feel. Simone wouldn't let herself fall prey to Abby again.

"What do you think's going to happen, Abby? We're going to hug and kiss and giggle about what amazing bitches we were back then?" Simone shook her head. "We'll never be those people." The ones who fall into each other and laugh about a shared past and awkward adolescence. She had wanted Abby so much then she could barely function when she was near. And after all the time and distance, Simone was dismayed to learn Abby still had the same effect on her equilibrium.

Abby stepped closer, until her body was flush with Simone's. "No, you're right. I don't want to talk either. What I want is for you to stop acting like a scared little girl. It's been ten years, Simone."

"And what?" Simone shook her head. "I'm not the scared sixteen-year-old you used to push around." She let her mouth curve into a cruel half smile. It felt sickeningly familiar. It'd been so long since she'd been this heartless person who used her words carelessly as a weapon. The rush of power made her sick to her stomach, and she swallowed it. Simone squared her shoulders and straightened her spine, forcing her body closer to Abby, invading her space. She traced the line of Abby's jaw with her fingers, then moved her hand around until she had a firm grip around the base of Abby's neck. If she was going to play with fire, she might as well go all in. After all, she'd already kissed Abby. What more did she have to lose? "Or is that what you want? For me to show you how different I really am?"

"Yes." The word escaped on an exhale and Abby's eyes slid shut in the same moment. "Please."

"I bet your boyfriend would love that." Simone laughed. She sounded bitter and aged even to her own ears.

Abby's eyes flew open. "I told you, Gavin isn't my boyfriend."

Simone growled, an honest-to-God growl deep in her chest, and it exhilarated her. Hearing Abby say his name made Simone want to push all memory of him from Abby's mind. She stopped herself from kissing Abby again, barely. Their shared kiss on the patio wasn't enough to satisfy years of simmering want, but Abby wasn't hers to take.

Abby laid her hand on Simone's chest. "I wouldn't do this if he was." Her voice was tinged with laugher as she brought her lips to Simone's. Abby delivered a sweet, searing kiss that robbed Simone of all thoughts.

Everything in Simone lasered in to one primal point. This might be her only chance to have Abby, and she wouldn't surrender it now, consequences be damned. She wrapped her arms tight around Abby's waist and dragged her to the rear of her car, deeper into the shadows. Nothing she could do—save driving to her apartment, and there was no way she would take the time to do that—would shield them from view completely. The shroud of darkness was the best she could hope for under the circumstances.

Simone wrenched her mouth from Abby's even as her hands were gathering Abby's dress, drawing it up around her waist. "Are you sure?"

"Yes." Abby's head rolled back, opening the line of her throat to Simone. Simone licked from Abby's clavicle up, up, up along the smooth skin and ended with her face buried in Abby's hair, her tongue worshipping the sensitive hidden place just behind Abby's ear. "Yes, please," Abby repeated.

Simone lifted Abby onto the trunk and dropped to her knees between Abby's spread legs. The gravel bit into knees, reminding her this wasn't a dream. It was very real, and everything that came after this point was a memory she wanted to savor. Still, she would not take without Abby's permission. It was bad enough that Simone showed no regard for Abby's boyfriend, but she wouldn't violate Abby completely. She raised Abby's leg and rested Abby's ankle on her shoulder. She pressed her lips to a small heart tattoo on the inside of Abby's left foot, just above the leather strap that held her low heels in place. She couldn't see the tattoo in the dark, but she remembered the first time she saw it right after Abby turned eighteen. It was during one of the small pockets of time during high school when they were more friends than enemies. Simone raised her face to meet Abby's gaze. "Tell me this is okay?"

A shiver worked its way through Abby's body and Simone could see her delicate body tremble and quake. "This is so much more than just okay." Abby shook her head in wonder. "Please."

"Okay." Simone nodded, surrendering to her desire. She was no longer strong enough to hide from herself, from Abby. "Just this once." Simone knew, even as she said the words, that one time with Abby would never be enough to slake her desire for her. Yet somehow it would have to be.

Simone ran her hands over the soft, smooth skin of Abby's inner thighs, and Abby spread herself open wider. Her dress draped modestly over the sacred apex, the place Simone most wanted to know. Simone watched as her hands, then her arms, disappeared beneath the fabric, exploring Abby by touch alone. She closed her eyes and reveled in the touch, the feel of goose bumps rising on Abby's hot flesh.

When Simone reached the juncture, the moist heat that had called to her from the moment she'd first spotted Abby across the crowded room, she opened her eyes. She needed to see Abby, to memorize her face as Simone spread her apart and entered for the first time. She wouldn't rush. The moment was too important to lose to haste.

Abby stared down at her, heat coloring her neck and cheeks. Her eyes blazed with barely contained need, and Simone reflexively dug her nails into the sensitive flesh beneath her fingers. Abby gasped, but she held Simone's gaze. Simone released, then strengthened her grip. She loved how Abby responded to her touch. With Abby's needy stare burning into her skin, it took everything in Simone to not push the fabric of Abby's panties to the side and stroke into Abby swift and deep.

"Show me." Simone spoke low and sounded far more needy than she would have liked.

Abby inched the skirt of her dress higher by incremental degrees until she was exposed to Simone. She pushed her legs open wider and Simone whimpered. She could smell Abby's need and it swamped her senses. The strip of material covering Abby was drenched. Simone eased her fingers beneath the fabric, running them along the edge and pulling it away from Abby's sex. Heat flared through her at the feel of Abby's wetness coating the backs of her fingers despite her effort not to make contact.

"Simone…" Abby sucked in a shaky breath. She thrust her hips gently, rocking shamelessly into the night air, but finding no purchase. She whined. "Please."

"Yes." Simone carefully removed Abby's ruined underwear. She wanted to keep them, a souvenir of their time together, but she had no pockets and her purse was still inside. She folded the scrap of lace and laid it next to her.

Finally, after years of longing, Abby was bared and open before her. The sharp sting of gravel biting into her knees, the cool nip of night air on her skin, the faint noise of the party all faded to a gray state of nothingness. All that existed in that moment of time was Simone crouching before Abby. Simone felt unworthy of Abby's beautiful perfection. Simone inhaled and forced herself to wait, to savor the essence of their inevitable coupling. Soon she would taste Abby, feel the warm tang as it coated her tongue and mouth. She needed every detail etched in perfect relief and captured forever in her mind.

Abby's skirt rippled on a breeze, and the goose bumps that had receded sprang back to life, eternal and waiting just below the surface. The muscle high on Abby's inner thigh, right at the juncture between leg and torso, trembled. With her tongue, Simone traced the contours of muscle, tendon, and the vein coursing with vitality. She licked and kissed and sucked the flesh, worshipping with her mouth, so close to where she wanted most to be.

Abby's fingers wove through her hair, drawing her closer to Abby's center. Her touch was insistent, yet gently coaxing. Simone pulled back, ending the contact from her mouth to Abby's body. She was on her knees, willing to please, but she would not be controlled when Abby hadn't earned that right. Abby whimpered but eased the pressure. She left her hands on Simone's head, her fingers kneading and digging into her scalp sharply, but no longer attempting to force her movements.

Simone placed her hands on Abby's thighs and urged her to open herself even further. There was no conscious thought to her movements. Simone let her hands roam as they wished, with the tactile sensation of Abby to guide her. Her fingers found Abby's center and she spread Abby's labia with her thumbs. She was slick and so very wet. Simone moaned and lapped at Abby's opening.

"Yes," Abby hissed quietly, and her hips jerked forward. Abby's grip on Simone's hair increased, and fire bursts of pain prickled over Simone's scalp. She was too lost in the taste to care.

"So wet." Simone moaned the words, too overwrought to remain silent, but too involved to stop working her tongue against Abby.

Simone wrapped her arms around Abby's thighs and pulled her roughly to her. She would wait no longer. She thrust her tongue into Abby, burying the sleek muscle as deep as she could. It wasn't nearly enough; she couldn't reach far enough to truly feel Abby. Her palms and fingers itched with excitement. She longed to climb inside of Abby, to own her from the inside out. For now, she'd content herself with the use of her mouth, with the feel of Abby's desire coating her face, dripping down her chin.

Simone thrust in and out, encouraged Abby to meet her rhythm with her hips. She wanted Abby above her, riding her face, fucking her mouth.

"Oh, God." Abby groaned as her body quaked. It was too soon for her to orgasm. Simone wasn't ready. Again she pulled away. Abby cried out. "No. God. You're killing me."

Abby tried to thrust her hips again, but Simone held her firm. Simone adjusted her hold until she was able to again use her thumbs to pull back Abby's hood and leave her exposed. Her clit gleamed in the dim starlight, hard and proud and demanding attention. Simone laved it with her tongue, and Abby bucked against her so hard Simone couldn't control it.

Abby clutched Simone to her and begged, "Don't stop. Please don't stop."

Simone wouldn't. She circled Abby's clit, sloppy and without rhythm. She usually had fabulous technique, controlled and precise. With Abby, all she could hope was to hold on and take Abby all the way through release. She flicked her tongue against the tight bundle, then scraped her teeth lightly against the tip.

Abby keened, her body drawn tight and pulsing. She was so very close. Simone sucked, gently at first, then hard and relentless. She drew Abby into her mouth and worked her with her tongue, the warmth of her mouth, the hard edge of her teeth. She used everything, including force of will, to bring Abby off.

As Abby quaked and shook, her hold on Simone tightened until suddenly it was gone. Abby slumped against the car, her hands slack in Simone's hair.

Simone rose swiftly. "Oh, no, you don't." She drew Abby up and wrapped her left arm tight around Abby's torso. Simone kissed her hard, forcing her tongue, and Abby's essence, into Abby's mouth. At the same time, she entered her with two fingers. Simone pushed inside as fast and deep as she could go, and Abby bucked to immediate awareness. Simone withdrew and pushed in faster and deeper.

"Simone, God, I'm not—" Abby protested only to have her words swallowed by another intense, deep kiss.

"Don't tell me you're not ready." Simone thrust again and again; then she stilled. She held her hand perfectly, painfully, immobile. Then gently, she fluttered her fingers against the back wall of Abby's vagina. She drew her fingers forward, scissoring open and closed. Abby pulsed around her. "I can *feel* you. You have so much left to give."

She removed her hand from Abby's cunt and brought her fingers to Abby's mouth. She traced Abby's lips, coating Abby with her own wet desire. "Taste." Abby's lips parted slightly, her breath ragged and hard. Simone pushed her fingers inside, sliding along Abby's tongue. She groaned at the coarse texture as she pulled out and fucked inside Abby's mouth again. There wasn't a single part of Abby that Simone didn't want to own, but they had so little time. She withdrew and thrust one last time. "Do you taste it? How much you want me? How ready you are for more?"

Simone replaced her fingers with her mouth and tongue. Abby sucked her inside, and Simone nearly collapsed at the sensation of being pulled deeper into Abby's hot mouth. She fucked Abby's mouth, once again reaching as deep as her tongue would go, plunging in and retreating only to plunge in again. It wasn't enough.

"God, Abby, you taste so good…feel so good. Let me please you." Simone circled Abby's entrance and licked at Abby's lips, teasing with her fingers and tongue.

"Yes, please." Abby wrapped one hand around Simone's wrist and gripped Simone's neck with the other. She claimed Simone's mouth even as she pushed Simone's fingers into her. "Oh, yes."

Simone fucked Abby using every ounce of power, every ounce of harbored desire. She thrust with her hips, shaking the car and slipping in the loose gravel. She adjusted her position, her fingers working without fail. Abby needed to come. Simone needed to see, to feel, to *know* she was the cause.

The muscles in Simone's arms and hips flared hot with exertion, and rivulets of sweat wound down her arms and back. She pushed harder, feeling Abby grow tighter and tighter around Simone's fingers. She curved her fingers, drawing out and pressing hard against Abby's G-spot. It'd grown hard and prominent, and Abby flailed when she touched it. Simone stimulated it again, pumping in and out, slower but deeper and more completely. She stroked every part of Abby, reaching inside her and drawing out her pleasure. Abby orgasmed in her hand, coming hard and long, and drowning Simone in her desire.

Simone held Abby close to her as she gently removed her hand. Abby pulsated and fluttered, then released her fingers. This time,

Simone would let her rest, even though her own desire was far from being satisfied.

Abby slumped against the car and waited for her body to recover. Mush replaced both her brain and her bones, making it impossible to think or stand. She registered when Simone pulled out but couldn't respond with more than a grunt of dissatisfaction.

After a few moments, Simone untangled herself from Abby and stood a few feet away. She brushed off her knees and legs. Pebbles fell to the ground. She had a small gash on her left leg that had stopped bleeding a while ago but clearly wasn't there before tonight. Next time they really needed to find a room with plush carpet and a nice soft bed instead of a driveway.

Simone regarded Abby, and all evidence of desire drained from Simone's eyes, from her countenance. If Abby hadn't been there, if she wasn't still recovering from the experience, she never would have believed that Simone had been filled with fire just moments ago. Simone held her right hand stiffly to the side. She flexed her fingers and released them. Simone clearly didn't like the physical leftovers coating her fingers.

"Are you okay?" Abby asked. From the look of things, Simone wouldn't let Abby help even if she wasn't. Their time together was over.

Simone held her hand aloft and laughed uncomfortably. She shrugged and said, "Sticky." She examined her fingers, then brought them to her mouth. Her tongue darted out and tasted the minutest amount. Simone's eyes darkened again and Abby almost went to her. Before she could, Simone dropped her hand and said, "I'll have to wash them when we get back inside."

"Oh, you're going back?" Abby sounded more disappointed than she wanted. Simone was clearly done here. Her interest in Abby had disappeared the second she finished taking what she wanted. Abby wasn't going to humiliate herself by begging for more.

"I'd rather not, but I forgot my keys and purse." Simone took a couple of steps, then turned back toward Abby. "Are you ready?"

Abby wasn't ready at all. She'd just had not one, but two amazing orgasms, and she didn't trust that her legs wouldn't collapse beneath her. "So this is it? Will I see you again?"

Simone looked away, her gaze landing on Gavin's car. "I don't think that's a good idea." She walked toward the house without waiting for Abby.

❖

Abby didn't follow immediately. She'd have to face Simone, and everyone else, soon enough. The trip back to real life didn't appeal to her. She'd rather enjoy the solitude and moonlight alone, and imagine that Simone hadn't bolted immediately after sex. Simone had been a staple in Abby's sexual fantasies since high school. She'd rather not admit that the real Simone didn't live up to her imagination. The sex had been amazing, life-changing, better than her dreams. But her fantasy Simone always held her afterward. They drifted to sleep together, woke up in each other's arms the next morning. She'd never once run away at the first opportunity. Abby didn't like the prospect of reconciling her hot fantasy with the cold reality that had played out.

The chill in the night air finally pressed at her more than her wish to hold on to her fantasies for a while longer. Abby smoothed her hands over her skirt. It was a wrinkled mess with no hope of fixing it, and her underwear was nowhere to be found. Oh well. She straightened her hair, concentrated on not looking freshly fucked, and went in search of Gavin. She wanted to go home.

When she entered the house, she found Gavin just inside the door talking to Simone. "Abby tells me the two of you were friends in high school."

Simone looked calm and in control, her eyes completely shuttered. Abby wanted to see fire in them again. Now.

"Friends isn't exactly the right word," Simone replied smoothly. "We ran in the same circle."

Simone was together enough to be charming, which Abby found utterly annoying.

Gavin spotted Abby and held out his hand. He drew her to his side and slipped his arm around her waist. No wonder Simone refused to believe her. She and Gavin were too good, too accustomed, to the pantomime of lovers. Abby had to find a way to convince Simone it was all a charade.

"Abby, look. I found your friend, Simone." Gavin had apparently decided to ignore Simone's denial of friendship.

Abby regarded Simone. For a brief moment, her eyes were filled with tortured anguish, then instantly changed to calm, placid stone. No hint of approval or disapproval. She was a blank canvas as she smiled expectantly at Abby. Abby returned the smile and hoped it didn't betray her wish to tear down Simone's walls. This wasn't the place, after all. "Hello, Simone."

"Abby." Simone nodded tersely, then turned back to Gavin. "I really must be going. It was nice getting to know you better."

Simone shook Gavin's hand and retracted her hand with a grimace. She rubbed her fingers against her thumb. It was the exact movement she'd made just a few moments ago right before her tongue darted out to taste Abby on her fingers. Abby imagined that perhaps she hadn't found a sink after all, and the idea was completely mortifying, yet deliciously scandalous.

"Good night, Abby." Simone pulled Abby into a brief hug and whispered in her ear. "I wish…" She left the rest unsaid and pulled away.

"It was nice seeing you again, Simone." Abby held firm. She wouldn't allow herself to chase Simone a second time in one night, no matter how much her instincts yelled for her to do so.

Simone left without another word, and as the door closed behind her, Gavin asked, "What was that all about?"

"Mmm, miscommunication." It was a continuation of every other experience she'd had with Simone. They circled one another, crashed into one another, but never quite connected. "I'll call her later, see if I can straighten it out." If she could find Simone's phone number. Somebody had to have it.

Abby had been waiting since she was sixteen. She could wait a few more days to convince Simone there was more between them than just angry memories.

CHAPTER THREE

Beige. Simone loathed the color, and everything in Dr. Donovan's office was covered in it. The walls, the shades, the couch, the chairs, even his suit. Every last bit of it was calm, soothing beige. Simone didn't find it calming in the slightest, but after years in therapy with more psychologists than she could count, she was willing to overlook the beige for Dr. Donovan. He was the first therapist she'd seen who didn't make her want to punch a wall. That was invaluable.

"You realize you've been glaring at that lamp for the past twenty minutes?" Dr. Donovan tapped his pen against his yellow legal pad restlessly.

The lamp was beige, too. Simone redirected her gaze from the furniture to the good doctor. "Better?"

"Simone," he leaned forward slightly, "this is your time. You can do whatever you want. It's just been a long time since you spent the entire fifty minutes silent and angry. Do you want to talk about what triggered this?"

"Not really." She was being petulant and it was annoying, even to herself. She'd called and scheduled the impromptu visit rather than waiting for her regular appointment. She'd graduated to seeing Dr. Donovan once a month. One evening spent with Abigail, and she was thrown backward to the time in her life when she needed nearly constant hand-holding.

Dr. Donovan made a note on his tablet, then relaxed back into his chair. "Okay."

And that was why she liked him. He didn't try to convince her how she should spend the time she was paying for. It was her money. She could spend it however she wanted. He also didn't see a lot of value in dragging up shit she wanted to leave buried. He believed she would deal with things as she needed. If a memory wasn't keeping her from functioning, why pick the scab?

"She was at Gavin's promotion party." Simone stared at the wall to the left of Dr. Donovan's shoulder. She knew she needed to talk, but that didn't make her happy or willing.

"She?" Dr. Donovan scribbled a few more notes. He used a yellow, no. 2 pencil, and she debated snapping it in two. The one big downside of therapy was all the damn note-taking. It unnerved her.

"She." Simone gripped the arms of her chair until her knuckles hurt. "Abigail Nelson."

"Oh. And what did you do?"

Simone remembered the feel of Abby clenching around her fingers, her body drawn tight on the verge of orgasm. "I fucked her against the trunk of my car."

For once, Dr. Donovan didn't write down her response. He stared at her patiently, then asked the patented therapist question. "And how did that make you feel?"

She smirked at him. "Really fucking horny."

He rested the tablet and the pencil across his lap and waited.

Simone stared at him, but he didn't blink or look away. He'd heard all about her kinky sexual trysts. Fucking against a car didn't faze him. She should have known better. So much for shocking him out of demanding the real answer.

When she was in high school, her parents had sent her to a string of different therapists, all of them female. They thought talking to a woman would help her to open up. As soon as she turned eighteen, she demanded to be allowed to choose her own therapist. She wasn't foolish enough to think she could get away with not going at all. Her parents would have cut off their funding for school if she'd tried that.

She'd selected Dr. Donovan on a whim, not because she thought he'd actually help, but at the time she thought it would be fun to screw with a middle-age guy. Turned out, he was unflappable. It didn't matter how many salacious details she threw at him, he never so much as adjusted his collar. For a while she thought he must be gay, but now she didn't care either way. He'd earned her respect and she trusted him enough to try.

Finally, she took a deep breath and slumped slightly in her seat. "I don't know."

He nodded. "So let's talk about that. Did she want you to fuck her?"

He said the words so matter-of-factly, Simone was jealous. No matter how much training she received, she'd never be that placid when asking a question like that.

She started to answer and he held up his hand. "And let's focus on emotions for now. I don't need a play-by-play of her bodily reactions."

Simone nodded. "She wanted me to. I left the party and she followed me outside. She kissed me and…" She was going to say "begged me to fuck her," but she wasn't sure if that was an emotional reaction. She let the answer hang.

"How did you feel when you first saw her?"

"Overwhelmed. Excited. Confused. And like I'd do anything to make her happy." Anger and disappointment had quickly replaced those feelings when she'd spotted Gavin.

"So very similar to the way you felt for her in the past."

She'd spent too many hours to count dissecting her need for Abby, her deep-seated emotional attachment to her.

"Exactly like that."

"Then what?"

"Then I saw her boyfriend." Simone forced her voice to remain flat. The memory of Gavin's fingers playing through Abby's hair, his arm around her waist, his possessive, loving smile, all of it was too sharply close to the surface for her to properly evaluate the emotions it evoked.

"Boyfriend? How did that make you feel?" Dr. Donovan arched his eyebrow but gave no other indication of surprise. Simone was impressed. She was pretty sure they'd worked through her need to fuck straight girls, too, but apparently she'd been wrong.

"She told me he's not her boyfriend, but I'm not sure she told him."

"What do you mean?"

"He touched her constantly, very much like a boyfriend would do."

"And how did that make you feel?" Dr. Donovan asked yet again. Simone wondered if he ever grew tired of asking the same question over and over.

"Jealous. Disappointed. Angry." That was the nutshell version of her emotions, but it didn't come close to describing the swamp of emotion she'd felt when she'd realized Abby wasn't available.

"Is that when you decided to, ahem, *pursue* her?"

"You mean fuck her? No. That's when I decided to walk away. She followed me."

"And what did you do then?"

"I kissed her." Simone had tried, really tried, to just leave, but the open pleading on Abby's face had been too much to ignore. She'd immediately regretted her decision, but the regret didn't stop her from wanting more.

"And then?"

"Her boyfriend walked up on us."

"The boyfriend she says isn't a boyfriend?"

"Yes, that's the one."

"And what did you do?"

This teeth-pulling approach to extracting information from her was painful, but Simone didn't know any other way. It wasn't in her nature to spill everything at once. She couldn't manage anything but bits of information.

"I walked away. Again."

"And she?"

"Followed me. Again." If she'd remembered to grab her purse and keys, she'd have been long gone by the time Abby reached the driveway. The scent of Abby had lingered on her fingers long after their encounter. She wasn't sure if that was a good thing or not.

"And that's when…" Dr. Donovan gestured vaguely with his hands.

"Yes."

"Did you, at any point, stop and actually talk to her?"

"Not really, no."

"Yet you fucked her."

"Right." Simone gritted her teeth. She knew where this was going, and she didn't like it.

"Do you think that's a healthy alternative to communication?"

"I think it's a form of communication." She looked directly at Dr. Donovan as she spoke. They disagreed on this one point, and that wasn't likely to change.

"What did you communicate?"

Simone clenched her jaw but didn't respond.

Dr. Donovan waited a few moments, then reviewed his notes. "Let's go back to the boyfriend. She said he's not, but you believe he is."

"It doesn't matter."

"It seems to."

Simone nodded. "No matter what, she's lying to someone."

"Explain."

"If he is, she's lying to me about him. And to him about me." Simone paused. She hadn't considered the second half. She'd cast herself as the other woman, a role she'd tried to avoid in recent years.

"And if he's not?"

"Then she's lying to everyone else, because they definitely act like a couple."

The timer on Dr. Donovan's desk went off and he stood with a smile. "That's it for today, Simone. Why don't you think about what all this means and we can discuss it again…next week?"

Great, he'd decided she needed more-frequent visits again. Just…great. She nodded and extended her hand as she stood. It was reflex to shake hands at the conclusion of any meeting. "I'll schedule something on my way out."

Simone made an appointment for the next week as suggested. Her conversation with Dr. Donovan hadn't clarified anything for her, but her emotions were no longer running close to the surface. She felt better in control.

She refused to let Abigail Nelson unravel her like she had in the past.

CHAPTER FOUR

Simone sipped her drink and checked her watch. The ice had long since melted, leaving her with the watered-down remnants of her martini. Top-shelf wasn't enough to save it. She'd been here too long, and the piped-in instrumental covers of top-40 crap were giving her a headache. She'd like a few minutes alone with whoever had conceptualized this bastard-child of the music industry. That person needed to feel her pain.

Simone dropped her drink on the closest shelf and admitted defeat. As she turned to excuse herself, the only reason Simone had wanted to stay walked in the door.

Abigail Nelson. Blond, aloof, statuesque, bitch. In a word, perfect. Except she wasn't really all that bitchy any more. She was still blond and looked like she was carved to perfection rather than born and grown into adulthood like the rest of the planet. And the aloof thing wasn't really happening anymore either. In high school, she wore it like a protective layer, like she was afraid of the unwashed masses getting too close and rubbing off on her. Now she smiled, greeting people warmly.

Simone hadn't seen Abby since Gavin's promotion party over a month ago and had been both hopeful and afraid Abby would escort Gavin to the Christmas party. She desperately wanted to see Abby, but knowing that her relationship with Gavin hadn't changed left her deflated. The anticipation she'd felt sagged into defeat.

Abby had called more than once. Simone answered the first time because she didn't recognize the number. As soon as she realized who it was, she hung up. She hadn't answered again. Abby was toxic for Simone. Regardless of how she looked, how much Simone wanted to believe the change she saw was real, she knew it wasn't true. Either Abby had a boyfriend, who also happened to be her boss, or she was lying to *everyone* about it. Neither option appealed to Simone.

"Jesus, Simone, just fuck the girl already so you can stop glaring at her." That bit of advice came from Simone's not-quite-sober best work friend, Marco.

Simone swirled the gin-soaked olive through her fresh martini, then snatched it off with a snap of her teeth. "If only it were that simple." Simone left out the part where she'd already fucked Abby and it hadn't stopped the glaring.

Abby met Simone's gaze from across the room and gave her a half smile. Abby's hand rested in the crook of her boyfriend's arm. Gavin was gallant like that. Rather than holding her hand, he offered his arm like he was living in a *Leave It To Beaver* era movie. As much as Simone hated Abby with him, she had to admit he was good to her, boyfriend or not. They shared a comfortable intimacy and Simone was jealous. She wanted that for herself.

Simone saluted Abby with the oliveless pick and turned her body, if not her attention, back to Marco. "Why are you slobbering your drunk ass all over me rather than rescuing your wife from Stevens?" Simone inclined her head toward the corner where Marco's wife was boxed in by the ever-persistent Stevens. Unlike his partners, who tried to pretend to have some socially redeeming qualities, Stevens had no indication of humanity. In his opinion, the milk of human kindness was an obscure concept best left to folk musicians and Buddhists. He wanted money and all manner of shiny things. The shiny thing that had caught his attention at the moment was Belinda Lewis. That she was married to an associate was irrelevant to a motivated and highly intoxicated Stevens.

Belinda's smile strained at the edges as she tried once again to navigate around Stevens's arm. She was unsuccessful.

"Son of a bitch." Marco was off on his white horse to rescue his fair maiden. Belinda's smile when he arrived was real. And Simone's requisite good deed for the day was done. Another ten minutes and she would be clear to leave.

Abby materialized beside her, an ethereal dream come to life. "Hi, Simone." Gavin was nowhere in sight.

"Hey." Simone sipped her martini thoroughly enough to border on gulping. This woman unraveled her. Always had.

"What'd you do with Gavin?" Not that Simone wasn't happy Abby was alone, but it seemed the obvious conversation starter. Besides, it was dangerous for Simone to be alone with Abby at company parties. Abby belonged to Simone, whether Abby and Gavin knew about it or not. And that feeling of ownership made it unsafe for Simone to spend time with Abby. She was likely to do something rash. Still, she lingered.

"Why won't you answer my calls?" Abby tipped her drink to her lips and evaluated Simone over the rim, her eyes dark and curious. "I can't stop thinking about you," she murmured between sips.

Simone liked Abby's conversation starter better than her own, but it only led to disaster. Fucking straight girls with boyfriends had lost its appeal for Simone a long time ago. Except for this girl, apparently. As much as her brain said this was a bad idea, Simone's body was at full attention, rapt and ready to act if given a chance.

Simone edged nearer to Abby—close enough to be suspect if anyone was paying attention. "Don't let your boy hear you say that." Simone wanted to press her lips to Abby's ear, to let her breath caress Abby's skin, but she held back.

Abby stiffened. "I told you, he's not my boyfriend."

"Right. I forgot." Simone couldn't afford to believe Abby. She'd watched the two of them together. She might not be his lover, but she definitely loved him. Simone didn't want to learn exactly where the line was drawn in Abby's heart. "Maybe you should tell him that."

"He knows." Abby spoke with the conviction of truth. "What can I do to make *you* believe me?"

Simone shook her head. She leaned in closer to Abby, unable to avoid temptation. It was such a bad idea, but just as she'd thought, once hadn't been enough. Abby was so deeply infused in Simone's consciousness she feared she might never be able to remove Abby's mark. She lied to herself, promised she could control the fall if she could just keep Abby from talking about *real* things. For Simone, it didn't get much more real than her decade-old, unrequited love for Abby. Her only hope was to walk away, but her feet refused. And her mouth betrayed her as well. "Tell me what you've been thinking about me."

"About you, the way you feel." Abby took a breath and her eyes slipped shut. "The way you make me feel."

Simone waited. She wanted more from Abby. She wanted to hear Abby say that she was unraveling, that Simone made her fray at the edges, the same as Abby did to her. She said nothing and they stood together, breathing each other in, capturing the other's exhaled breath.

"God, Abby, I want—"

"There you are," Gavin said, relief in his voice. "I thought I'd lost you." He slipped his arm around Abby's waist, pulling her into his bubble and out of Simone's. Simone was getting goddamned well tired of him interrupting their near-intimate moments.

"I was just catching up with Simone." Abby smiled, her mouth a tight, small line, and inclined her head in Simone's direction. The dark edges of her eyes cleared as she spoke to him, re-casting herself as devoted girlfriend.

"Oh, yes. I forget the two of you know each other." Gavin squeezed Abby indulgently, then his hand edged upward toward her breast. "Remind me how?"

"High school." Simone answered for Abby, leaving out their recent exchange of bodily fluids in the Holts' driveway. "If you'll forgive me, I'm going to head out. I've absorbed as much holiday cheer as I can take."

Simone slipped out with a wave to Dmitri and Holt, who were propped up together at a table with several empty bottles of champagne. As the newest associate, Simone had to attend these events. Fortunately, staying long enough to see the three senior partners make complete drunken asses of themselves was not. She'd seen more than enough for one night.

Simone glanced toward Abby one last time as she collected her coat. Abby stared at Simone from across the room, her gaze never wavering despite Gavin's presence at her side. Simone wanted to look away, to prove she was unaffected. Instead, she maintained eye contact until the doors closed on the elevator, a physical barrier reminding her of the distance between herself and Abby.

❖

The phone was ringing when Simone entered her apartment. She answered without checking the caller idea and instantly regretted it. She'd momentarily forgotten she was screening her calls.

There was no response when she said hello.

"And that was fun, but now I'm hanging up." Simone had her finger on the END button when she heard a faint voice.

"No, wait." Abby sounded distant, hesitant.

"Where did you get this number?" Prior to this point, Abby had limited her stalker behavior to Simone's cell phone. "Gavin would have my cell, but not my home phone."

Abby laughed. "I didn't ask *Gavin* for *your* number." Abby's answer was a slap in the face to Simone. Why wouldn't she get it from him if they weren't lovers?

"Why not?"

"He's my best friend. I'm not exactly eager to admit that I keep throwing myself at you, even though you've said you're not interested. More than once. It's embarrassing."

"Best friend?" Simone blew a raspberry between her lips. It just looked and sounded like bullshit.

"Yes, Simone. We're friends. How many fucking times do I have to say it?" Abby was angry and Simone thought it was sexy.

"He's all over you. Every time I see the two of you. Tonight he practically copped a feel with me watching." Simone was still pissed about that move.

"And that bothered you?" Abby's voice was full of hope that Simone thought she didn't deserve to have. Their relationship, for lack of a better term, was a non-starter.

"Of course it bothered me. Jesus, Abby. I don't want anyone else to touch you. Ever." That was more honesty than Simone had prepared for. It left her throat raw and her heart vulnerable.

"Why not?"

Simone focused on her breathing, one slow, easy inhale followed by a metered exhale. This conversation just needed to end.

"Simone?"

"I need to go." All she had to do was hit the disconnect button. It was so simple and yet she couldn't bring herself to do it.

"We need to talk about this." A soft breath. "Please."

Simone wanted to hang up. She *needed* to hang up. Maybe she could force Abby to do it for her. "Let me change out of this dress first." She sighed and dropped the phone onto her bed without putting it on speaker. She needed a few minutes to clear her head. Perspective came with distance, and with Abby she needed a lot of distance, more than a few minutes' reprieve from a phone call. Simone slipped out of her dress and into a well-worn T-shirt and shorts. She left the phone sitting long enough to remove her makeup and brush her hair and teeth. If she left it long enough, maybe Abby would give up and disconnect the call.

"I'm back." Short of simply hitting the disconnect button—which she knew wouldn't work because Abby would just call back—Simone had no choice but to push forward with the conversation.

"Good. I was beginning to think you'd forgotten about me."

"I was hoping you'd think that." Simone settled into bed. Unable to admit she hadn't been able to forget about Abby for the past ten years, she figured a few minutes while she changed for bed was no threat to her memory.

"You never answered my question."

"And I'm not going to. Where are you now?" Simone had left Abby at the party, but there weren't any telltale party noises in the background.

"I just lay down. It's been a long day." Simone heard a light rustling of fabric and pictured Abby settling into her bed.

The image of Abby stretched out wearing something small and black and lacey with her hair down, probably mussed, hit Simone in the gut. She'd worked hard after high school to put Abby out of her mind. But all that work unraveled a little bit more every time Abby so much as exhaled in Simone's direction.

"Tell me what you wanted to talk about." Simone hated how soft her voice was, how needy. She purposely thought of the threat Abby posed to her well-being, to how close she was to falling apart completely. It didn't help.

"Simone…" Abby paused. "I just…"

"Yes?" God, she sounded so eager. It was embarrassing.

"I just can't stop thinking about you."

Simone refused to jump on the statement. She already sounded like an eager puppy begging for more. It felt far too familiar, and she refused to relive the fantasy created by her sixteen-year-old self. It was bad enough that she was once again on the phone with Abby, listening to her breathe and trying to build up the courage to ask for more.

"What about me?" Simone shifted her phone to her left hand and gave her right permission to roam. If Abby was going to call her up and revive a long-dead fantasy, Simone was going to take full advantage. Besides, whether her brain wanted to do this or not, her hands and body were fully engaged. "Tell me what you think about, Abby. Do you think about how we used to be friends? Or do you think about the kind of friends you'd like us to be now?"

Abby gasped, her breath ragged, but still she didn't speak. Apparently she'd called Simone up to let her do all the heavy lifting. And that pissed Simone off.

"You want to know what I think about?" Simone stopped playing. She twisted her nipple between her thumb and forefinger. They were really doing this, and by the sound of Abby's breathing, Simone was behind. "I think about how it felt to finally get inside you."

"Oh, God."

"Are you touching yourself, Abby? Are you touching yourself and imagining it's me?" Simone pushed her shorts down, and they got caught around her ankles. She kicked hard but could only get one side to come off. She left the other hanging and shoved her hand inside her panties. She hissed as her fingers slid over her clit. It had been at attention for the past month, since first seeing Abby again. "Jesus, Abby, the things I want to do to you."

"Yes, please." It came out more a moan than words, but it was enough. Simone wanted to hear her shudder through a climax.

"What are you doing? Tell me." Simone tried to sound stern, commanding, but she was too desperate to pull it off. Instead, she sounded like she was pleading for her life.

"Touching myself." Abby's voice came to a stuttering stop between "touching" and "myself." Two words and she could barely get them out. Thank God she was having just as hard a time focusing on the conversation as Simone was.

"More." The lack of details wasn't working for Simone. She wanted to know all the dirty, naughty thoughts in Abby's head, and she wanted to hear Abby say them over the phone while touching herself. "Tell me how."

"My...ugh...clit." Abby gasped, and Simone pressed her fingers in tighter circles over her increasingly hard bundle of nerves.

"Go inside." Simone dipped her fingers lower, teasing herself, remembering the feeling of her fingers sliding into Abby, hot and wet and so, so open. She pushed inside with two fingers. "God, you feel so good."

"Yes." It came out as a long, heavy groan. "Thank you."

"Do you want to come?" Simone slowed, letting her fingers explore but not push. "Do you want me to make you come?"

"Please, yes." Abby's voice was honey-heavy, dripping with desire. "I want you so bad."

"Not yet." Simone sat up in bed and wiped her fingers on the bedspread.

"Simone..." Abby whimpered. "Please, Simone, I need..."

"Here's what I want you to do." Simone leaned into the phone, her lips pressed close to the receiver. It was the only kiss she could get from Abby at the moment. "Either finish by yourself..."

"No," Abby said, a bare, desperate whisper. "Simone."

The way she said Simone's name was hypnotic, a whisper through the trees in the summertime—lulling, beautiful, promising. As always, it left Simone wanting more.

"Or you can put your clothes back on and get your ass over here. Do that and I'll fuck you so hard you'll forget everything but my name." Simone finished in a whisper, her finger over the END button.

Simone disconnected the call and threw the phone onto the bed. She pushed her hands through her hair and blew out a frustrated sigh. Her thighs were sticky, her cunt needy, and her brain foggy. No part of her agreed with the words that had just come out of her mouth, and a full-scale riot was guaranteed if she didn't get a little release. She pushed herself to her feet. First, she'd take a cold shower to cool off, not that she thought it would help, and then she'd wait.

CHAPTER FIVE

Simone poured herself a glass of wine and sat on the sofa sipping it. Either Abby would show up and be impressed with the wine selection—it was a damn fine bottle—or Simone would move from sipping to gulping and finish off the damn fine wine by herself. Nothing pathetic about that. Not at all.

She'd debated waiting naked, but the possibility that Abby would be a no-show compelled her to dress. She'd rather have Abby take her clothes off than have to get dressed alone later when she was drunk on a bottle of wine she also drank alone. When she'd told Abby to get her ass to her place, Simone had felt brave. The sound of Abby on the verge of release, the heady power of knowing she'd caused the desperate way Abby gulped air, her breathing choppy and uneven, had made her overconfident. The longer she waited, the more foolish her demand seemed. An orgasm with the woman who twisted her insides, even via phone, was better than not having one at all. Wasn't it?

She was on her second glass of wine when she heard a faint almost-not-there knock at the door. It was so soft she wondered if she'd imagined it out of desperation. A few seconds passed and she heard it again. Definitely not a hallucination.

Simone finished the glass of wine in a final gulp before opening the door. She needed the brief reprieve before she crossed the point of no return. When she opened the door, there'd be no turning back.

Abby looked as uncertain as Simone felt, like she wasn't in complete control of the actions her body was taking, but she knew it probably wasn't the smartest thing she could be doing at midnight on Thursday. Simone invited her in before either one of them could change her mind. Again.

"I wasn't sure you'd come."

"Neither was I." Abby clutched her long overcoat tight around her body. Her knuckles were turning white.

"You want me to hang that up?" Simone touched her fingers to the lapel of Abby's coat, just let them rest there lightly for a moment. She'd demanded Abby's presence so she could touch her with a lot more than just two fingers skimming along fabric, but the action still felt overly intimate to her.

Abby chewed her bottom lip. "Ummm…" She unknotted the belt slowly. "I think so."

What the hell was the big deal? It was just a coat, for Christ's sake. Abby's hesitance confused and annoyed Simone. What did Abby think would happen when she took it off? She'd be trapped in Simone's apartment forever?

Then Abby parted the front and let it slide off her shoulders and Simone was staring at breasts. And legs. Perfect breasts and legs that made her want to prostrate herself in worship.

Every thought in her head shuddered and ground to a halt. Abigail Nelson was standing naked in her foyer, and all Simone could do was gape, open-mouthed, and wait to wake up. No way was this real.

"Simone? I need you to say something or do something or… something." Abby shifted her weight from foot to foot, her hands moving restlessly. "This was a bad idea. I knew it was a bad idea, but I couldn't help but hope. I'm just going to get my coat and go."

Simone didn't register her words until she bent to collect her coat from the floor. Simone growled when she realized that Abby was gathering herself to leave. "No." She took the coat with a little too much force and pulled Abby into her arms as well. She caught her easily, the coat between them. Abby here, in her home, was a *great* idea. She held Abby for several moments and stared into her eyes. She had so many questions, but there was no clear answer in sight. Every thought led her to the same conclusion. A relationship with Abby spelled disaster. The tenuous grip Simone had on her own emotions would slip and fall into the abyss with one wrong move.

"Let me take that." She released Abby and moved back a careful half step. She wanted to stay and simply *look* at Abby. She was perfection, and any time spent with her was pure decadence. The smooth line running from the base of Abby's neck to the top of her ass begged Simone to touch, to caress the flesh and run her tongue along the trail of her spine.

Simone snatched the coat from Abby's hands and turned abruptly toward the coat closet. She needed to clear her head, to stop herself from thinking about this moment like a scene from a bad romantic comedy and figure out what to do next. Clarity would never happen while she was looking at Abby. All that skin was way too distracting. Who could be bothered with mundane things like thinking? Simone kept her movements metered and slow, taking her time to carefully hang the garment on a wooden hanger, then place it on the bar in the closet. Each movement gave her another moment to collect herself, or so she hoped.

When she turned back to Abby, whatever calm she'd managed to scrape together was lost. She swallowed once, but it did nothing to clear the desertscape in her mouth and throat. She needed a drink.

"Wine?"

Simone started pouring before Abby could answer, and the glass was half full before Abby spoke.

"I really didn't come here for wine, Simone." Abby took a slow, shaky step toward Simone, and then another, until the only thing between them was Simone's half-full wineglass. Abby took it from Simone's fingers and set it on the coffee table. "And that's not why you invited me here, is it?"

"Definitely not." Simone wanted to ask about Gavin, about Abby's willingness to lie on his behalf, but if she did that, she'd be forced to think about reality. That wasn't nearly as appealing as the very naked Abby. Instead of speaking, she closed the gap completely, moaning when her lips met Abby's. This was such a bad idea. A perfect, disastrously bad idea, until the "disastrously bad" part fell away under an onslaught of kisses and all she was left with was "perfect."

"God…" Simone moaned into Abby's mouth, desperate to say more, share how she felt, how the sensation of Abby's skin against her fingertips, her tongue sliding along Simone's, how just the sight of her vulnerable and needy standing in Simone's entry made Simone willing, how it made her want to take self-destructive chances with her career, with her life, with her heart.

"I can't believe I'm here." Abby fumbled with the fabric of Simone's T-shirt, pushing it up but not all the way off. She stopped when her fingers skimmed over Simone's nipples, making Simone groan, then gasp at the sharp pinch-twist. "I've always, *always* wanted you. Even in high school when you were sleeping with everyone else but wouldn't give me a second glance." Abby forced Simone's T-shirt up and over Simone's head. It fell to the floor and was soon joined by Simone's shorts.

"You know why I wanted you to come here?" Simone remembered her goal, her ultimate reason for demanding Abby make the trip across town rather than finishing over the phone. "I wanted to be able to touch you. I wanted to be able to take my time and really make you feel it. And," Simone took a deep, steadying breath, "I wanted to have as many options as possible while doing it."

"Options?" The word shivered over Abby's skin, and a trail of bumps followed in the wake.

The first time they'd fucked had been amazing, the fulfillment of a fantasy for Simone. It had been everything, yet it hadn't been enough. Simone had cut the hell out of her knees on the gravel driveway and ended up with a dent in her trunk. To top it off, Abby had gotten off twice, but Simone hadn't.

Even without orgasm, their frantic, desperate, borderline violent fucking in the crisp November air had left Simone dazed. If it was all Simone ever had of Abby, she would cherish the memory. It would carry her. But if they were going to do it again, and thank Jesus they were, Simone wanted this experience to be everything the first time wasn't. She didn't want a repeat of the desperate, clothes-still-on, one-sided finger fucking. She wanted to make sure Abby really knew what it meant to be fucked by—to make love to—a woman.

"Come with me." Simone led Abby slowly down the hall to her room, each step steady and easy. Just because Abby showed up naked didn't mean she couldn't change her mind. Simone wanted her to have plenty of time to do that before they got to the bedroom, because once inside, Simone wasn't letting her leave for days. The rest of her life could kiss her ass.

Abby didn't hesitate. She matched Simone step for step, pausing before entering the room to give Simone a deep, lingering kiss that started gentle and sweet, until Simone couldn't stand the tenderness any longer and she deepened it until it was a desperate, inelegant, and sloppy grinding of tongues and teeth.

Simone tugged Abby's hand and led her impatiently to the bed. She invited her to sit, and when she looked comfortable, Simone opened the bedside drawer.

"Options," she said as she laid out objects one by one. A leather harness. Several dildos in varying shape and size, including her favorite, which was bright purple, only eight inches long, and thinner than the others. It fit into places the larger ones wouldn't go without a lot more coaxing. A box of condoms. Vibrating finger massagers. Flavored massage oil. A string of beads. Three different bottles of lube. A leather paddle that left the impression of the word SLUT when swung just right. A pair of nipple clamps.

Abby stopped her with a gentle hand covering hers when she began to pull more out of the drawer. "I've seen enough."

"Yeah?" Simone had all sorts of delicious, wonderfully naughty ideas of what she wanted to do to Abby and in what order. In that moment, however, she was more interested in hearing about what Abby wanted. "Anything appeal to you?"

Abby started replacing items in the drawer. "Let's just keep it simple." Back went the nipple clamps and the paddle, followed by the flavored massage oil and the vibrating finger massagers. She stopped when all that was left was the harness, the bright purple dildo, and a bottle of lube. Her eyes were dark and wide. "This is what I want."

Simone ran her finger along the stiff leather edge. She had other, softer harnesses—like the black nylon that felt like it was barely there when she wore it—but she liked the hard edges of the leather. She liked the feel of it digging into her skin. She liked that it was solid and heavy. She liked a little—and sometimes even a lot—of pain to go with her fucking. The imprint the leather left behind was a favored reminder of what she'd done. Simone wasn't a nice girl when it came to sex, and her life became much simpler when she was finally able to admit that to herself.

"It'll take me a second to get this on." Simone undid the buckles.

"No." Abby reached for the harness. "I want to wear it."

Simone released the harness to Abby's hands. Her mouth went instantly dry with Abby's comment, and she realized that, while Abby had technically been in her apartment and naked for at least fifteen minutes, Simone was still partially clothed. She swallowed and removed her bra and panties. "Okay." The word came out scratchy and barely there. She swallowed again and said, "Do you know how to put it on?"

Abby didn't answer. She stared at Simone's breasts, a bit of drool forming in the corner of her mouth.

Simone smiled and pointed to Abby's lip. "You have a little something right," she brushed against the corner of her mouth with her thumb, "there."

"Right." Abby surged forward and captured Simone's lips in a fierce kiss.

Seriously, Simone could stay just like that all night long, just getting lost in Abby's kiss, the taste of her lips, her hot breath mixing with Simone's, the demand of her tongue as it pushed deeper into her mouth. It was intoxicating. The hot pressure low in her belly begged for more. She wrenched her mouth away. "Do you know how to…" She gestured at the harness and made a series of one-handed pointing/buckling motions.

Abby looked dazed, her pupils blown wide and her eyes half closed. "Ummm…I've never…not any of this…"

Simone gently removed the harness from Abby's grasp and knelt at her feet. She was uncertain about how she felt about Abby wearing the cock instead of her. It was definitely a departure from what she expected and what she usually did, but that didn't make it a bad thing. She was nervous, apprehensive, and turned on as all fuck. The thought of Abby above her, pushing into her…it wasn't a bad thought at all.

"Let me." Simone released the buckle she'd already loosened, then held the harness low in front of Abby. "Just step in."

"Okay." Abby's voice was shaky, but she stepped into the harness without hesitation. She placed her hand lightly on Simone's head, presumably for balance. Her fingers were long and smooth, and Simone couldn't wait to do something to make those fingers dig in and grip hard.

Simone guided the leather into place, sliding her hands along the smooth skin of Abby's legs and thighs. When she reached the top, she caressed Abby's ass, then kneaded the firm muscles. Abby moaned, and the pressure on Simone's head increased slightly so she did it again, more firmly the second time. Abby had a perfect ass—tight, round, and well muscled. Simone couldn't wait to get behind it and make Abby beg. "Perfect," she whispered.

Before she let herself get further distracted—she was on eye level with Abby's cunt, for God's sake—Simone tightened the straps and buckled them in place. The desire to stay there on her knees just feeling Abby's skin, breathing in her essence, was overwhelming. Simone leaned back onto her heels, once again trying to use physical distance, however small, to gain a little mental clarity. And once again it didn't work. She fastened the purple dildo in place. Eight inches didn't sound very long when said aloud, but with it strapped to the woman who'd given Simone a hard-on for over a decade, it didn't seem small at all.

Simone poked out her tongue and touched it to the tip of the dildo. She'd been in this position before, but never with a partner who hadn't explicitly placed her there. That she was here, on the verge of giving Abby a serious blow job without being forced, surprised Simone. That it made her crazy wet was enough to make her follow through without prompting.

She wrapped her lips around the purple head, and Abby tensed to the point of trembling. "You don't have to…"

"I know." Simone looked up and met Abby's curious gaze. "I want to. Just relax." She gripped Abby's hand, the one that wasn't already gripping her head, and led it to the side of her face. She kissed the palm, then guided it farther back until both hands cupped the sides of her head, just above and behind her ears. She knew from being in Abby's position that she was going to want a good grip when Simone got started for real. "You're going to enjoy this."

Simone wrapped both hands around Abby's legs and gripped the back of her thighs. She parted her lips and pulled Abby toward her. Traditional blow jobs where it was all tease and tongue did nothing for a dildo. The imagery was great for about ten seconds, but after that the person strapped in needed to fuck something. Simone wanted Abby's hips in motion, guiding her to thrust before she even realized herself that she wanted to. Soon enough, Simone knew, she'd be mentally begging Abby to stop and simultaneously to never stop. Having her throat fucked felt awful and yet oh so fucking amazing all at the same time. And she wanted Abby to feel the power of holding her face and forcing her cock—Simone's cock—down Simone's throat.

She pulled Abby into her mouth until she felt the cock brush her uvula, then paused. She swallowed and collected herself, holding Abby in place while she tamped down the urge to vomit. It would pass. She just had to be patient and let her body work through its reflexive response. When her stomach settled, she pressed forward again, pausing when she felt the tip of the cock push against the back of her throat.

"God, Simone." Abby choked on whatever she was going to say as Simone gripped her thighs and pulled her back. She needed another moment to recover. The cock went in only about halfway, but four inches was a lot when it was causing a gag reflex.

Before Abby could collect her thoughts, Simone pulled her forward again, working her through the speed and force she wanted her to thrust. She paused again when Abby hit the back of her throat, raised her eyes to meet Abby's gaze, then pushed farther. There was initial resistance, then the cock slid down Simone's throat. She held it there long enough to swallow. She doubted Abby could feel the vibration of the motion through the silicone, but old habits die hard, and when Simone decided to give a blow job, she refused to half-ass it.

Abby's grip in her hair tightened, her fingers scraping Simone's scalp and pulling her hair in the most delicious way, and then she released the pressure. She left her hands in place, weaving into Simone's hair. Simone guided one hand to her throat. She wanted Abby to feel herself inside Simone. With Abby's fingers stretched along the length of her throat, Simone pulled back slowly, letting Abby feel the cock retreat bit by bit.

"Jesus." Abby groaned and the grip in her hair returned, and she dug her nails into Simone's throat, chasing the path up the cock as it traveled up. "Fuck."

Simone didn't allow Abby to pull out completely. She didn't want her to have time to think, to decide this was too scary, too *manly* for her to continue. She jerked Abby's hips forward hard and quick, forcing the cock down her throat again. She swallowed quickly, letting Abby's fingers feel the muscles of her esophagus work against the cock. Without pausing, she pulled her back out, then jerked her forward again. Simone was ready. Abby was ready. Simone wanted Abby to take her. She wanted her to fuck her like it was the only thing that mattered, like it was the only thing on the planet to do.

That was enough for Abby. She grabbed hold of Simone's hair, holding her head tight in place and began to thrust on her own. She moved slower than the pace Simone tried to set for her. Simone wanted frantic. She wanted Abby to come undone. She wanted Abby to come down her throat and collapse on top of her. And she wanted to suck the come from between Abby's legs when she did and then kiss Abby with the flavor still on her lips.

Simone held herself firmly in place. She didn't rush forward to meet Abby's hips, nor did she shrink away. She held herself open and receptive to whatever—and however—Abby wanted to give to her. She reflexively dropped her hands from Abby's hips and clasped them together behind her back. Years of training taught her that's where they belonged in this situation. But this *wasn't* that type of situation. Abby wasn't even close to being in control. She was taking what Simone offered, but she wouldn't know how to take it if Simone resisted. She hadn't earned the kind of submissive acquiescence that kept her hands behind her back in the past.

Not to mention that Abby was getting desperately close to coming, if the near-frantic snap of her hips was anything to judge by. Last time they were together, Abby had gotten off and Simone was left wanting. She wasn't about to let that happen again. She redirected her left hand to her own clit. She was right-hand dominant, so using her left on herself would slow her own progress toward release. And given how hard she was at the moment, she needed that minor road bump.

Besides, that left her right hand free to pursue other things. She let the fingers of her left hand work through her own folds, teasing her clit and pussy. God, this woman made her wet beyond belief. How much of that was leftover high-school fantasy, and how much was real in the moment? Simone decided she didn't care when Abby thrust particularly hard and a thrill traveled sharp and fast from her mouth straight to her cunt. She was going to come soon.

Abby's face was strained, her eyes fluttering, half open and staring at the cock as it slid between Simone's lips.

They slid shut for a moment, only to open again seconds later. Her mouth was open in a perfect "O" to match the forced shape of Simone's. Sweat beaded at her temple and ran in rivulets down her face and neck.

It wasn't enough for Simone. Abby was still too much in control, resisting the pleasure Simone offered. Simone wrapped her right hand around Abby's thigh again. She considered, very briefly, snaking it lower and letting it play in the juices running down Abby's leg. No, she wanted to lick it all away later, when she'd make Abby come a second time with her tongue.

Instead, she kneaded the firm muscles of Abby's ass, digging her fingers in hard to match the power of Abby's thrusts. She wanted Abby to feel the impression of her fingers for days after. She wanted Gavin to see evidence of her time with Abby. More than that, though, she wanted Abby to come.

Slowly, she worked her fingers toward the crack, the line separating the perfect cheeks of Abby's behind. When she reached her goal, she pulled hard, digging her fingers in and separating the flesh, exposing her goal—Abby's anus—to the air. Abby gasped and her thrust stopped mid-stroke, her cock deep in Simone's throat.

Simone met her gaze, watching her eyes as she worked her finger slowly toward the opening. When she reached it, she felt the puckered opening flex and tighten against her fingertip. Abby's grip on her hair tightened, pulling Simone to pinpoint prickling attention. Simone tweaked her own clit hard, twisting it between her thumb and forefinger. She needed to last just a little longer, to enjoy the reward of reaching her destination.

Simone circled her finger slowly around Abby's anus, teasing and gentle. Abby's eyes slid shut and still she held herself perfectly still, the cock not moving. Simone needed to get her going again before she choked for real. Simone pushed inside of Abby, one finger, just the nail, barely breaching the opening, and pulled her head back. She needed air and Abby was frozen-statue still.

Jiggling her finger just inside the rim felt impossibly good for Simone. She knew how good it felt for Abby, the barely there teasing that felt so much larger than it really was. And the delicious, dirty raunchiness of it made Simone want to push all the way in, to spread Abby open in one clean thrust. It was too soon, though. Abby wasn't ready. But she could take just a little more.

Simone spread her palm wide against the skin of Abby's buttock, keeping her finger steadily working. Gentle, slow, yet persistent movements. She pulled Abby's hips forward and opened her throat to the intrusion, once again guiding Abby through the motions, showing her how to fuck her. Abby remained still, unmoving, and Simone nudged Abby's hips back, releasing the cock with a pop and kissing the tip of it.

"Abby..." Simone jiggled her finger again, a little more assertively, her other hand still working steadily on her own clit. "Abby, baby, please, I'm so close. Please."

Simone spread her lips, holding her mouth open millimeters from the cock but not taking it in. Abby finally, slowly, slid the cock in, pausing when she hit the back of Simone's throat like Simone had taught her. She was a quick learner and Simone would reward her for that later. And then Abby pushed the cock home. Simone pressed her finger deeper, entering up to her first knuckle. Still not deep, but clearly far more than Abby was accustomed to.

Abby pulled back and thrust forward again, and again, not pausing between strokes, and Simone worked her finger deeper with every thrust until she was fucking it in and out of Abby's ass in rhythm with the stroke of the cock entering her throat.

Simone let her fingers dance across her own clit, urging herself higher. Abby was close and Simone wanted to come with Abby's cock still in her throat and her finger buried in Abby's ass. If she timed it wrong, Abby would come before her, then come to her senses and make Simone withdraw before she was ready. Abby felt too deliciously dirty and perfect for Simone to want to give that up before her orgasm.

Finally, after several more thrusts, and at a moment when Simone was sure Abby would pull out all her hair, Abby came with a high growl. Simone held her finger deep inside Abby's ass, vibrating it as fast as she could to match the tempo against her own clit. She needed to breathe, but the cock was buried deep in her throat and Abby was collapsing on top of her.

Simone's orgasm ripped through, racing out from her clit, up through her belly and chest and down through her legs. Her thighs trembled as she pushed the cock out of her mouth and removed her finger from Abby's ass.

Abby slumped to the floor next to her and Simone tried to collect her as well as she could between gasping for breath and waiting for her extremities to start working again. Abby's breathing was rough and uneven, and shudder after shudder ran the course of her body as Simone held her.

"You okay?" Simone was barely able to whisper, her vocal chords protesting the recent abuse. She swallowed, cleared her throat, and tried again. "Abby, are you okay?" It didn't come out any louder.

Abby stirred against her, turning her face farther into the crook of Simone's neck. "I'm good. Great." She rose up to look Simone in the eye. "Are you?"

Simone wanted to say she was better than okay. She was lying naked with a woman she'd fantasized about since high school, and she'd just had a killer orgasm. That *always* added up to better than okay. She settled for nodding out of respect for her voice. It needed a rest.

"Good." Abby dropped her head back to its home on Simone's shoulder. "I've never done," Simone could hear Abby blushing as she spoke, "anything like that before."

Simone kissed the top of Abby's head. "I figured." She played with the loose strands of Abby's hair and wished they'd moved to the bed before getting this comfortable together. "Do you want to talk about it?" Simone hoped Abby's answer would be no. Her throat hurt like hell and she could barely manage a croak. An entire conversation would be murder. Still, what they'd done, what she'd guided Abby through, was not standard, run-of-the-mill, vanilla sex. Abby was going to need to process it. And if she needed to do that by talking her way through it, then so be it. Simone had created the situation when she took the dildo between her lips the first time. She could face the fallout head-on.

"Is it okay if we wait?" Abby kissed Simone's clavicle. "Right now I just want to bask."

Simone nodded, her movements big enough that she knew Abby could feel her answer. Eventually they'd have to talk about what they'd done tonight, but more importantly, about what they were doing overall. They'd moved past a one-night-only event, and Simone needed to know what that meant.

For now, however, she was content to hold Abby. She eased Abby up until they were both able to stand, then led her in to bed. She was exhausted, needed sleep, and as soft as Abby's skin was, it wasn't enough to make up for the hard floor. Simone pulled Abby under the covers with her and snuggled in.

She'd put off thinking about what it all meant until tomorrow.

CHAPTER SIX

Abby was blanketed in warmth, safe and sheltered. Snow fell lightly from the ceiling, or the sky? Abby watched as the textured surface morphed into sleek, endless stars. Simone took her hand and they reached up to catch the falling snow together. They spun in circles until Abby was dizzy, but Simone held her securely in her arms. Simone eased her down until she was lying, arms still stretched over her head, on a blanket of snow. Rather than the bitter cold of winter, she felt the heat of the tropics. The snow drifted slower, sparkled brighter until Abby realized it wasn't actually snow at all. Glitter!

Simone kissed Abby slow and sweet, with gentle passion. She nipped and teased, and Abby arched up to meet her.

"Abby?" Simone pressed her lips to the small patch of skin behind Abby's ear, the one that made Abby melt.

Abby moaned and reached for Simone, but her arms wouldn't move. Abby struggled. She wanted to hold Simone, to pull her into her arms and keep her there forever. No matter what she tried, her arms wouldn't work. They were bound immobile.

Panic bloomed in her chest and she cried out. "Simone."

Warmth enveloped her. She could feel Simone pressed against her, shielding her from the night. She relaxed and Simone kissed the spot behind her ear again. Her panic receded, replaced by rising passion. Abby tilted her head, offering her neck to Simone. Her body strained for more, awakening under Simone's insistent touch.

"Abby?" Simone spoke into Abby's ear, then licked around the rim. "Wake up, baby."

Abby searched the sky for signs of her snow-glitter, but all she saw was inky blackness.

Simone licked and sucked at Abby's neck, and Abby moaned. Once again she tried to reach Simone, but her arms wouldn't respond. She arched her body into Simone, her only way to get closer. "Yes, so good..."

Abby drifted, the blackness transformed to muted gray in the same moment that Simone's lips closed around her nipple. With the sweet suction, Simone pulled Abby from sleep to awake and deep, painful arousal. Simone released her nipple, and Abby sagged against the bed and groaned.

"Good morning." Simone's breath was hot against Abby's ear. She spoke directly into it, and the heat traveled directly to Abby's cunt. God, this woman set her on fire.

"Morning." Abby spoke softly, her voice rough with sleep. Simone hovered over her, braced on one elbow. She caressed Abby's body, letting her hand roam easily but consistently lower. Abby reached for Simone and realized she couldn't move her arms for real. It wasn't just part of the dream. She jerked her hands sharply to free them, but they didn't budge.

"Careful." Simone blanketed Abby's body, her mouth at Abby's neck. She stretched one hand along the sensitive plains of Abby's arms until she reached her wrists, where they were bound. Simone held both of Abby's hands and the knot binding them together in her own. She abandoned her leisurely pace and used her other hand to cup Abby intimately. She slipped her fingers between Abby's lips and teased her clit. "I've got you."

"Oh, God." Abby strained against Simone, against her bonds, and against the fleeting tendrils of sleep still holding her mind. Abby was confused and so very turned on. Excitement flooded her and she wanted desperately to touch Simone, to feel her body beneath her fingers. She writhed under Simone, overwhelmed and speechless. "Simone? Please."

"Please what?" Simone's words were teasing and hot against Abby's throat, blurring Abby's thoughts even further.

"Please, I want to touch you." Abby again tried to free her hands.

"Shhh." Simone massaged Abby's wrists and hands, but didn't loosen the hold. "Just relax. Let me please you."

Simone continued to play with her clit, her fingers sliding without pattern or urgency.

"Why?" Abby squirmed in lustful anguish.

Simone slid one finger inside of Abby. She entered with painfully slow precision, so gentle Abby feared it was her imagination.

"Why what?" Simone asked, her eyes dark, intense, and demanding.

Abby watched as Simone lowered her mouth to Abby's chest, laving the skin with her tongue. Simone sucked Abby's nipple into her mouth and twirled her finger inside Abby's cunt at the same moment. Abby moaned, awash with heat and want. When Abby didn't answer Simone's question, Simone curled her finger against Abby's g-spot and hummed against her nipple. "Hmmm?"

"Why can't I touch you?" Abby gasped the words, unable to find her voice properly as Simone brought her body to life.

Simone sucked harder and deeper, drawing the wire of lustful intent tight between Abby's breast and her cunt. She released Abby's nipple with a loud pop, and Abby drooped into the bed and panted. The wire still buzzed, encouraged by the motion of Simone's fingers working between her legs, but not with the same urgency. The momentary reprieve made her whine with disappointment.

"Because I want you like this. Helpless and at my mercy." Simone kissed Abby, forcing her mouth open with her tongue.

Abby opened herself, enjoying the dual intrusion of tongue and fingers. God, Simone knew how to fuck, to make a woman forget everything but the sensation of the moment. She'd never been tied up before; it was another on a growing list of firsts with Simone. The fabric dug into her wrists and stung in a low ache that echoed the divine pressure building deep in her belly. Abby focused on how being restrained made her feel. Infinitely frustrated because she wanted very much to touch Simone, to chase the ripples of excitement over her smooth skin, but beyond that, she felt exhilarated. Being restrained was beyond the fringe, beyond the scope of her safe history with sex. It fell in the category of paddles intended to brand words on flesh, of deep-throating strap-ons, and of fucking against a car while a crowded party continued a few feet away. In a word, it was Simone, and that thrilled Abby. She pulled against her restraints and moaned.

"You like this." Simone's smile was smug. She pressed her forehead to Abby's and said, "I like it, too."

Simone withdrew her hand, leaving Abby empty and adrift. Abby whimpered. God, she wanted those fingers back inside her. "Please." It seemed she said little else to Simone.

"I want to show you. You're *so* wet," Simone said.

Simone brought her fingers to Abby's mouth and traced her bottom lip gently. Abby's mouth fell open and she darted her tongue out to taste Simone's fingers. Abby licked her lips, then curled her tongue around Simone's finger. She sucked it into her mouth. The memory of Simone fucking her fingers—coated with Abby's desire—into Abby's mouth had haunted Abby since their first time together. She'd never experienced something so primal and sensual and invadingly intimate prior to that night. She wanted Simone to push into her again, to make her feel deliciously violated all over again.

"Ah-ah! Greedy." Simone shook her head, an amused smile on her lips. She removed her hand when Abby tried to suck her fingers into her mouth. Simone held Abby's gaze, her eyes hooded and her pupils blown wide, as she slipped her fingers between her own lips. She sucked them in deep and groaned, then retracted them. She licked and sucked the skin at the base of her fingers, then massaged her tongue over the length, all the while staring into Abby's eyes.

"God." Abby arched off the bed, her hands held immobile by Simone's binding, and captured Simone in a sloppy, wet kiss. Simone's fingers were trapped between them, and she licked them inside of Simone's mouth. It was hot, tangy, and highly erotic.

Simone moved her fingers into Abby's mouth, gliding them against her tongue, and ended the kiss. She sat up so no part of her body touched Abby's save the fingers owning Abby's mouth.

With Simone in full view for the first time, Abby was immediately aware of only one thing: Simone was wearing a strap-on. It was much larger than the one Abby had selected the night before, and Abby gaped. Simone withdrew her fingers and chuckled. How had Abby missed *that*? She forced herself to look away. She sought out Simone's eyes and was stunned by the force of desire she found there. Simone's face was heavy with lust and need. Abby gasped.

"Hi," Abby said. She needed something to break the building tension.

"I'm going to fuck you, Abby." Simone's voice was deathly serious. "Okay?"

Simone was a sexy, dark goddess. The long, lean lines of her body glowed in the early morning light that streaked in around the curtains. She settled back onto her heels and regarded Abby. The muscles in her abdomen twitched and Abby's mouth watered. What she wouldn't give to trace the ridges with her fingers at that moment.

Abby nodded, dazed. Simone was going to fuck her. Abby couldn't think. "Please."

Simone stood and walked to the end of the bed. Abby could feel Simone's eyes on her, traveling over her body, as sure and steady and as arousing as Simone's touch. Bumps rose on her skin as her excitement bubbled to the surface. She shivered and squeezed her thighs together. Just a little pressure, that's all she needed.

Simone gripped her ankles and forced her legs apart. She stretched them wide and pinned them in place with her hands, her fingers flexing and releasing like a pulse.

"I'm tempted to untie you so you can show me how you touch yourself." Simone stared at Abby's pussy and Abby's skin flared with heat. She squirmed and tried to fold her legs together. Simone strengthened her hold on Abby's ankles and held her open. "Stop that." Simone's voice was cutting, and Abby felt like a scolded child.

"I'm sorry." Abby struggled to hold herself open. She'd never felt so exposed and vulnerable. Simone's scrutiny was unnervingly intense.

Simone moved her gaze up and met Abby's. She looked confused. "Why are you trying to hide? You're beautiful."

Abby swallowed. She tried to look away, but found she couldn't. "I've never…"

Simone shook her head with a bemused smile. "Oh, the things I want to do to you."

Abby couldn't breathe. Her lungs pulled tight and burned, and still all Abby could focus on was Simone and her unholy influence. Abby would do anything for this woman. She finally gulped air into her lungs, and the pinpoint black dots receded from her field of vision.

"Okay." Abby nodded. Whatever Simone wanted, Abby would give it to her. "Okay," she said it again, her voice stronger the second time.

Simone smiled and crawled onto the bed. She placed small, fleeting kisses along the length of Abby's legs and stopped when she reached Abby's pubis.

"For now, I'm going to do this." Simone found Abby's clit with her tongue. She circled it a few times, then flicked over the very tip. The barely there touch made Abby gasp and strain for more.

Simone forced her legs farther apart and held her firmly in place. She continued to tease and lick Abby's clit, never touching solidly enough to be truly felt. Abby grew harder and she could feel moisture pooling between her thighs. She was so ready, all it would take was one purposeful caress and Abby would fly apart. Simone was teasing her.

"Simone, please."

"Yes." The heat of Simone's answer washed over her and Abby quivered in anticipation. Simone spread Abby open with her fingers but didn't touch Abby where she needed it most. After a moment, Simone asked, "Are you ready?"

"Oh, God, yes."

Abby hadn't finished answering before Simone was on her. She enclosed Abby's clit inside her lips, enveloping her in warm, wet heat and suction. Abby arched off the bed. Simone wasn't strong enough to hold her down and she moved with Abby, riding the wave of her desire. Simone sucked gently and flicked her tongue relentlessly over Abby's clit. Abby's body drew tighter and tighter, and she pulled hard against her restraints, and her body pulled into itself.

When she thought she could take no more, Simone licked over her one last time, and the tension pooling inside Abby released. Her body fractured and fell. She floated on a cloud of bliss, peripherally aware of Simone pressing an easy kiss to her mons.

"So beautiful." Simone's repeated words skimmed Abby's consciousness. She was too deeply awash.

Simone's hands were everywhere, smoothing over her body and extending her pleasure. Then she gripped her at the waist and flipped her onto her stomach. Abby had barely registered what had happened when Simone pulled Abby onto her knees and then thrust cleanly inside of her.

Abby's face smashed into the pillow, and though she was still recovering from her first orgasm, her body rose to meet Simone thrust for thrust. Pressure, barely released, started to build again, and when Simone placed her hand on Abby's shoulder and pushed her into bed, Abby cried out with excitement.

"Stay down like that." Simone grunted out the words, her grip firm on Abby's neck. She dug the fingers of her other hand into Abby's hip and heaved her ass up. She thrust into Abby, the dildo reaching deeper than Abby had ever felt. "Okay."

Abby nodded and gulped air. She couldn't speak.

Simone pressed against her neck one last time, then placed both hands on Abby's hips. She withdrew and slammed home over and over with such vehement power that Abby's hips collapsed into the bed and she moaned ceaselessly.

"I said like this." Simone pulled her ass into the air again and spanked it hard. She gently rubbed the sting, and the tender touch soothed and confused Abby. She didn't know if she wanted Simone to do it more or never again.

It didn't matter because Simone didn't ask what Abby wanted. She dug her fingers into Abby's hips and resumed her pounding, relentless pace.

"Abby, can you come like this?" Simone voice was strained and Abby wanted to see her face. The soft fabric of Simone's sheet grew rough as Abby's face rubbed over it again and again.

"Abby, answer me." Simone continued thrusting and Abby couldn't think. What was the question? Could she come?

"Yes, God, yes." Abby was close. So very close.

Tension built inside her, driven higher by Simone's frantic rhythm, until she couldn't take another exquisite moment. She shuddered and came hard in wave after wave of pleasure. Abby collapsed, beneath Simone, spanking be damned. She couldn't remain on her knees if the devil himself were in the room with them.

Simone thrust a few more times, then cried out. She fell on top of Abby and panted into Abby's neck. She lay there for several moments until her breathing calmed. Abby knew Simone would move soon and she didn't want her to. She groaned in protest.

Simone chuckled and said, "That was awesome." She squeezed Abby's waist gently, then kissed her cheek. "I'm going to pull out now, okay?"

Abby nodded, but she wasn't happy about it. "Okay."

Simone withdrew slowly, but she didn't move off Abby. She lay there, her cock dangling between Abby's thighs, and stretched her hands up to where Abby was secured to the bed. As she worked the knots loose, Simone pressed lazy kisses to Abby's neck and chin. Abby felt the moment the bind slipped away, but Simone held her hands in place. She massaged the skin around her wrists, over her hands, then back up her arms.

"Roll over?" Simone lifted her weight off Abby and Abby moved onto her back. She wrapped her arms around Simone's waist and pulled her body flush again.

"Mmmm." Abby ran her hands over Simone's skin, touching to her heart's content now that she was allowed. "Good morning."

"I'd really like to stay and do this all day," Simone adjusted her position until the dildo was once again snuggled between Abby's thighs. She eased it back and forth, teasing along Abby entrance. "But I need to get to the office."

With that, Simone was gone and Abby was left stretched on the bed, cold and not nearly ready to get up.

Simone showered and dressed in a smart, sexy suit that made Abby want to undress her again. The closer Simone got to leaving for work, the further she moved away from Abby. By the time they left her apartment, Simone was a closed door to Abby. The fire that had been surface level earlier was so deeply buried, Abby questioned if it'd ever really been there.

Simone held the door open for Abby but wouldn't look her in the eye. Abby stopped and put her hand on Simone's arm. "Can I see you again?"

Simone's smile was small and controlled. "I'll call you."

CHAPTER SEVEN

Simone didn't even wait for the door to close behind her before she started talking. "I saw her again."

"Oh?" Dr. Donovan collected his tablet and pencil. He started writing notes as he settled into his seat. "How did that go?"

Simone sank into the couch. She didn't even try to hold herself upright. "I don't know."

Dr. Donovan stared at her, his pencil poised over the paper.

"She was at the Christmas party with her not-boyfriend again. I left as soon as they arrived, but she called my house."

"You answered?"

She'd told Dr. Donovan about the string of unanswered phone calls.

"I didn't realize it was her. I'd just walked in the door and didn't check caller ID." Prior to that, Abby had always called her cell phone. It hadn't even occurred to her that it might be Abby calling her home phone.

"What did you do when you figured it out?"

"We…talked." She'd have to disclose what they talked about at some point, but she'd opened with fucking against the car a few visits ago and gotten no response. There was no reason to lead with phone sex this time around.

"About?"

She laughed dryly. "Sex. I think she called just to get off."

"Do you really?"

It had definitely been the end result of their conversation, but had that been Abby's only goal?

"I don't know. Maybe?"

"I see."

Simone shifted in her seat, and the leather creaked as she moved. "Can't you just skip the head-shrinking bullshit and tell me what to do?" She knew the answer but had to ask. Dr. Donovan was the smartest man she'd ever met. He had to have some insights into her fucked-up-ness. If he didn't, she was right and properly screwed.

He stared at her a long time, then eventually set the tablet and pencil on the table between them.

"I think you need to decide how you feel about her and what you want to do about it."

She started to speak and then stopped. She shook her head and tried again. "I really have no idea."

"You have a deeply connected link between sex and power and love. The three are tightly interwoven for you, more so than average. That's neither good nor bad, but it is insightful. You've taken certain actions with Abby. With that correlation in mind, what do you think those actions mean?"

"I don't understand."

"When you had sex, was it the same as with other women? Or was it different? Did you demand control like you normally do?"

Simone suspected Dr. Donovan already knew the answer, which was good. She wasn't prepared to tell him that she'd dropped to her knees willingly and without being made to submit. She'd allowed Abby to fuck her mouth, practically begged her to do it. And then she'd fucking snuggled afterward. *Snuggled!*

She'd tied her up and fucked her the next morning just to prove to herself that she could. It'd been more about reclaiming herself than claiming Abby.

"You don't have to answer that, Simone, but you do need to think about the answer."

"But none of that matters if I can't trust her."

"Are you sure it really bothers you?"

"Of course it does. Honesty is important to me."

"Let me ask a different way. Are you sure you haven't grabbed onto this as a point of contention, as a way of drawing a metaphorical line in the sand? Are you sure it's not just a distraction to keep you from evaluating how you really feel?"

Simone spent the remainder of her visit staring at him. Not out of defiance as she'd done in the past, but rather because she had no idea what to say.

She had no idea how she felt about Abby beyond the knowledge that the woman commanded all her attention whether she was in the room or not. Was that an emotion or an obsession?

CHAPTER EIGHT

A re you sure this is a good idea?" Gavin asked the question for the fiftieth time, and if he didn't hand over his phone soon, Abby was going to snatch it from him and clobber him over the head with it.

"For the love of God, Gavin. Give me the damn phone already." Through an act of extreme effort, Abby didn't yell. Gavin had questioned her because he loved her. He wasn't trying to stand between her and true love. At least that's what she told herself.

Not to mention the true-love bit was a stretch. It'd been two weeks since she'd seen Simone. The last thing Simone had said to Abby as she showed her the door the next morning was, "I'll call you." It was too clichéd for words. No matter how hard she tried, the total radio silence hurt Abby's feelings.

"I know, but she said she'd call." Gavin spoke kindly, patiently, but it didn't curb Abby's desire to club him if he didn't stop trying to protect her. Gavin smiled and said, "Don't you think she'd do that if she wanted to see you?"

Abby understood the words Gavin was saying. She'd said them to herself over and over. And she believed them enough to keep her from calling Simone before now. This morning she'd reached her breaking point. She was tired of being a stupid, afraid little girl. She wanted Simone, and instead of going and getting her, she was sitting by like a princess waiting to be rescued. It was time for her to rescue herself. If she was lucky, then Simone would agree to be a part of that. If not, she'd move on. This was it. Make or break for their relationship. She was done waiting.

Abby looked out the glass wall that encased Gavin's office. She had a clear view of Simone at work in her office on the other side of the bullpen. Simone leaned into her computer, elbow on the desk, fingertips pressed to her temple. Deep lines creased the middle of her brow. Whatever she was reading wasn't making her happy. Abby wanted to talk to her, but she wasn't quite brave enough to take the few steps from Gavin's office to Simone's. The phone was the next-best option.

"Gavin. For the last fucking time, I'm sure. Dial the number." Abby bit out the words. Gavin had frustrated her to the point where her mood matched Simone's.

"As long as you're sure." Gavin dialed the number and turned over his office phone.

"Privacy?" Abby knew she was pushing her luck, but damnit, Gavin owed her for years of playing the happy, devoted girlfriend. You'd think a girl could get a little sex in exchange for that.

Gavin shook his head and walked out of the office right as Simone picked up.

"Simone Davies." Simone looked across into Gavin's office a half second after the greeting. "Abby." She whispered the name.

"Hi, Simone." Now that Abby had her on the line, she couldn't remember what to say. She'd outlined an entire script, but it escaped her in the moment.

"What are you doing?" The momentary softness in Simone's voice disappeared.

"You didn't call." Perfect. Abby sounded like a jilted lover, exactly what she didn't want.

"Abby. I wanted…" Simone sighed and shook her head. "I'm at work."

"So you wanted to call?" And now she sounded like the clingy girlfriend.

"I can't do this." Simone moved to hang up.

"Wait!" Abby yelled loud enough that Simone probably heard her through the glass walls, as well as the phone.

Simone put the phone up to her ear again but didn't speak. She looked pointedly at Abby. She was not amused.

"I don't understand what the problem is. You know he's not really my boyfriend. I'm single. You're single. We're great together. What's holding you back?" Abby spoke in a rush. She'd convinced Simone to listen, and she didn't want to waste the opportunity.

"You really don't get it, do you?" Simone stared at Abby, her eyes hard and angry.

"Tell me. Whatever you need. I'll do it."

Simone pressed her fingers to the bridge of her nose and muttered under her breath. When she met Abby's gaze again, she spoke clearly and carefully. "You really want to do this? Here? Where I work. Where Gavin works?"

"You've given me no choice." That wasn't entirely true. Abby could have gone to Simone's house again. In fact, she had. She'd sat in her car across the street for almost an hour. Ultimately, she'd driven home without knocking on Simone's door. At the time, it'd seemed more important that Simone chase her for a change. Now that logic just seemed silly.

"Fine. You lie."

"What? No. I haven't lied to you." Abby hesitated. She'd lied to Simone routinely in high school, but surely Simone was able to get past that. It'd been a full decade since graduation. Abby had grown since then, changed for the better. Simone had to see that.

"Maybe."

"Simone, you have to believe me."

"Okay, I believe you. You haven't lied to me recently. But that doesn't change anything."

The relief Abby felt when Simone agreed was destroyed by her next sentence. A sinking feeling settled in her chest.

"What do you mean?" It took a couple of tries, but Abby finally forced the words out. Simone looked far too calm, like she wasn't about to tear Abby apart from the inside out.

"If you're not lying to me, that means that you're lying to every other single person in this firm. Either way, you're lying to someone."

"He's my friend, Simone. I *help* my friends."

"Then Gavin's lucky to have you."

"What about you?" They could see one another, but two layers of glass and a multitude of office activity obscured the view. It felt like they were much farther apart.

"What about me?"

"You have me." Whether Simone wanted her or not, Abby belonged to her. "Are you lucky?"

"I don't." Simone's voice trembled slightly, but otherwise she looked and sounded unaffected. "I don't have you. I can't. I don't trust you, Abby. It's that simple."

"Simone, please." Abby was out of words. Her heart was breaking. "Let me try. One date. Just let me see you. Please."

"Good-bye, Abby." Simone held up her hand, and Abby wasn't sure if she was signaling Abby to stop or if it was an aborted attempt to wave. Simone hung up the phone.

Abby held the handset to her ear and listened to the dial tone. She started crying and couldn't stop. Tears slid silently down her face as she watched Simone return to her work.

Gavin stood just outside the door. He smiled and asked, "How did it go?"

"Not great." Abby sniffled.

"What happened?"

"She doesn't trust me."

"Oh, honey." Gavin wrapped her in a hug. "I'm sorry."

"It's over." Abby wiped her eyes with a tissue Gavin supplied. She was done crying when Simone didn't care enough to even stop working. She'd begged and it clearly wasn't enough. Now it was time to get on with the moving on. Besides, she could cry later, without an audience.

"Come on. I'm taking you to lunch." Gavin guided her to the elevator with his arm snug around her shoulders. And as good as it felt to have him on her side, she couldn't silence the voice that lived inside that sinking feeling as it whispered it was a mistake. Every time she acted the part of Gavin's devoted girlfriend, she galvanized herself as a liar in Simone's eyes.

Abby glanced toward Simone's office one last time while she waited for the elevator. Simone didn't look up from her work.

❖

Gavin knocked on Simone's open office door and said, "You have a minute?"

Fucking perfect. She'd told his *not*-girlfriend that she couldn't see her again, and now Gavin decided to visit. How polite did she need to be? Whatever he was about to say, she was certain, would cross professional boundaries but could have a profound impact on her career nonetheless.

"Yes, of course." Simone smiled as she stood and gestured to the open chair. If they were going to talk, she preferred to do it seated like civilized people.

Gavin nodded, tightly and succinctly, and closed the door behind himself. Apparently he preferred to keep their conversation private as well. He sat in the offered chair and spent a few moments inspecting his cuticles. From Simone's vantage point, they looked perfectly manicured.

Simone reclaimed her own seat and resisted the urge to rush into the conversation. Waiting for Gavin to speak first was the only smart play. If she was patient, eventually he'd say whatever he came to say.

Eventually, Gavin raised his eyes to meet Simone's gaze and said, "This isn't easy for me, but you need to know certain things. Abby needs you to understand."

Simone nodded and folded her hands on her desk.

"No one in this office is aware, and be very clear, I'll fire you if you tell anyone." Gavin spoke with the passion of a litigator, and Simone believed every word. "I'm gay."

Simone let Gavin's confession sit between them like an unexploded mine. Under-reaction was in her best interest. The less she acted like it was a big deal, the less threatened he'd be. And the words "I'll fire you" came far too close to his declaration for Simone to dismiss them. Simone knew he couldn't fire her as easily as that.

It'd take some serious campaigning and negotiating, but ultimately he'd be able to make it happen.

Besides, she already knew he was gay. His big reveal was a non-event.

"So am I." Simone said it as conciliation. Even though Simone was pretty certain everyone in the office knew about her at this point, she hoped Gavin would see it as a bargaining point. Why would she care if he was gay when she was herself?

"I know." Gavin looked at her like she was an idiot who left a bad taste in his mouth.

He sat there, silent and evaluating her. Simone had work to do, work that made him money, and he'd rather she sit quietly while he stared. It was unnerving.

"Gavin, how can I help you?"

"Abby is a good woman." Gavin was entitled to his opinion, skewed though it might be by his friendship.

Simone didn't have to agree with him. "Okay."

"But you don't agree?"

"I'm not sure why that's relevant." Simone was a reluctant participant in this no-win conversation. She damned well wasn't going to volunteer any information.

With that statement, Gavin resumed staring without speaking. Simone debated returning to her brief, but somehow, winning their staring contest seemed more important. She folded her hands over her desk and regarded him impassively. She'd wait.

Gavin broke first. "She loves you and you're totally blowing it."

Fuck. That wasn't what Simone expected. Certainly not what she wanted. She arched her brow and tilted her head to the side. If she waited long enough, he'd say more and the chance of her making an ass of herself would go down exponentially.

Gavin shook his head, and the calm facade slipped a little. "She's not the first person to beard for a friend."

Simone shifted in her seat. She wasn't sure which was worse, Gavin pretending to be nice or his burst of temper. "It's still a lie."

"Do you really think that? I value my privacy. Abby knows that and helps me keep my personal business personal. Surely you can understand that."

She could understand it in theory, but she'd never been afforded the luxury of a closet.

"I'm not going to out you, Gavin." As much as his cowardice pissed her off, she wasn't foolish enough to put herself in jeopardy for the sake of disclosure.

"Don't make this about me."

"But it is, isn't it? She's lying to protect you." She was dangerously close to crossing a line and needed to remember the influence Gavin wielded over her career.

Gavin's face flushed red and he took several deep breaths before speaking. "My family life is…complicated. She wants me to be able to come out when I'm ready."

"Why?" Simone stood and placed both hands flat against the surface of her desk. "Why is she willing to let you decide? To go to such an extreme to protect that right when she threw me out long before I was ready for that kind of exposure?" Simone had been scared, uncertain, and desperate for her friend to understand. Instead she'd been betrayed and laughed at.

Understanding flashed on Gavin's face and he stood. He stared at Simone like he'd uncovered a great secret and it was a great disappointment. "That's what this is about? You're still mad about something she did when she was a kid? Seriously?" He straightened his jacket and headed toward the door, a look of disgust on his face. He paused at the door and turned back to her. "Grow up, Simone."

Then he left.

Chapter Nine

The call to Dr. Donovan went to voice mail. Rather than leave a message, she hung up and dialed again. She repeated the process until he finally picked up on the fourth call. His voice was as calm as ever. "Malcolm Donovan speaking."

"She's his beard."

"Yes." Dr. Donovan didn't hesitate. He went with the conversation even though Simone didn't bother to introduce herself first. "I thought you understood that."

"Gavin thinks I don't care about the fact that she's lying. Because no matter what you call it, she's still lying."

"Who's Gavin?"

That's right. She hadn't mentioned him by name yet. She didn't want him to have that much power over her. "The pretend boyfriend."

"Okay, and what do you care about, according to Gavin?"

"He thinks I'm still mad about high school." Simone felt silly saying it aloud, but it didn't change the depth of her emotions. Abby had cut her very deeply in the past. She wasn't sure she was ready to forgive that.

"Are you?"

"Yes, I think so." It felt good to say it. It took some of the pressure off her chest, like a release valve had been activated.

"But?" Dr. Donovan's voice held that unaffected, yet still interested quality. She pictured him with his pencil furiously scribbling notes about her possible breakthrough.

"I still want her." Her desire to have Abby—to be with her, to touch her, to possess her, to make her submit, all of it—pressed in on Simone until it was so thick she could taste it on her tongue.

"Which do you want more?" He asked the question gently.

"What do you mean?" She was still heady from the realization that she held tight to old resentments she thought she'd released years ago.

"You have to choose, Simone. Do you want her or your anger? You have to let one go in order to fully have the other."

The pressure in her chest increased and she feared she might black out. Hopefully someone would find her and call 9-1-1 if that happened.

"Those are my only choices?"

"That's it."

"Okay. Thanks, Dr. Donovan. I'll let you get back to work." She wanted to keep him on the phone, demand a third, less painful option, but knew he was right. There was no point delaying good-bye.

"Good luck, Simone. I look forward to learning what you decide."

She disconnected the call. She looked forward to learning about her decision as well.

CHAPTER TEN

"Gavin came to see me after you left." Simone entered Abby's apartment and set a bottle of cheap champagne on the table.

"Oh?" When Abby had left Simone that afternoon, she hadn't expected to ever see her again. And here Simone was, standing in her kitchen.

"Glasses?" Simone peeled away the foil from the cork and pulled a corkscrew from her breast pocket.

Abby shook her head. She wasn't quite ready to forgive and forget. It wasn't okay for Simone to show up and expect everything to be fine.

"You don't have glasses?" Simone looked pointedly at the rack of crystal stemware hanging beneath the cupboard. She pulled the cork from the bottle. It foamed slightly but didn't overflow.

"I have glasses. I'm not sure I want to drink with you. Why are you here?"

"I told you, Gavin came to see me."

"And what did he say?"

"That you and I should spend some time drinking."

"He said that?" Abby wasn't convinced. Gavin was a poor drinker and generally didn't encourage it in others.

"More or less." Simone held out the bottle, but Abby refused to take it. She needed a better answer. Simone sighed. "He said you love me. He said I'm blowing it. And I'm still not sure what I'm doing here because nobody has ever come close to hurting me as much as you did."

"That was high school. Let it go already." Abby took the champagne and set it on the table. She didn't plan to drink any until this conversation was done, one way or another.

"I'm trying. I thought I had. And then I saw you again, and you're still lying to people in order to be popular."

"It's not the same, Simone." Abby shook her head sadly. If this was how Simone really felt, they had no hope as a couple.

Simone looked like she wanted to believe her.

"The things I did back then were so…hurtful. And I'm sorry about that. But this is different. I'm protecting Gavin, not hurting him."

"That's the first time you've said you were sorry."

"Really?" Abby had thought about apologizing so many times. Could this really be the first time she'd said the words to Simone?

Simone nodded and looked down. She studied the floor and Abby studied Simone.

"I am. Sorry. If I could take it all back, I would. I regretted it at the time, and I've regretted it every day since."

"Okay."

Abby met Simone's probing gaze, her eyes raw with emotion, sadness, grief, wanting.

"Okay? You believe me? That easy?"

"Of course it's not that easy. But I haven't been able to get over you for more than a decade. I don't think more time will help."

"So what does that mean?"

"It means…" Simone grabbed the bottle and picked at the label. "It means that I want to try, and I think that calls for a drink."

"Really?" Abby took the champagne from Simone and drank straight from the bottle.

Simone nodded and kissed Abby before she could swallow. Champagne trickled from her lips and into Simone's mouth. Simone laughed again and licked the drips from Abby's chin. "Oh my God, that's nasty shit."

"Why did you buy it?" Abby took another drink. The bubbles tickled, which she liked, but the alcohol tasted too sweet. She forced it down, then took another swig. Simone could afford a better brand, but this suited Abby. A day like today deserved a nice cheap drunk.

"Because..." Simone took the bottle from Abby and stared into Abby's eyes. "The last time we drank together, this is what you liked."

"You remember that?" Abby trembled under Simone's intense scrutiny. Simone was right. It was the brand she drank in high school. It was cheap and easy to get her hands on.

Simone set the champagne on the table without looking away. It hit with a ring of finality. She scanned the length of Abby's body, pausing briefly at Abby's chest, then resuming the upward climb until she held Abby's gaze once again. She took a visible breath and said, "I remember everything."

"Oh."

Simone worked the buttons on Abby's shirt free. She kissed low on Abby's neck and Abby melted inside. Her thoughts went from scrambled to completely absent with the briefest touch of Simone's lips.

"You don't think we should talk more?" Abby dropped her arms to her side to make it easier for Simone to slide her shirt down her shoulders.

Simone nodded and took a step back. "If that's what you want."

Abby's head cleared. "It's important."

"Okay. You go first." Simone slid a chair out and sat at the kitchen table. Every move was practiced and graceful. She sat upright, her spine straight and at attention.

They needed to discuss so many things. Their history, their future, and all the things Simone made Abby feel. She had no idea where to start. She decided to go with the most pressing need—the ever-present fire in her body when Simone was near—and leave the past for later.

"Sex." Abby blurted out the word, then felt her body and face flush with heat.

Simone smirked. "Yes, please."

"I've never…" Abby took a deep breath. There were certain things she needed to say. "The things we've done…I've never—"

"Done anything like that before? I figured." Simone folded her hands in her lap and waited.

"No. I mean yes, you're right, but what I was trying to say was I've never felt like that before. It was very…intense." Abby was flustered. She needed to sit but wanted to remain close to Simone. She settled on her knees at Simone's feet and looked up into Simone's eyes.

Simone smiled and caressed Abby's cheek, then tapped Abby's shoulder. "Back straight."

Abby lengthened her spine in her best mirror of Simone's posture. She wasn't sure how much she was allowed to say, to ask, but she needed to know more. "Will it always be like that?"

"Intense?" Simone played idly with Abby's hair. "I hope so."

"What about…" Abby searched for the right words. "You have a lot of accessories."

"I like toys." Simone kissed Abby languidly, and Abby opened herself to Simone's exploring tongue. Simone had a way of making Abby feel like she was completely inside of her. Before Abby was ready, Simone ended the kiss. "So do you."

Abby did. Very much. But before Simone, she'd had no idea.

Simone looked at Abby closely and seemed to come to a conclusion. "Abby, I like certain…elements to be included during sex, and that doesn't always mean toys."

"Tell me what to do." Abby was poised on a precipice. On one side lay safety and the known. The other held the answer to why Simone moved with such power, carried herself with such precision, and why Abby yearned to please her so desperately.

"How about we take it day by day and see where that leads us?" Simone stroked Abby's hair with one hand, and with the other she caressed Abby's cheek with the backs of her fingers.

"Yes." The words escaped her as a breathy whisper. Abby felt light-headed, like her very ability to breathe depended on Simone's next words.

"Okay." Simone smiled and kissed Abby gently.

"What else?" Abby asked. There had to be more than just Simone's easy willingness to let their relationship happen. The growing pulse that traveled through her demanded that she learn all Simone's secrets, every place on her body that made her shiver and moan.

"Now you make me come." Simone stood and removed her pants and panties with perfunctory movements. She folded them both neatly and laid them on the table next to the forgotten champagne bottle. She unbuttoned her shirt, but left it and her bra on. Abby watched with her mouth open. The out-of-control urgency was completely gone. Simone was calm and precise. Perfectly in control.

Simone reclaimed her seat and spread her legs obscenely wide. She was positively dripping wet. Abby whimpered and reached out to run her fingers through Simone's folds. Simone's legs closed before Abby could touch.

"Your mouth only, please." Simone spread her legs again.

Abby had fantasized about Simone a thousand times before, and none of those fantasies took place in her kitchen. The cold tile pressed hard against her knees, and she shifted to ease the pressure. Simone watched her with feigned disinterest. She didn't encourage Abby to hurry, but waited patiently, like sitting with her thighs spread and her cunt on display was perfectly comfortable. If not for the slight tremor and the stunning amount of wetness, Abby would have thought Simone was bored. That needed to change.

"Am I allowed to talk?" Abby edged closer. She asked the question, then licked the length of Simone's labia.

"That depends." Simone's legs tensed, but her voice remained even. "Would it turn you on more for me to say you can't?"

Abby clenched with a new wave of arousal. "Apparently so." She licked Simone again, flicking her tongue over Simone's clit before sitting back.

"I think we should save that for another time. For now I want you to be able to ask questions when you have them." Simone placed her hand lightly on Abby's head and guided her forward. "Continue, please."

"Yes."

With Simone's hand on the back of her head, Abby wanted nothing more than to please her. It was a simple, unassuming touch, but so much rested on that contact. Abby took it as a sign of Simone's breaking control. She was no longer content to sit back and wait, and Abby was thankful for the admission.

Abby licked along Simone's length again, edging her tongue between the outer lips. She moved slow and steady, savoring every moment. She slipped easily in Simone's desire, the taste hot and perfect on her palate. Abby rolled her tongue over Simone's clit, circling it, then flicking the tip rapidly until she heard Simone's breath hitch and felt her legs clench. Then she started over again, lapping at Simone's opening until the pressure on her head increased ever so slightly. One more sign that Simone was unraveling, and it drove Abby to work harder. She made her way to Simone's clit again and sucked it into her mouth. Simone was hard and exposed in her excitement. Abby held her gently between her teeth, letting her jaw work easily. She continued to manipulate her tongue over the sensitive nub, flicking and circling until Simone trembled on the verge of release.

"Inside, please." Simone gripped her own leg with her left hand, and her fingernails cut white, crescent impressions into her flesh. Abby envisioned a similar set on her scalp.

She continued to lick, testing Simone's limits. She brought her fingers to Simone's opening, and the thought of filling her made Abby weak with desire.

Simone grabbed her wrist in one hand and stopped her from entering. She pulled Abby's mouth from her, forcing her head back until she looked Simone in the eye.

"Hands behind your back, please." Simone dropped to her knees between Abby and the chair. She guided Abby's hands where she wanted them and demonstrated that she should clasp them together like a soldier at ease.

Simone was close and her breath was hot against Abby's bare neck and shoulders. Abby clasped her right hand in her left as Simone requested, and her breasts jutted out, pressing into Simone urgently. "Like this?" she asked, her voice a raspy whisper.

"Hmmm." Simone tilted her head to the side. "Let me help you remember." Simone brought both hands between them and cupped Abby's breasts through her bra. She squeezed and massaged until Abby was on the brink of begging for more. Then Simone slid her arms around Abby's body and released the clasps. Her bra sagged but remained in place.

Simone slowly, patiently snaked her finger under the bottom edge of the fabric and circled to the front. She moved with leisurely ease that was at odds with the urgent fire filling Abby. When Simone reached the front again, she slipped the cups up until Abby was fully exposed. Simone lifted the fabric over Abby's head and eased it down her arms until it met at her clasped hands. Abby started to remove it completely and Simone stopped her.

"No, keep your hands like that."

Simone kissed the side of Abby's neck, and the sensation traveled over her skin like a wave. She almost collapsed with joy. Then she felt Simone's hands in motion, tying the bra snug around her wrists. She couldn't move her hands now even if she wanted. The thrill of being restrained caught Abby off guard. She wasn't supposed to like any of this, but it felt amazing. She struggled lightly to test the bond and Simone cinched it tighter.

Simone pulled back until Abby could see her eyes, then quietly asked, "Okay?"

Abby nodded, jerky and so very certain. "Yes."

"Good." Simone kissed Abby again. Gentle approval washed over her with Simone's touch, followed by pressing need.

Simone cupped her breasts again, her touch bordering on reverent. She dropped her head to kiss first one nipple, then the other. Abby arched as Simone opened her mouth and sucked her nipple inside. She was gentle at first, but the pressure gradually increased until all Abby was, all she would ever be, was captured in that one pinpoint perfect place in time. Heat pulsed through her like a firebrand, and she almost ruptured when Simone took the other side between her fingers and squeezed hard enough to match the pressure of her mouth.

Abby screamed. Or she thought she did. Or maybe she didn't make a sound at all. She was lost to the sensation, to the rushing blood in her body. All external sound faded to oblivious periphery. And then Simone sucked harder, squeezed harder, and Abby flew apart. She was so wet, her panties and slacks ruined, as her desire overflowed. Simone whispered in her ear, indistinguishable words that eased her through the tide of orgasm. She came back to herself slowly, and the ocean roaring in her ears receded until she was left quivering on her floor, held upright by a smug-looking Simone. Abby closed her eyes and rested her head against Simone's shoulder.

"Fuck," Abby moaned. She struggled to regain her posture.

"Easy. It's okay." Simone stroked her hair as she held her. "Have you ever done that before?" Simone cupped her breast and softly grazed her thumb over the nipple.

Abby yelped. "No. But I'd like to do it again some time." She smiled and forced her body to relax into Simone's touch. Simone continued to stroke her nipple through the pain until Abby was panting and ready for more.

"Good." Simone kissed Abby lightly on the lips. Then she grabbed the bottle of champagne from the table. "Thirsty?"

"Yeah." Abby was parched.

Simone took a drink, then brought her mouth to Abby's. She shared the liquid through their kiss, and Abby licked at Simone's mouth to consume every taste. The next drink, Simone offered to Abby directly from the bottle. She held it to Abby's lips and tipped it back. Abby gulped down swallow after swallow, until she could hold no more. The excess flowed down her neck and chest, and still Simone kept pouring.

Simone finally pulled the bottle away and set it on the floor next to them. She licked her way over Abby's throat and chest, flicking her tongue gently over Abby's nipples. She worked her way back up to Abby's neck, sucking hard on the skin there. The sensation of her blood being pulled to the surface, disrupted from its normal flow by the demanding suction of Simone's mouth, excited Abby. Abby could only imagine how much makeup it would take to cover the mark for work the next day, yet she didn't want Simone to ever stop.

This woman had proved herself capable of sucking an orgasm out of Abby from two different points on her body—first her clit, then her nipple. She'd gladly give her body up to experimentation to see if they could expand the list of successes. Simone released her evenly, then licked over the mark with the flat of her tongue.

Abby was still recovering as Simone returned to her seated position above her. Once again, she tapped Abby on the shoulder.

"Finish, please."

Simone sat before Abby, statue perfect, poised and unflustered, as Abby gasped for breath. The sight of Simone spreading herself open, wet desire clinging to her lips and glistening over her inner thighs, excited Abby further. How did Simone manage to look so calm? It irritated the hell out of Abby, and it was her personal mission from this moment on to upend Simone's composure.

"Are you always in control?" Abby asked the question as she leaned in to suck on a small patch of skin high on Simone's inner thigh. It was much harder to balance with her hands tied behind her, and she wavered for a moment. She sucked harder than she intended. Simone's answering flood of new arousal pleased Abby.

"With you?" Simone gasped, the first verbal sign she was feeling the energy between them as acutely as Abby. Simone threaded her hands into Abby's hair and held her firmly in place. "I don't feel like I'm in control at all."

Abby licked and sucked and worried the sensitive skin at the juncture of Simone's thighs. When she felt Simone relax marginally, Abby pulled the skin between her teeth and clamped down. She bit much harder than she'd ever dared to with any other lover and worried she might have pushed too far with Simone as well. Simone's hold on her hair increased to the point of being painful, and her legs shook. She held Abby in place until the tremor subsided, then forcefully moved Abby until her mouth was pressing hard into Simone's clit.

"Here, please." Simone had been painfully polite with all of her commands, including the requisite *please* with each one. This time, Abby felt the plea deep inside her. She could feel Simone straining to not thrust against Abby's face. Simone was still well in control.

Abby licked Simone's clit, amazed at how very hard Simone was beneath her tongue. She smoothed the rough part of her tongue over it in broad, sweeping circles, over and over until Simone jerked on her hair, hard and insistent.

"Stop teasing me." Simone ground the words out through gritted teeth. She was desperately close.

Abby sucked Simone into her mouth. She cradled Simone's clit between her teeth and flicked her tongue relentlessly. This time she wouldn't stop until Simone came.

Simone's legs shook and her body was strung so tight she barely remained seated. Abby lapped at an endless stream of wetness and was lost in the experience. Simone had glorious orgasms, if the moisture between her legs was any indication. She released her grip on Abby's hair abruptly and slumped back into the chair.

Abby sat back on her heels and waited. Simone's essence coated her chin, and the thought of her entire body being slathered in Simone made Abby smile. It was something they could try another time.

When Simone's breathing evened out, Abby asked, "How are you doing up there?"

Simone immediately sat up straight, all signs of recovery erased. "Fabulous. You?'

"Never better." Abby was surprised to find she meant it. They still had a great deal to sort out between them, but she was confident they would make it work.

"Good." Simone stood, bringing her crotch within range of intimate contact. Abby's mouth watered. She was ready for more. Simone laughed and side-stepped until she was clear of Abby and the chair. Simone asked, "Can you stand or do you need help?"

"Depends." Abby angled her arms to the side to show she was still restrained. "Are you planning to leave me like this?"

"For now, yes." Simone removed her own shirt and bra as she spoke. They joined the stack of clothes on the table.

"Then I might. Let me try, though." Abby leaned to the left and brought her right leg forward until she could get her foot under her. So far, so good. She shifted and moved slowly until she was able to do the same with her left. It wasn't pretty, but she stood on her own.

"Nice job." Simone stroked her face and then kissed her softly. Abby didn't understand how she could transition so easily from red-hot sexy to almost chaste.

Simone worked quietly to remove Abby's slacks and panties. She knelt before her and kissed the inside of Abby's knee. With her palm cupped gently around Abby's calf, Simone encouraged her to step out of her pants. She collected the clothes and folded them as well.

"What now?"

"You should know I'm not great at relationships," Simone said.

Simone's confession caught Abby off guard. It wasn't surprising so much as out of left field. Abby had expected further direction for their sexual encounter, not emotional disclosure.

Abby wanted to hug her, but her bound wrists prevented the contact. Instead she leaned into Simone, pressing their bodies close together. "We can take it slow."

Simone looked Abby up and down and grinned. "It's a little late for slow, don't you think?"

Abby imagined she looked quite debauched.

"I meant emotionally. There's absolutely no reason for us to slow down as far as sex is concerned."

Simone drew Abby into the circle of her arms and held her. "I meant emotionally, too, Abby. I've been falling for you since tenth grade. There's no way I could turn back now."

As she spoke, Simone freed Abby's hands. Abby felt a sense of loss as the bra fell away from her wrists.

Simone winked and said, "Don't look so disappointed. I can always tie you up again later."

"Do you mean it?" Abby wrapped herself up in Simone's embrace. Maybe having her hands freed was a good thing after all.

"That I can tie you up? Test me." Simone bit out the last two words, and Abby instantly straightened. Simone's voice evoked the most wonderful visceral response in her.

"No, I meant the emotionally-falling-for-me part. Do you mean it?"

Simone swallowed and nodded. Her eyes were clear and vulnerable. "I do."

Abby laughed because her only other option was to cry. She had too much happiness inside her to not release some of it. Simone scowled at her.

Abby raised herself up and kissed Simone on the nose. "Then we'll be okay."

She led Simone down the hall toward her bedroom. She still had a mountain of unanswered questions, but she felt a certainty she'd never known before. Finally, after years of separation, she and Simone were together. And for the first time, they were on the same track. Abby planned to keep Simone around for a long time to come. They would sort out the details together.

Hollis

CHAPTER ONE

Jude Lassiter stepped off the bus and dropped her bag at her feet. She should have rented a damn car when she had the chance, because arriving at the FBI training facility via bus felt a little too much like boot camp. She'd hated boot camp. She'd given the marine corps her required four years, then promptly joined civilian ranks. She didn't want to relive it twenty years later.

"Are you Detective Lassiter?" A woman wearing reflective-lens aviator glasses and a FBI windbreaker greeted Jude. The name Hollis was printed on the front of the jacket, opposite the FBI logo.

Jude pushed her own glasses onto her head. She preferred to look people in the eye. "I am."

"Special Agent Hollis. I'm in charge of your training." Hollis didn't offer her hand in greeting.

Jude nodded. She couldn't say *nice to meet you*, as she was undecided.

"You're a day late." Hollis kept her glasses on, and the rest of her face gave away nothing.

"I was wrapping up a case." It was unfortunate that the murderers in Portland didn't take the FBI's training schedule into account when committing their crimes. She wouldn't apologize for doing her job well.

"We've already started. Come with me." Hollis turned on her heel and left Jude gaping at her.

"Wait. I need to drop my bag and get changed."

Hollis stopped and waited for Jude to catch up. She regarded her carefully, her eyes still hidden but clearly traveling the length of Jude's body. "Bring the bag with you and your clothes are fine." She resumed her journey.

They passed a building labeled Housing Unit C, the unit Jude was assigned to, according to the detailed itinerary sent to her by the FBI.

Jude stopped following. "My room is here. I'm going to drop this off." She tugged on the strap around her shoulder.

Hollis stopped a second time, her back ramrod straight. She turned and lowered her sunglasses, and Jude saw her eyes for the first time. They were bright, angry blue. "Are you sure you want to do that?"

Jude was forty-two fucking years old. "Absolutely."

Hollis slammed her glasses back in place and gestured toward the door with a broad sweep of her hand. "By all means."

Jude carried her bag into the barracks, knowing with certainty that Hollis would find a way to punish her for the delay. Her gut clenched at the thought, and she hoped this didn't turn out to be a case of all bark and no bite. She wanted to feel what kind of damage Hollis could inflict with her teeth.

Jude found her room with the help of a man who seemed to like the role of tour guide more than his paid position of maintenance engineer. She dropped her bag on the unused bed—her roommate had clearly checked in on time—and changed into the FBI-issued shorts and T-shirt that were waiting for her. Regardless of what Hollis said, slacks and a button-down were not appropriate when a good portion of the training promised to be physical, according to the agenda.

Hollis stood exactly where Jude had left her, with her glasses firmly in place and her face placid. She held the clipboard lightly in both hands like an afterthought.

"You're ready now?" Hollis greeted her with cool professionalism. All the heat that had bubbled to the surface was gone.

"Yes, sorry it took so long." Jude's shorts rode up and she refused to adjust them in front of Hollis. God knew she'd been in much less comfortable positions for much longer. The fabric might have been annoying, but it wasn't enough to break her.

Hollis evaluated her and Jude wanted to remove those damn glasses, regardless of the consequences. Hollis smiled, and a cool bolt of energy worked its way up Jude's back.

"The others are waiting." She turned and continued on her previous path.

This time Jude didn't try to walk beside her, but rather stayed a step behind. The pull of Hollis's slacks around her ass as she walked was mesmerizing. Until she was commanded not to look, there was no reason not to enjoy the view, so she indulged herself.

"Here we are." Hollis stopped at the exterior entrance of a small building. "Try not to be too disruptive." She said the words like she knew the inevitable outcome from Jude would in fact be large-scale commotion. Not that Jude was particularly unruly, but with Hollis staring at her like she was a massive disappointment, Jude was willing to fill the role of troublemaker.

"I'll do my best." She stepped into the semi-dark room and waited a moment for her eyes to adjust. The other trainees were seated facing forward at small rectangular tables in groups of two. All together, she estimated around twenty participants. They were watching a training video. She headed toward the only available seat as discreetly as possible.

"Hey, you must be Jude." The person already seated at the table leaned closer to Jude and spoke in a whisper. "I'm your roommate, Reeva."

Reeva was at least twenty years younger than Jude and dressed in slacks and a blouse, similar to the outfit Jude had just changed out of. The air conditioning in this room was cranked down to arctic, and Jude suppressed a shiver. Hollis was watching.

"It's nice to meet you." Jude went through the niceties of introduction. She'd be sharing a room with Reeva for the next three weeks. Civility would go a long way toward making that work.

"Do you want to borrow my jacket? You look cold." Reeva had a standard-issue FBI windbreaker, just like Hollis's, draped over the back of her chair.

Jude looked at the jacket. It had a soft inner lining that promised warmth. Hollis cleared her throat and Jude looked in her direction. She was staring right at Jude, one eyebrow arched in challenge. Jude really, really wanted that jacket. More than that, she didn't want Hollis to know how badly that was true.

"I'm fine, thanks." Jude folded her hands on the desk in front of her and smiled at Hollis. She was willing to play any game Hollis had in mind.

Hollis dropped her eyebrow, but the challenge remained on her face. The dim lighting prevented Jude from seeing her eyes clearly. At least she wasn't wearing those damn glasses anymore. Hollis stood straight, hands behind her back like a soldier at ease. She needed to relax.

An explosion sounded in the front of the room, an on-screen bombing that Jude wasn't prepared to hear. She flinched at the noise before she could stop herself. Hollis smirked.

Jude sat up straighter and forced her eyes to the front. The film depicted a prisoner being questioned. They were using techniques that would get Jude fired, and probably sued, for even thinking about. Clearly this was the "what not to do in the real world" section of the training.

"I could never do that." Reeva whispered in her ear, her voice strained. Jude looked in her direction. Her face was unnaturally pale.

"Don't worry, you won't have to." Jude could think of a couple of people she'd arrested over the years that she'd like to torture violently. The scene they were watching paled in comparison to what she'd mentally acted out on some of her detainees. She'd spent a lot of hours with the department shrink working through those inappropriate urges a few years back after she'd shot a suspect. It was her first and only time firing her weapon at another person, and she preferred to keep it that way.

"I hope you're right." Reeva gripped the arms of her chair tight and swallowed. Jude had spent enough time breaking in rookie detectives to recognize when someone was trying not to hurl. She hoped like hell that Reeva made it to the trashcan if she couldn't hold it back.

The video ended and the lights came up. Hollis went to the front of the room and said, "Thoughts?"

"We're not going to have to do that, right?" a man toward the front asked. He looked as unsettled at Reeva.

"Not likely." Hollis's tone gave nothing away, but something in the way she held herself, the barely contained sneer that almost rode to the surface, told Jude that she judged him unworthy and weak if he couldn't do this in case his country needed it.

The man nodded and Reeva exhaled a little too loudly.

"Thank God."

Hollis regarded Reeva with that same placid yet somehow judgmental expression. Jude almost felt bad for her.

"Tell me," Hollis looked directly at Jude, "has anyone in this room ever actually interrogated a suspect?"

Jude dutifully raised her hand. She was the only one.

"And what are your thoughts on it…" Hollis referenced her clipboard. Jude was certain she didn't need to. "Ms. Lassiter?"

"*Detective* Lassiter." Jude bit out the first word a little harder than she intended. Certainly harder than Hollis expected, and the raised eyebrow returned.

"Yes, Detective, pardon me. Can you share with the rest of us what it's like to interrogate someone?"

"Nothing like that." She waved toward the still-motion frame on the screen, one man captured in agony, the other in restrained superiority. "I give them every reason to trust me, and that usually gets them to talk." Sometimes it didn't, but there was no way she was sharing some of the things she'd done in order to get a confession in front of a room full of strangers.

"And if they don't?"

"If they don't, they don't. You go back to the evidence." Forensic science was a goddamned miracle. The lab techs had saved more than one dead case for Jude, and she respected them for it.

"Which department do you work in, Detective?" Hollis twisted her title out to make it take up far more time and space than required. By the time it reached Jude, it was sharp and pointed. It hit her low and hard and she liked it.

"Homicide."

Hollis nodded and crossed the front of the lecture area. She set a slow, deliberate pace, then retraced her steps when she reached the end. "You're smart to trust your forensics. But tell me, why wouldn't that work most of the time when dealing with terrorist threats?"

"In homicide, the crime is done. It's already been committed, so there's evidence to find. With a terrorist threat, you're looking at a potential crime that hasn't yet happened. That tends to make evidence a little lean."

"Good. So what do you do in that situation?" Hollis stopped pacing and stared at Jude deliberately.

"What do you mean?"

"When there's no evidence to follow, where do you turn next? Do you wait for the next event or do you work to prevent it?"

Jude nodded and Hollis looked pleased. The look of approval vanished when Jude started speaking. "I understand what you're saying, but I don't agree."

"Why?" Hollis narrowed her eyes. Reeva gasped.

"It's not foolproof. You could *question* someone in a very persuasive manner, as depicted in your film, and that person will tell you *anything* to get you to stop. How much time is wasted chasing dead information?"

Hollis picked up a small stack of papers. She rolled it into a tube and smacked it softly into her hand over and over as she said, "But what if you *know* they know something?"

Jude felt every smack the paper made as it connected with Hollis's palm. It resonated against her skin, traveled down her spine, and landed deep in her gut. And then slid a little lower. Hollis raised one side of her lips in a near-smirk, then dropped it again before Jude could be certain it really happened.

"If you *know*, then you already know what they know and you don't need them to tell you."

Hollis's smile was tight and controlled, and absolutely terrifying. If Jude wasn't on her shit list before, she definitely was now. Her goose bumps from the cold stood up a little higher with fear and anticipation.

"So you would never interrogate someone in this manner." It wasn't a question.

Jude shrugged. "I don't know." She'd learned long ago not to underestimate how her desire to get things done often overrode her other sensibilities.

"But you don't think it's right."

"I think a lot of things aren't right, but that doesn't mean I don't do them anyway."

Hollis nodded and hit a button on the open laptop at the front of the room. The video resumed and the lights dimmed.

Jude tried to focus on the film, but her eyes followed Hollis as she skirted the room. She lost track of her when she passed out of Jude's field of vision, and the only way to maintain visual would have been to turn in her seat. She wasn't ready to be that obvious. Yet.

She felt Hollis behind her a split second before warm breath hit her ear. Jude's muscles tightened and she sat up straighter, but she kept her eyes facing forward. There was a reason Hollis chose to approach her this way, and Jude wasn't about to challenge her on it at this point.

Hollis stayed there, crouching behind Jude's chair with her face pressed close for several moments. Jude felt the unmistakable trace of fingers against her skin, dancing along her neck between the loose tendrils of hair that escaped her ponytail.

"I want you in my office." Hollis whispered into Jude's ear, low enough that Jude could barely hear it, let alone her classmates. But she definitely felt it. "After class."

Jude managed a stilted nod and then Hollis was gone. Jude sucked in a breath, and her heart started beating a punishing rhythm.

Holy fuck. She'd been summoned straight to hell, she was sure of it, and she couldn't wait to get there.

❖

"I am so glad that is over." Reeva was a tad dramatic with her excitement. It was only a video, for Christ's sake.

"Mmm." Jude kept her answer noncommittal. She was still operating under the premise that she and Reeva needed to get along to some degree

"A bunch of us are going to grab a drink in the cafeteria. You want to join us?" Reeva asked with such open-faced interest Jude wanted to forgive her for being squeamish.

"Rain check? I have something I need to take care of." Jude almost wished she could join them. Not because she particularly enjoyed the company of twenty-somethings. Comparatively, they were babies. But she did like the idea of forming some alliances. Police work had taught her many important lessons about life, not the least of which was to make allies carefully and quickly when isolated without her regular backup.

"Sure. Come by when you're done. Maybe we'll still be there?" Reeva smiled like she was flirting with a boy, and Jude wondered if it was intentional.

"Maybe." Jude slipped on her sunglasses and headed off in the other direction.

The office was easy to find, listed on the directory along with countless other Special Agent so-and-so instructors. Her entire name was printed on the nameplate next to the door. *Special Agent Beverly Hollis*. Jude smiled. Now she knew the instructor's first name, a name she planned to be moaning later, whether under her own efforts or with help from the challenging Agent Hollis.

She knocked, but there was no answer. She tried the doorknob and the door opened easily. Hollis said she wanted Jude in her office, so Jude took the liberty of showing herself inside. The office was small by any account, but certainly larger than the space her desk took up in the bullpen of the homicide department. Still, she would use the size against Hollis if it promised to be fruitful. She didn't have a good-enough read on her to know what her tastes were. She guessed, based on Hollis's tone, her forward way of looking and touching without permission, that Hollis was a dominant. But she'd been wrong about that too many times in the past. She'd learned to be patient, to let a woman show her what she wanted.

She had a choice between a plush leather couch along one wall or a straight-backed wooden chair. It was simple, utilitarian, and placed Jude center stage when Hollis entered the room. There was no contest. Jude selected the chair.

She sat, back to the door, spine rigid, palms flat against her thighs. With her feet squarely on the floor and her body weight evenly distributed, it was easily one of the most comfortable positions Jude had been made to wait in. She relaxed into the posture and took a deep breath. She'd learned the easiest way to survive the boredom was to not allow it to set in. First she found a focal point—the nameplate on Hollis's desk—and then focused on her breathing, on keeping it deep, even, and well regulated. She let her thoughts roam, but not her eyes. She kept her attention facing forward as she let her mind wander.

The small window behind Hollis's desk had horizontal blinds that had been raised to the top, letting the afternoon sunshine and light the room. As the sun began to set, the light in the room dimmed. Jude hadn't turned on the light when she entered. It was fully dark when she heard the door handle engage.

A soft snick and the room filled with light. Jude blinked for a moment to let her eyes adjust.

"You waited." Hollis's voice adopted a warm, honeyed sweetness.

"Of course."

The door clicked shut behind her, and then Hollis entered Jude's line of vision. She closed the blinds before turning to face Jude. "I'm pleased."

She still wore the same FBI-issued slacks and shirt. She carried the jacket in her hand and slipped it over the back of her ergonomic office chair. It looked decidedly more comfortable than the one Jude was seated on.

"Do you know why I asked you to come here?" Hollis circled the desk and perched against the corner, her ankles crossed, hands resting on the edge of the desk. She tapped her index finger against the polished wood surface as she regarded Jude.

Jude nodded. She was absolutely certain why she'd been summoned and then left to wait. And the prospect of it made her light-headed and giddy. She loved this stage of a new encounter, one where boundaries were tested and established.

Hollis raised her eyebrow. "Well?"

"You wanted to see if I would come." Jude chose her words carefully. She wanted to say everything, but not too much. Similar to Hollis. *I want you in my office.*

Hollis nodded, the fingernail tap-tap-tapping. "Yes, I suppose I did."

It was clear at this point that Hollis liked words. She wanted Jude responsive and vocal. She'd watch carefully to see when that leeway ended.

"And you left me here as a test, to see if I would wait."

Hollis smirked then, her lips raised without fully committing. "And you did."

"I did." Jude relaxed into the chair, the first time in the hours she'd been there. Yes, she was pushing, but that was the fun of it. "I'm hoping it was worth it."

Silence grew between them as Hollis stared at her without speaking, the smirk softening. Finally, she pulled away from her perch and circled back around. She took a seat, opened a file, and slipped on a pair of reading glasses. They made her look smart. And sexy.

"You're forty-two?" She said it like a question even though she was no doubt looking at the answer on the piece of paper in front of her.

Jude decided to play along. "I am. How old are you?"

Hollis glanced at her while still studying the file. It was an impressive trick. "Forty-six."

She was in damn good shape. Jude approved of her workout routine, whatever it was.

Hollis continued. "You do not report to me. Outside of this training session, I have no influence over your future or your career. Do you agree?"

"Sure." Jude sat up and leaned closer to Hollis. Things were getting interesting.

"I want to be very clear about that before we go any further. Please say it." Hollis engaged her "I'm in charge" voice and Jude snapped perfectly upright. No more relaxing back or pushing forward. It was a matter of reflex, and until she was told otherwise, she had no choice but to follow her training. At this point it was engrained in her at a cellular level.

"You do not have the power to ruin my career." Her sodden underwear and her sanity in that moment? Absolutely. Her future as a detective with the Portland Police Department? Not in danger at all. Jude didn't point out that Hollis was the only one at risk in this scenario.

Hollis nodded and closed the file. She removed her glasses but didn't return them to her desk. She held them in her hand like an accessory, using them to gesture when appropriate, occasionally chewing on the stem that made her teeth flash white in a way that drew Jude even tighter in her seat. At forty-two fucking years old, Jude Lassiter was officially hot for the teacher. God.

"Tell me, Jude. Why do you think I asked you to my office?" Hollis chose her words too carefully and Jude smiled in spite of herself. She'd already given this woman too many little acts of disobedience to use against her. She didn't need to add fuel to the fire.

"You didn't ask." Despite her self-preservation instinct, Jude poked at Hollis once again.

"No, I didn't."

"You said *I want you in my office.* I took the order at face value. You want me. In your office." She left a long, pregnant pause between the first and second half of that sentence. "And I very much like the idea. So here I am."

"And here you are." Hollis echoed Jude, her eyes growing darker with every passing moment. Still she didn't move. Jude had made it very clear that she understood. And that she was willing. She would continue to wait until Hollis was ready for the next move.

Finally, after staring at Jude with those dark, probing eyes for so long Jude was certain she'd leave a wet spot on the chair when she stood, Hollis spoke again. "Do you have a safe word?"

"Of course." Jude was a little insulted. Even experimenting college students had a safe word. And she'd made it pretty damn clear that she was well beyond amateur status. She might have let her irritation show in her tone of voice.

Hollis raised an eyebrow, perfectly manicured and arched without interrupting the flow of her face. Her skin was flawless and beautiful, and her eyes flashed hot and cruel. A lesser person would have squirmed in her seat, but Jude sat fast.

"Would you care to share it with me?"

Oh, yes, she very much would. "Strawberry jam."

Hollis folded her glasses and returned them to the case in her desk drawer. She moved with controlled precision, every gesture economized and flowing into the desk, like office tai chi.

"Strawberry jam?" Hollis nodded as she said the word, her face tilted, contemplating the worthiness of a word chosen so long ago that Jude rarely thought of the circumstances anymore. It'd seemed poetic and ironic at the time. Now it just seemed functional. Like every other part of her training, it was ingrained. She would not forget, no matter how much Hollis might try to break her.

Hollis moved to Jude's side and leaned over her, her stature comforting and intimidating and commanding. Jude's breath hitched when she felt Hollis's fingers caress the length of her cheek, then dip inside her collar to graze the smooth skin of her upper chest. She spoke directly into Jude's ear, her voice low and dangerous. "Good. I'm going to make sure you need it."

CHAPTER TWO

Jude slept for shit. It was a strange bed, in a tiny, strange room with a roommate she didn't know. Reeva, for all her awkward charm and beauty, had a respiratory problem that made her lungs work fine most of the time, but then they'd stop at random intervals while she slept. As a result, she had a machine to make sure she stayed alive through the night, and it made her sound like Darth Vader.

And really, she could have slept through all of that if Hollis hadn't been such a fucking tease and left her with the biggest case of blue balls ever. Hollis had promised to push Jude to breaking, and then she'd left. That was it. Jude was flooded with arousal, her panties embarrassingly wet, and Hollis had simply walked away with a command that Jude wasn't allowed to take the edge off herself.

It was a test. And Jude hated tests, especially this one. No matter what she did, Hollis won and Jude lost. Except she didn't. If Jude jerked off, Hollis would know. Of that, Jude was absolutely certain. She probably had some heightened sense of smell and could detect self-induced come on a woman's fingers. And she would definitely punish Jude for disobeying.

If Jude waited—which was what she chose to do—she got to sport an over-sensitized clit with no idea when Hollis would take mercy and bring her off. Either way, Hollis got off on the control and Jude's discomfort. Fucking manipulative Dom.

She'd squirmed in bed, rubbing her thighs together miserably and cursing Hollis. Not that she could have done anything about it anyway, with Reeva and her mechanical lung four feet away, but being told she couldn't made her want it that much more.

After a quick shower, she and Reeva made their way to the cafeteria together. Jude was barely awake and stumbling, and Reeva was far too awake and chipper. If the girl asked her one more question before she found the coffee machine, Jude would honest to God choke her to death with the plastic tubing that led from her breathing machine to the mask she wore on her face as she slept at night.

"What's it like to be a detective?" Reeva asked with bright-eyed curiosity. "Have you ever shot anyone?"

Jude squeezed the bridge of her nose tight between her fingers. God help her.

"How is it possible that you actually work for the FBI?" How this absurdly naive girl from fucking Topeka managed to land a career with the FBI was a mystery to Jude.

"Oh." Reeva paused for a moment. "They recruited me."

"Of course they did." She didn't even want to know why.

They arrived at the dining hall and Jude could smell coffee, but she couldn't actually *see* it. Except, of course, in the hands of other people. It seemed everyone but her had a paper cup filled to the brim with glorious black coffee. And Reeva chose that moment, the one time Jude needed her all morning, to disappear. Fuck. She was on her own to find the coffee.

Reeva returned before Jude could truly orient herself and pressed a cup into Jude's hands. "You look like you need this."

"Oh my God, I love you."

Jude took her coffee hot and black. Beyond that, she didn't care about the particulars, and the cup Reeva brought her was perfect.

Reeva smiled at Jude, all open and confident like Jude had no choice but to like her. As she gulped black coffee, Jude could almost agree.

"Want me to show you around?"

Jude nodded. She needed more than coffee to fill her stomach and help her make it through to lunch.

"Good morning." Hollis's smooth voice registered at a visceral level long before Jude realized that the woman walking past with a filled tray was their instructor. Her spine straightened reflexively. She was too tired, too unprepared to stop the reaction before it happened.

Reeva didn't notice, but Hollis did. She smirked at Jude and continued to a table filled with other instructors. She sat too close to a cute blonde, who was almost as bubbly as Reeva, and Jude choked down the rising bile in her stomach. Hollis winked wickedly and took a loud, crunching bite of an apple, then casually draped her arm over the back of the other woman's chair, brushing her shoulders with her fingers as she did. The woman smiled at Hollis, then went back to her bowl of oatmeal and her conversation.

Reeva grabbed Jude's arm, and coffee sloshed over the rim and burned her skin.

"Come on, it's this way."

Jude shook the coffee from her fingers and dutifully followed Reeva with only a mumbled "Shit!" as admonishment. She glanced over her shoulder at Hollis one last time to discover that Hollis was no longer paying her any attention. She was fully engaged in the conversation at her table, leaning forward and speaking with great passion.

Reeva led Jude through the options with too much ease for a person who'd only arrived the day before. Jude selected a simple protein smoothie. It was easy to consume and even easier to digest. The less she had to think right now, the better.

They joined a group of their classmates at a table on the other side of the dining room, too far away for Jude to truly see Hollis, but close enough to track her outline. She felt like a stalker.

"Tell me why they recruited you?" Jude asked after she'd finished her first cup of coffee and started on her second. She felt a little more human after her initial intake of caffeine and therefore more willing to try at playing nice.

"Because I remember things." Reeva added jam to her toast from a small square packet, the kind that was always too much for one piece, but never enough for two. "Well, everything, really. I remember everything." She said it with the same uncertain cadence that she'd used for every communication so far, and Jude found it both endearing and annoying.

"Don't be late for class." Once again Hollis snuck into their conversation before Jude realized she was coming. She smiled directly at Jude with too many teeth and *I dare you* in her eyes. It was terrifying and yet Jude was irresistibly tempted. She definitely would dare.

"What happened to you yesterday?" A man whose name Jude couldn't remember asked the question.

Jude watched Hollis walk away until she rounded a corner and dropped out of sight. Then she turned to the group and shrugged. "I had a few things to take care of." She wasn't about to tell them what she'd really been up to.

"I was worried. Special Agent Hollis looked like she was ready to kill you when you argued with her." Same guy again. He regarded her like he knew something she didn't. Too bad he wasn't interesting enough for her to care.

"I didn't notice." Jude sipped her coffee.

"Seriously?" Reeva gaped at her. "She was livid. And when she walked over to you during the movie, I about shit. I'm glad I'm not you."

Jude snorted. "What do you think she's going to do?" Jude was certain that with all of Reeva's goofy, Bambi-like sweetness, the worst she could think of wouldn't even come close to the truth.

"I don't know. Fail you?"

Jude switched to her smoothie. She had too much caffeine in her stomach without a buffer, and she'd pay for it if she didn't change that soon. "This isn't high school, Reeva. I'm not being graded."

Everyone stopped eating and stared at her.

"You're not?"

"You are?" Jude looked closely at her classmates. They all wore identical FBI-issue T-shirts with the agency emblem on the front right. "Oh, shit. You are? Am I the only person here who doesn't work for the FBI?"

"At this table, yes. In the class, no," Reeva said.

"You'd know that if you'd arrived the first day with the rest of us." Suddenly, Jude was very interested in knowing this man's name.

"I'm sorry, who are you?"

"Tim." He stuck out his hand gamely.

Jude shook it because that's what cops did all day long, shake hands with people they'd rather not touch. She'd learned long ago to use the experience to help her read other people.

"Okay, Tim, you're right. I would know if I'd been here. But I figured that learning your name and vocation on day one wasn't quite as important as scooping up a sick fucker who likes to kill women and then fuck their skulls." Jude took a long drink of her smoothie.

Tim turned a satisfying shade of green. So did Reeva.

"If you'll excuse me." Jude pushed away from the table and stood. Dramatic exits aside, she really didn't want to be late. It was too early in the day to provoke Hollis. "I'm going to head to class."

Reeva chased after her. "Is that true?"

"What?"

"That part about...skulls."

"Yeah." Jude tossed her trash into the bin with too much force. It didn't budge and that made her feel foolish. Her outburst had no place here. She scrubbed her hands over her eyes. "Sorry. It's been a rough week."

Reeva squeezed her shoulder. "I can't imagine." Maybe Reeva would be okay after all.

"You shouldn't have to."

They walked out of the building and were halfway across the compound before Reeva spoke again.

"So what's the deal with you and Special Agent Hollis? For real?"

Jude smiled. "Nothing."

"That was convincing."

Slumber-party confession wasn't Jude's style. She knew better than to share anything tangible. Especially with a person who "remembers everything."

"What do you think's going to happen? I'm here for three weeks to *learn*. Then I go back to Oregon."

"But she's hot, right? You noticed that?"

"She's definitely hot."

"I knew it!" Reeva did a ridiculous little hop clap that made Jude mildly nauseous.

"Jesus, calm down."

"I can't. You have a crush!"

Jude stopped walking and stared at Reeva. "What are you? Like twelve?"

"No, but I saw you watching her yesterday. And she is hot. And now we're bonding because you talked to me about it." Reeva clapped again.

"Are you kidding me?" Jude shook her head and started walking again. Reeva laughed and skipped to keep up.

"Yay!"

"Stop it. You're a federal agent. Have some decorum."

"They didn't hire me for my decorum."

"Right. I forgot. You remember things."

"That's right. Like yesterday you wore workout clothes for classroom time, which means you didn't check the itinerary beforehand. Obviously you were a little tied up with the whole apprehending-a-psychopath thing. And you were cold, with goose bumps and everything, but you wouldn't take my jacket. You were watching Special Agent Hollis and obviously didn't want her to know you were cold. And, just so you know, she was watching you just as closely."

"And?"

"And since the sun was bright enough the blinds didn't block it out, the light switch, which should have been on the opening side of the exterior door, was actually located in the middle of the back wall. And Hollis tapped her fingers against the wall heating unit sixty-seven times after you joined the class, but didn't do it once before. And you smelled like bus even though you obviously took time to change. Your shoelaces were tied perfectly in the middle, but your hair was coming undone. And the video showed two people on the screen, but there were at least six in the room, based on the shadows and background noises—"

"Enough. What do I have to do to get you to promise to never, ever do that again?"

"Admit she's hot."

"She's hot."

❖

"What were you talking to Reeva about?" Hollis scraped the sharp edge of her nail along Jude's spine.

"When?" Jude stood naked and blindfolded in Hollis's office. The combination was so disorienting she wasn't able to track Hollis's subject change.

"A few days ago when you were leaving the cafeteria."

Hollis's voice floated into her, disembodied and soothing. It wove Hollis into Jude's subconscious, fixing her in place with sense memory of pleasure and pain. Memory recall of any event that took place prior to Hollis securing the scarf over her eyes and saying "Trust me" was a complete loss.

A sharp, stinging blow landed across her backside, in that crease too low to be ass and too high to be thigh. The cutting line caught her off guard. Hollis's gentle touches had lulled her into relaxing. She sucked a breath through her teeth and straightened instantly. She'd been sloppy, and Hollis had called her on it.

"I don't remember."

"Let me help." Hollis traced her fingers over the fire-hot line where she'd just struck her. Jude wondered what she'd used. The ruler from her desk? It definitely wasn't her palm. Her touch was cool and comforting, taking the heated bite from Hollis's skin. "Reeva said 'she's totally hot,' and you agreed. Now do you remember?" Hollis held her mouth close to Jude's ear as she spoke, and the word "hot" shivered down her spine and further fanned the flame building inside her.

Jude vaguely remembered the conversation. It'd been Jude's first trip to the cafeteria and they'd just finished eating.

"I remember. She was talking about you. She thinks I have a crush on you."

Hollis laughed, a weird mix between surprise, amusement, and cruelty. "How cute."

"She's young." Jude couldn't remember a time when she'd been so staggeringly naive, but she imagined she must have been at some point. Maybe when she was twelve.

"Yes, she is, but is she right?" Hollis resumed her slow tactile exploration of Jude's body.

"About what?"

"Do you have a crush? Should I get you a collar and make it all official?"

Jude couldn't stop the snort that escaped at Hollis's question. It was just too absurd for her to do anything else. "That won't be necessary."

"No?" Hollis circled her neck with her hands where a collar would go. She pressed in tight to close the circle. It was snug, but not suffocating. Jude focused on her breathing and waited. "You wouldn't like that? A snug band of leather around your throat to remind you who owns you?"

Hollis squeezed hard enough to cut off airflow, and Jude's head swam. It didn't matter that she had plenty of oxygen in her lungs; the action both excited and frightened her. Something to explore later, perhaps.

She shook her head no, and Hollis loosened her grip but kept her hands in place.

"Have you ever worn a collar?"

She nodded. "But only for play. Not as part of a commitment."

"Why not?"

The same reason she'd never gotten married. As clichéd as it sounded, she just hadn't met the right person. "I don't know."

"Do you want to?"

"Maybe, some day. With the right person."

Hollis dropped her hands. "Isn't that sweet. Reeva is rubbing off on you."

"Have you?"

Hollis laughed, a brittle, dry sound that communicated everything except amusement. "Once. It was…interesting."

Before she could ask any further questions, Hollis circled her body and snaked her arms around her waist to palm her breasts. "Wait right here. I'll be back."

Jude heard Hollis's soft footsteps as she crossed the room, followed by the sound of the door opening and then closing. She shifted her stance into a military at-ease pose. With her hands clasped together behind her and her legs spread slightly, she was more comfortable.

She hoped the shades were closed but couldn't be sure. They had been when she'd stripped, but after Hollis had applied the blindfold, she'd heard too many sounds to keep track of everything that had happened in the room. For all she knew, the blinds were open and an audience was seated on bleachers outside the window.

Her nipples perked at the thought. Something else to explore. She'd never been a fan of audiences in the past, but tastes change, and her body definitely liked the idea of others watching her with Hollis.

The door opened and closed again, but Hollis didn't speak. Rather, Jude hoped it was Hollis. It would be difficult to explain her current position to anyone else. She waited a few moments, straining to hear even the slightest sound. It had to be Hollis. Anyone else would have gasped or yelled or said something. Wouldn't they?

This was a test, she was sure of it. She wouldn't blow it by calling out. Hollis would speak when she was ready. Jude started to count. She reached four hundred and twelve before Hollis broke the silence.

"You're very good." Hollis's voice caressed her. "So beautiful, so controlled."

Jude felt the moment that Hollis stepped near her. Her body recognized her energy and reached out for it.

"You're back." Her voice was breathless to the point of embarrassing, but all Jude could focus on was the promise of Hollis's body so close to her own.

"Did you miss me?"

"Yes." She didn't even try to hide her arousal. Hollis dismantled her without even trying. She didn't mind sharing.

"I brought you a present. Spread your legs."

Jude stepped out wide, opening herself with the stance. She heard a tinkling noise, like an empty drink glass with only ice left in the bottom. Then she felt it, something so cold it felt like fire being pressed between her lips and up into her cunt.

She gasped and clenched to keep it in place. The sensation of being penetrated and burned flashed through her like a wildfire.

"Okay?" Hollis asked. She played in Jude's folds, rolling her fingers and knuckles through the wetness. It was the first truly intimate touch since Jude entered her office, and the sensation overwhelmed her.

"Yes." She forced the answer. Hollis liked her questions to be answered.

"Good girl. Can you hold it there?"

"Yes." Another stilted answer was all she could manage.

"Excellent." Hollis moved her fingers to her clit, circling easily to awaken the parts of Jude that threatened to freeze and burn to ash at the same time. "Can you come?"

Come? Jude hadn't even thought about it. She'd been so focused on controlling the slippery, melting cube inside her that the rising tide of arousal had built without her recognizing it. Her body responded though.

"Yes, please."

"Whenever you're ready." Hollis continued to play with her clit without urgency. Her fingers slipped smoothly through the growing wetness, drawing Jude's clit out until it was fully exposed and hard.

The careful, steady touch drew Jude higher until finally, blessedly, her orgasm washed over her. Every ounce of control drained from her muscles as she rode her release through to completion. She felt what was left of the ice cube slide out of her as she slumped against Hollis. She didn't have the strength to stop it.

The bright light from the fluorescents overhead blinded her when Hollis removed the blindfold. She blinked to give her eyes opportunity to adjust.

Hollis smiled at her, a smirking satisfied smile that said she was well pleased with herself. Jude hoped that satisfaction extended to include her.

"Thank you."

Hollis nodded. "You should get dressed. I'm sure you have homework to finish tonight."

Jude nodded, too. This part of their relationship was odd to her. As familiar as the actions were, something about Hollis watching her gather herself to leave unnerved her.

As she was about to go, Hollis stopped her at the door. She placed a simple, chaste kiss against Jude's cheek and said, "Thank you. I enjoyed tonight."

Jude nodded once more and stepped out the door, unsure exactly which part Hollis had enjoyed.

Chapter Three

Sweat rolled down Jude's back and saturated the waistband of her federal-issue gym shorts. Her heart pounded as she gulped air. She'd been warned. Squad mates who'd previously attended the FBI anti-terrorism training session had told her it wouldn't be all book learning. They hadn't, however, prepared her for the sadistic instructor whose singular goal was to make Jude's lungs bleed. She'd been there for just over a week, and Hollis seemed to enjoy making her suffer during class almost as much as after hours in her office.

Seven miles, for fuck's sake. When she chased perps, which wasn't very often, they ran for a block or two. Half a mile, tops. They didn't race full out through the woods, over trees, splashing through streams for seven fucking miles. She was here to learn how to catch terrorists, not rabbits.

For now, though, she'd settle for catching her breath.

"Move it, people." Hollis smiled. "Get a drink of water and let's go. The American people don't want to waste their tax dollars paying you to breathe."

Jude pictured Hollis in a leather corset snapping a whip at their heels. It wasn't an entirely unpleasant image, even if the timing was crap. Forget the fact that they were surrounded by Jude's classmates. The brutal, slipping-toward-middle-age truth was she was too damn tired to enjoy the fantasy.

"You're staring again." Reeva handed her a cup of water and collapsed on the grass next to her. "And you have a little drool right there." She pointed at Jude's chin.

Jude swiped her hand over her mouth and chin just in case Reeva wasn't kidding.

"Thanks." She took a long drink, then poured the rest over her head. If the ice-cold water didn't cool her down, nothing would.

"Show of hands, people." Special Agent Hollis dangled a pair of handcuffs from her finger. "Who here has actually cuffed a perp?"

Jude raised her hand reluctantly. She was probably the only person in the group to have done a lot of things, but that didn't mean she wanted to be singled out. She had the sinking feeling that, with the admission, she'd volunteered for something.

"Really? Lassiter's the only one?" Hollis raised a brow and snapped the cuffs through the air to Jude, the chrome winking in the sunlight. "Bring your roommate with you."

"Great," Reeva mumbled under her breath as she followed Jude to the front. "I get to be strapped to your work-experience ass."

A trickle of sweat threatened to fall into Jude's eyes, and she hiked up her shirt to wipe her brow. The cool breeze against her skin was a revelation. She took her shirt off completely, used it to towel her hair to spikey submission, then tossed it to the side while she waited for directions. She doubted the FBI would approve of her change in wardrobe, but she wasn't a federal employee so she was willing push it. What was the worst that could happen? Special Agent Hollis would punish her?

Hollis's gaze lingered on Jude's abs. The run might have turned her into a sweaty, heaving wreck, but what she lacked in cardiovascular endurance, she more than made up for in muscular definition. She tightened her stomach. If Hollis wanted to stare at her for the remainder of class, Jude was fine with that.

"Lassiter, pretend you're an agent and cuff her."

"How 'bout I just *be* a detective and do it anyway." Jude turned to Reeva without waiting for a response. "Turn around, hands on the back of your head, fingers interlaced."

Like most people, Reeva did as she was told, and Jude snapped the handcuffs home on one wrist, guided both arms down behind her back, and secured the other side. She spun her around and stood, hand reflexively positioned low on Reeva's bicep. She didn't actually think Reeva would try to run away, but you can't undo almost twenty years of training and practice.

"Good." Hollis unlocked Reeva. "This time trade positions."

"Really?" Being restrained wasn't new to Jude, but she only yielded to those who proved worthy. So far, Reeva hadn't demonstrated the appropriate amount of strength to make Jude willing to slip into that role.

Hollis regarded Jude, her face placid, almost bored. "Really."

"Turn around, and put your hands behind you?" Reeva sounded uncertain. Until that point, the prescribed script had been words on a test, and she clearly struggled to get them in the right order.

"Yeah, about that," Jude took a step back, "I don't think so."

"Huh?" Reeva reached for Jude's wrist and Jude slapped her hand away.

"Not everyone goes down easily." Jude smiled at Reeva and took another step away. She felt bad for making things harder for her roommate, but not bad enough to acquiesce.

"No, not everyone does." Hollis spoke from behind her, her lips close to Jude's ear, her breath hot and teasing against Jude's neck. "But eventually, *everybody* goes down."

Before Jude could spin around, Hollis twisted her arm behind her, pressing her fingers high between her shoulder blades, and kicked the back of her knee, forcing her to the ground. Jude landed hard, her face muffled in the grass. "Fuck," she groaned.

Hollis twisted the arm a little higher and pressed her knee into Jude's back. The sudden pressure was sharp and wicked. Jude gasped, relishing the aggressive touch. It'd been forever since someone had commanded her attention through brute force, and the sensation was delicious.

The cutting edge of metal bit into Jude's wrists when Hollis snapped the cuffs in place, cinching them down tighter than any law-enforcement agency allowed. Jude struggled, pushing up against

Hollis, knowing she couldn't get away, but testing her boundaries anyway. Hollis shoved her down roughly, mashing her cheek into the sod. The rich, earthy scent of grass soothed her, a direct counterpoint to the harsh command Hollis issued. "Stay down."

"Yes, ma'am." Jude stopped squirming and held her body rigid, the urge to obey too deeply engrained to suppress. She averted her eyes, out of habit rather than need. She hadn't been able to see more than a glimpse of Hollis since she'd forced her to the ground.

"Good girl." Hollis rubbed her thumb lightly over the skin just above the handcuffs—a touch too intimate to be unintentional.

Jude remained facedown for the remainder of the training session. By the time Hollis helped her to her feet and removed the cuffs, Jude's hands were numb and her panties were soaked. She hoped her classmates couldn't see just how excited the encounter had made her, but she doubted she was hiding it well. And, at that point, she'd have done anything the instructor asked, regardless of the audience.

Hollis held out Jude's shirt and said, "Wait in my office."

Jude ached to rub the feeling back into her wrists and hands, work the stiffness out of her back and shoulders. Instead, she took the offered shirt with a curt nod and turned toward the building without a word, leaving Hollis behind to dismiss the other students.

She debated pulling her shirt on as she walked, then opted against it. Since Hollis didn't specify if she wanted her dressed or not, she ran the chance of being wrong either way, but if the decision were left to Jude, as it apparently was at the moment, she preferred fewer clothes for their meeting, not more.

Just like always, the door to Hollis's office was unlocked. She folded her shirt and laid it on a wooden chair. Should she remove the rest of her clothing? No, she decided as she dropped to her knees midway between the door and the desk as instructed during her last visit to this office. She faced the door, clasped her hands together behind her back, and settled in to wait for Hollis's arrival. She kept her gaze focused on the square of carpet directly in front of her. The temptation to explore the office was too great. If she allowed herself to glance around, she'd be up and snooping through the desk in moments. She did not want to be caught in that position.

That was her constant struggle, the balance between detective, the investigator who wanted to know everything, and the submissive, the woman who waited patiently, quietly, to be directed. Hollis, she was sure, would not appreciate her blurring the line between the two parts of herself by rummaging through her belongings.

When she heard the soft *rattle-click* of someone turning the knob, it could have been minutes or hours later. She'd learned long ago to surrender to the moment, allowing time to flow around her without trying to capture it or gauge the duration. She straightened her posture, wanting to impress Hollis.

"I see you're *capable* of obedience." Hollis skimmed one finger over Jude's shoulders and up, teasing the surface of her hair without coming close enough to actually touch it. Without warning, she gripped a handful of Jude's short locks and forced her head back, demanding eye contact.

Jude didn't respond. Speaking without permission was dangerous. Not that she minded pushing buttons, but she just liked to know the results before jumping in. Until she learned Hollis's proclivities, she would err on the side of caution.

"You can speak."

"Thank you." Jude tried to avert her gaze again, and Hollis gave a sharp tug on her hair. Jude wouldn't need a third lesson. Hollis liked to be watched.

Hollis released her hair. "Stand."

Jude rose fluidly, her movements graceful in spite of not moving for so long, first facedown on the field, then kneeling here on the carpet. She'd spent hours alone practicing how to move from feet to knees and back again. She wanted to be beautiful, and she'd been told many times that her efforts had paid off.

Hollis circled behind Jude, easing her nails beneath the edge of Jude's sports bra. She snapped the elastic across her back and said, "Strip."

As Jude removed her remaining articles of clothing and folded them carefully, her anticipation grew. Their last meeting had been filled with details, discussing the details, the rules, without any actual engagement. As good as she was at kneeling for long periods of time, waiting went against her nature. She wasn't a patient woman and all the delays, the denial, made her antsy. It also heightened her pleasure, so she'd learned to wait when directed.

Hollis pulled several items out of her filing cabinet and placed them on her desk in a line. A sleek wooden hairbrush, teak perhaps; a set of clamp-style paperclips; a manila folder; and a child's school ruler, wooden with a metal edge.

"Stand two steps from the desk, eyes on me. Bend at the waist and grasp the edge."

Jude followed the directions precisely, measuring out two steps before moving into position. She kept her head up, unsure if she should maintain eye contact or follow Hollis's hands as they worked to remove the metal strip from the side edge of the ruler. The steady, sure movements of her hands won out, as Jude found herself captivated, imagining the sting of the wood against her backside.

When Hollis finished removing the thin line of metal, she returned it to the desk and selected the manila folder next. She relaxed, sinking into her chair as she read, "Jude May Lassiter, homicide detective, North Precinct Portland, Oregon. Shot twice in the line of duty." Hollis looked up, her eyes searching Jude's body for evidence to support the information in the file. Her gaze lingered on the rough scar on Jude's shoulder, then continued the search of her body. She wouldn't find the one just below Jude's left breast as long as she remained angled over the desk. "Decorated as a hero for stopping a robbery in progress, and a second time for safely negotiating the release of a family taken hostage in their own home." She stopped reading, waiting for Jude to fill in the details.

Jude held her gaze but didn't speak. That day had been a horrible, crazy mix-up of luck and coincidence. The only reason she was here instead of dead was because the man's pistol jammed and she was able to tackle him before he cleared the chamber. The barrel had been pointed straight at her chest—covered in patrol-officer blue—when he pulled the trigger. At such close proximity, it would have done more than leave another scar to be catalogued in a file.

She'd been promoted to detective a week later. Her second promotion to detective investigator came after she brought in a serial rapist who had terrorized the St. John's area for months. After that she requested the transfer to Homicide, where the victims didn't cry when she found them.

Nothing in their exchange so far permitted Hollis to hear Jude's accounting of that part of her life, and if she continued to stare at Jude, entitlement and demand on her face, Jude would end the scene and leave. She wanted to get laid, not head fucked.

Jude eased her grip on the desk, already mentally removing herself from the room. As she was about to straighten and retrieve her clothing, Hollis finally spoke.

"Everything in here reads like a chief's wet dream." Hollis closed the file and set it next to the ruler, then picked up the metal clips. "So why are you down here being such a pain in the ass for me?"

"I..." Jude flexed her fingers, her muscles aching as she renewed her grasp. What could she say in her own defense? What would be good enough? "I'm sorry." She lowered her gaze, unable to keep her eyes forward during the apology. It wouldn't be enough for Hollis, she was sure, but it was the best she could offer.

"You're sorry?" Hollis was on her feet and by Jude's side quick enough to make Jude flinch. "You disrupt my class, embarrass your classmate, and that's all you have to say for yourself?" She spoke low and harsh in Jude's ear, her hand bouncing the metal clips up, just barely losing contact, then grasping them tight, her fingers loose and steady. Over and over. The rhythmic clicking lulled Jude.

"Umm..." Jude wanted to speak eloquently, to defend herself. All she could do was watch the flash of metal between Hollis's fingers.

Hollis leaned closer, her lips brushing against Jude's neck, just below her ear. "Sorry isn't enough. There are consequences for that type of behavior in my classroom." She sucked Jude's earlobe between her teeth and bit down hard.

Hollis pressed her fingertips against her shoulder, forcing her upright. She kissed and sucked her way down Jude's chest, taking first one nipple into her mouth, a barely there open-mouthed kiss, then moving to the other. "Your breasts are remarkable." As she spoke, she gripped both nipples between her thumbs and forefingers and squeezed.

Jude gasped, fisting her palms at her side to keep from grabbing Hollis and pulling her closer. The pressure increased steadily until all Jude could think about, all that mattered, was the urgent thrum of hot, lustful energy running from her breasts to her cunt. Her knees trembled and she felt herself slipping. She forced herself upright and braced herself. She would not fall over.

Just as the pressure reached the hard-enough-to-make-her-come level, Hollis released her. Before Jude could orient herself, return to a semi-normal state, Hollis slipped a clamp over her left nipple, then her right. The pressure rocketed, too painful, too decadent, too immediate, too jarring, too delicious, too…everything. Jude wanted more and she wanted less. Unable to decide, she whimpered and leaned closer to Hollis.

"I want you to make me come." Hollis slid out of her shorts and panties as she led Jude around the desk. "Then I'll decide on a suitable punishment for you." She reclined into her chair, forcing Jude to her knees and guiding her head between her legs in one smooth motion.

Jude eased her hands over Hollis's thighs, working her way up and inward, delighted to be allowed to touch.

"Ah-ah, hands behind your back." She rapped the ruler over Jude's knuckles.

"I'm sorry." Jude slipped her tongue between Hollis's lips. She fought to keep her balance as she stroked and swirled, experimenting with pressure and motion. She was determined to make Hollis forget her own name.

Hollis gripped the back of her head, the constant weight of her hand holding Jude steady. She thrust her tongue into Hollis, pushing as deep as she could, reaching to find Hollis's threshold for pleasure. She retracted and thrust again, building a steady rhythm that Hollis matched, her hips jutting into Jude's face. She wanted to grip Hollis around the waist, drag her close, pin her down, and tongue-fuck her until she came.

The tugging pressure on her scalp increased sharply in sync with the rising volume of Hollis's praise. "Fuck...God...Damn." Over and over, the same three words that started as a low, barely there whisper, then grew into a proud, desperate mantra.

Jude dragged her tongue up, applying direct pressure to Hollis's clit for the first time. She grazed it with her teeth, then sucked it hard between her lips, flicking the tip of her tongue over the tight bundle.

Hollis gripped her head tighter, her fingers tangled in her hair, pulling and pushing at the same time. She tensed, her body perfectly still, yet shaking from the strain as her body tightened. She teetered there on that edge, body quaking, until Jude couldn't take it any more. Fuck obedience. She slammed two fingers into Hollis's cunt, fucking her hard and fast.

"Jesus...Fuck...Fuck." Hollis buckled into the chair and tugged Jude up by her hair, covering her mouth in a demanding, invading kiss. "Damn, you're good at that."

As quickly as the kiss began, it ended. Hollis tugged on both nipple clamps, shooting fire to Jude's center. She almost collapsed in Hollis's lap.

"I want you on the floor, face down, ass up. Now." Hollis's voice held none of the languid recovery Jude expected. Her recuperation time was record fast.

As Jude moved into position, Hollis shoved the cushion from her chair under Jude's head.

"Keep your hands behind your back this time or I'll put the cuffs back on." She took a set from her top drawer and plopped them on the desk. "I have a hobby that you are likely unaware of."

Jude could hear Hollis moving around as she spoke, and she struggled to keep her head down. What else could she possibly have in her office to use on Jude? Either the ruler or the hairbrush would work nicely.

"I like to ride." Hollis's smile infused her voice, and Jude would have worried if given enough time. "English style."

A sharp crack from, presumably, Hollis's riding crop tore into Jude's rear end, and she bit her lip to keep from crying out. A second and third quickly followed.

"Feel free to count if it helps." Two more rapid strokes. "Or cry if you need to."

Jude ground her teeth together as another sharp blow caught her low enough to sting her pussy lips. "Six."

Jude counted fifteen before Hollis stopped. The cool counterpoint of Hollis's hand as she comforted the reddened skin relaxed Jude, and a tear slipped from her eye.

"So beautiful." Hollis praised her, her voice reverent and soft, as she massaged Jude's ass, alternating between gripping and pulling, and gliding softly. "You were splendid."

Hollis stretched her cheeks apart and a jolt of cool air hit Jude's anus, followed almost immediately by a slick, probing tongue. Hollis pressed into Jude, rimming her, as her hands continued to knead the abused flesh. Jude squeezed her muscles tight, all of them, her fingernails digging into her palms, her toes digging into the hard floor. Her tits dragged against the floor, amping up the fire from the clamps, as she strained against Hollis's tongue.

One last swipe and Hollis sat back on her haunches, still holding her cheeks open. Jude held herself rigid, fighting against the feeling of being exposed, vulnerable.

"God, I wish I had a strap-on here. I'd fuck your ass so hard you'd come for weeks."

Before the words could cool in the air, before Jude's pussy could stop clenching from the promise, Hollis pushed three fingers into Jude, so hard and so deep Jude wondered if it really was a strap-on. She set a fast, steady pace, increasing to four fingers before Jude was ready, and the stretching pressure-pain almost made her come instantly. She wasn't allowed yet, and she gritted her teeth and waited for permission.

Hollis grasped her hair, tugging her upright, flush against her, back to front, as she continued to fuck her. The new angle and increasing urgency brought Jude closer to the edge until she was staring down, trying not to fall into the vast chasm before her. She was barely hanging on, her grasp on solid ground tenuous and failing fast.

Hollis released her hair and wrapped her arm around her chest, toying with her nipples, one after the other, not letting either rest for more than a second before returning her attention to it. Then, blessedly, she licked the length of Jude's neck, still thrusting hard inside her cunt.

"Do you want to come?"

Jude's shoulders burned and ached, and her fingers itched to dig into the flesh of Hollis's belly. Her head swam, furling and dark.

"Answer me." Hollis tugged on one of the clamps, pulling and squeezing it tighter. "Do you want to come?"

Yes…yes…God, yes. Jude couldn't form the words. Her body was on fire, originating in her pussy and burning outward. She licked her lips. "Y…" She licked them again. "Yes, please, yes." She begged and cried, unable to think beyond the pounding fist in her cunt and the lightning-sharp pressure on her nipples.

Hollis released her hold on the clamp, leaving it in place but no longer adding to the pain. She moved her hand swiftly to Jude's mound, circling her clit with one soft, determined finger. "You can." She bit down on the meaty flesh of Jude's shoulder as she spoke.

Jude froze. Permission. She opened herself to the pressure in her cunt, her clit, her nipples, and the sharp tear of teeth at her pulse point. The dark, blurry edges of her vision overpowered the light and she surrendered, falling headfirst into the abyss.

CHAPTER FOUR

When Jude came to, Hollis was dressed and staring at her intently. The polished leather of her riding boots sat in stark contrast to the dull carpet. A tight, secret smile graced her lips.

She reclined on the sofa, one leg draped over the other, with the riding crop in her hands. She twirled it between her fingers and regarded Jude thoughtfully.

"You did very well." Hollis was a demanding lover but always remembered praise when they finished. It made Jude try that much harder. As much as she enjoyed the harder edge of sex, at her core, she wanted to please. Being punished when she failed, then praised when she did well fed her need at an absolute base level.

Jude pulled herself upright. She'd been out, sprawled unattractively on the carpet, long enough for Hollis to collect her toys and put them away. The hairbrush and ruler were no longer on the desk. And her nipples, while incredibly sore and sensitive, were decidedly clamp-free. After far too much effort, she positioned herself appropriately on her knees with her hands palm down on her thighs.

"Thank you." Her voice came out clearer than she expected. Jude was ruffled, destroyed by the demands Hollis placed on her body, first in class, then later in her office. Sweat had cooled on her body, and her inner thighs were tacky with leftover sex. She needed a shower desperately, but she held herself carefully, striving for placid beauty. For her part, Hollis looked completely put together.

"I hate to leave, but unfortunately I have a standing appointment." Hollis said it like her departure was eminent, but she didn't move.

"I understand." Jude felt shaky all over, her muscles weak and her ass screaming. It was a delicate balance to kneel appropriately and keep the pressure off her bottom and not tax her jellified thighs. She wanted to lie back out on the floor and take a nap, give her body a chance to process and enjoy what Hollis had put her through.

"But I want to take care of you first. There's a jar on my desk. Bring it to me."

Jude had missed it earlier, a small white plastic jar without a label. She rose carefully, thankful for the change in position, and collected the jar as requested. Hollis took the jar when Jude offered it, then held her hand out, beckoning Jude to come closer. Her touch, the smooth skin of her hand, was soft and gentle. She set both feet squarely on the floor, then guided Jude to lie over them, like a child awaiting a spanking. She clenched, fearful that Hollis was going to follow through on her promise to punish her for touching earlier when she'd been directed to keep her hands behind her back.

"Relax." Hollis soothed her hand over the sensitive flesh, and Jude tensed further.

The touch was tender, kind, and very arousing. And Jude had no idea what Hollis had planned next.

"This will help." She removed her hand, and Jude missed the cool touch immediately. When the touch returned, her fingers were covered in ointment. She massaged carefully, working the balm into Jude's flesh. By the time she finished, Jude was squirming with renewed excitement. And wet all over again.

"You really are insatiable, aren't you?" Hollis trailed her fingers through pooling moisture between Jude's legs and swirled her fingers at the opening of Jude's cunt. Teasing, but not really touching.

Jude nodded and pushed her hips back, encouraging Hollis to do more.

Hollis lingered there, her fingers stroking Jude with no real intent or purpose, and it was maddening. Jude drew tighter, the ball of heavy energy pulsing and expanding.

"Please." She gasped the word without really meaning to. So far, Hollis had wanted her vocal, but that didn't mean she wanted her to beg.

"Hmmm, you feel wonderful." Hollis pushed inside with what felt like only one finger. She withdrew just as quickly. "Tell me what you want."

She returned to the same lazy pattern as before, circling, dipping in, but never really touching Jude. She'd draw close, tease at something more substantial, then shift course. Once again, Jude was well past sloppy wet, and yet she had no idea what she wanted beyond just to come.

That wouldn't be enough for Hollis, she knew. Hollis was the type of woman who wanted specifics, details, and Jude was too fractured for that level of coherence. But she was damn well going to try.

"I want…" Jude swallowed, her head swam from the teasing pressure. "I want you to touch me."

Hollis laughed and the vibrations resonated through Jude. "I am touching you." She pressed inside again, still not enough to truly fill Jude. Just enough to make her yearn for more. Then she went back to her arrhythmic play, swiping her fingers, then massaging with her knuckles, always moving but never taking purchase.

"My clit. Please." Instant pressure on her clitoris, firm but unmoving, made Jude gasp, and her hips jerked.

Hollis pressed against her low back, holding her tight against her lap. "Don't move." She did not, however, move her fingers against Jude's clit.

The pressure grew but didn't shift, and it took all of Jude's willpower not to squirm. The slightest shift and she'd be gone, completely blown apart.

"What else?"

Jude was submissive by choice. She'd learned long ago that her body responded better to sexually aggressive and dominating partners. She didn't want to think. She only wanted to respond, to do as commanded without worrying about the right or the wrong of it. She didn't want to think about if she should do it, or if her body could handle it. She trusted her partner to take on all that burden. All she had to do was say yes and let go of her control. It was glorious and freeing.

And yet, prostrated emotionally and physically to Hollis, she struggled to do what was asked. Not because she didn't know what she wanted, but because she was afraid of how very much it excited her. She didn't know how much saying the words *touch me* would turn her on. She'd never been a dirty talker. Often gagged, sometimes literally, but most often figuratively, she wasn't accustomed to hearing her own voice in the middle of sex.

She groaned loudly but couldn't speak. What did she want? Hollis had asked the question, and she needed to find the words to explain her desires. "Please."

The pressure eased, then pulsed. "Please what? I want to give you what you want, Jude, but you have to tell me what that is."

Jude was absolutely certain Hollis knew what Jude wanted without Jude saying the words aloud. She took a deep breath and gathered herself. She could do this.

"Circles. Please." Said aloud, it sounded absurd, and decidedly unsexy. Jude tried again. "Make circles with your fingers."

Hollis massaged the muscles of her back with the hand that pinned Jude to her lap. She made tight, probing circles that felt amazing, but were nowhere close to what Jude needed. She sobbed with frustration.

"Like this?" Hollis didn't laugh aloud, but Jude could hear the amusement in her tone.

"No, your other hand, on my clit."

"Oh. You mean like this." All the laughter disappeared from Hollis's voice. She was suddenly all dark and intense and incredibly seductive.

She moved over Jude's clit with slow, deliberate movements, circling just like she asked, but never quite pressing hard enough.

"More, please." Jude tried to push against Hollis, to force more contact, greater pressure, but Hollis moved with her. She adjusted her legs and pressed even harder against Jude's back. It put amazing pressure on Jude's low abdomen that worked in tandem with the touch against her clit, and her arousal jolted through her.

"God, yes." Jude gasped. The sensation was unexpected, the pressure coming into her cunt from the wrong place, but it felt so very good. It overwhelmed her.

"Can you come like this?"

"Yes, I think…maybe." Jude shook her head and focused on the feeling building inside her.

"Rock against my knee."

Permission to move and so she did, humping frantically into Hollis as she continued to play with her clit. She teased it with her fingers—circling, flicking, massaging, and drawing it out—but her attention and pressure didn't wane.

"So good."

"You can come now."

Hollis twisted her clit between her fingers, pinching and tweaking hard, too hard, and Jude shouldn't have been able to come, but she did. In a great overpowering wave, her orgasm consumed her, starting low in her belly where Hollis's knee still drove into her, and radiating out until all she could do was shudder and whimper.

Smooth, calming strokes worked over her back, and she knew peripherally that Hollis was comforting her, easing her down.

"Wow."

"You liked that?" Hollis eased Jude into a kneeling position on the floor in front of her.

"Very much, thank you." Jude bowed her head, not as a matter of training, but out of pure exhaustion. Hollis stroked her hair.

"I'm going to get you a set of Ben Wa balls."

Jude clenched with anticipation. She'd used them one other time, and it had been a life-changing experience.

"I really do need to go." Hollis sighed and then stood. "Take your time and pull yourself together. You don't need to rush."

"Okay." But she really did. She had homework, of all things.

"Tomorrow," she said as she turned on her heel and headed out the door, "try not to disrupt my class again."

The door closed with a solid, final click, and Jude roused herself enough to begin getting dressed. Her body felt battered and spent. She pulled her shirt over her head, taking inventory of the tender and sore places.

Hollis was right. Tomorrow Jude would be the model student. But the next day, or perhaps the day after, when her body had recovered...well, that remained to be seen.

Jude slipped out of Special Agent Beverly Hollis's office and took one final glance around the room before closing the door. She wasn't too worried about the details of the room. She would be back again soon enough.

❖

Jude stretched and yawned. She still couldn't sleep as well as she did at home in her own bed, but the sound of Reeva's breathing machine no longer kept her up at night. She awoke damn close to refreshed.

Reeva's bed was already made and she was singing in the shower. It was her thing. She sang loud, off key, and with absolute joy in her voice. Jude would like to somehow replicate her enthusiasm for the day, but snarky cynicism had worked for her for this long. There was no changing it now.

A light knock sounded at the door, more a gentle *tap-tap-tap* than an actual answer-me-now knock that she'd grown accustomed to here. Everyone, it seemed, had an agenda, something to prove, and they were determined to start with their knock. It was obnoxious.

When she answered the door, Jude found a short woman she'd never seen before. She held both hands behind her back and glanced up and down the hall before speaking. "Are you Jude?"

"Yes," Jude answered reluctantly. This woman was skittish, which usually resulted in all sorts of bad things.

Before she could ask why the woman wanted to know, she thrust a package into Jude's hands, turned, and literally ran away. Jude was too tired to chase her to find out what in the merry hell that had been about. She shook her head and shut the door.

The box was small, maybe six by four by three, and covered in shiny red paper with a satin bow on top. In fine, solid penmanship, the words *Open Me* were written below the bow. She recognized the writing as Hollis's. She didn't find that comforting at all.

Still, she recognized a command when it occurred, even in writing. She pulled the lid off and stared, probably open-mouthed, as she was too dazed to really control herself. Inside lay two perfect silver globes, stainless steel, actually, each about an inch and a half in diameter.

Ben Wa balls. As promised.

Jude was so stunned she didn't notice Reeva had finished her shower until she asked, "Hey, what's that?"

Her voice was far too close, and Jude slammed the lid back on the box and shoved the whole thing under her shirt. "Nothing." She sounded like a guilty teenager, and she absolutely couldn't change that image with the box-shaped protrusion sticking out beneath her top.

"Okay." Reeva drew the word out and smiled, clearly confused and uncertain. She'd learned, however, that no amount of prying would convince Jude to talk if she wasn't in the mood. "Bathroom's open."

"Thanks." Jude grabbed her clothes, which she'd laid out the night before, and scooted into the bathroom.

Locked safely in there, Jude set the box on the vanity. She'd done a lot of truly debauched things in her life, and frankly Ben Wa balls weren't particularly scandalous. Unless, she realized, they were delivered to her room before breakfast with the possibility her roommate could have answered the door instead of her.

The ridiculous deviance of it all made her giggle. From Reeva's point of view, she probably looked and sounded like an idiot. That made her giggle harder.

A few deep breaths later she finally got hold of herself and stopped. She eased the top off the box, prepared this time for what she'd find inside. Along with the stainless-steel balls, she discovered a note, a piece of plain white printer paper folded into a tight, small rectangle with her name penned neatly on top.

She unfolded the note, clearly a communication of expectations from Hollis. It'd been a long time since she'd received directions in writing, and the process always thrilled her. It showed great forethought and care. There was nothing spontaneous about purchasing a gift, then printing out careful instructions for how to use it.

She spread the paper on the countertop, pressing the creases flat with her palms. The message was brief and simple.

Put these in now. I will remove them later.

Such benign, innocuous words had never excited her so much. The thought of going through her day with the balls rolling and shifting inside her made her squirm in anticipation. They should be easy to insert, but their size could be a problem if the day held too much physical activity. Easy to go in meant that they were also easy to come out. If Hollis had another seven-mile run planned, Jude would lose them before the first mile marker.

And really, how would she explain that to her classmates? "No worries, folks. Give me back my sex toy and go about your business, please. Nothing to see here." Yeah, right.

That scenario, however horrifying for Jude, would be equally exposing for Hollis, if not more so. She would trust Hollis to not place her in a losing situation that would embarrass them both.

She liked to linger in the shower, the feel of the water soothed her skin and eased her into the day, but she didn't have time for that, thanks to Hollis's gift and her giggle fit. She hurried through the basics and delayed inserting the balls until the last possible second.

She had her shirt on, shoes tied, and pants drooping around her thighs when she finally eased the first one inside. She didn't project a very sexy image in her bathroom mirror, but no one was there to watch. And the balls, while a lot of fun, quickly turned to too much stimulation. The longer she waited, the less likely she was to orgasm in front of her classmates.

The extra few minutes she gained by waiting until she was fully dressed wouldn't make much difference at all, but she felt slightly more in control because of it.

She inserted the second ball and shifted slightly, just to get used to the feel of them inside her. They moved within her, pressing against her vaginal walls in the most delicious way. She pulled up her pants, fixed her belt, and trained her expression in the mirror.

When she looked sufficiently placid, she stepped out, ready to face the day.

❖

The gun range was nicer than the one Jude used in Portland. Bigger, too. They'd issued her a Glock 19 that looked serviceable, but she preferred the feel and weight of her own Sig Sauer P226. She could have brought it with her, but the amount of paperwork required for her to bring it on the plane was staggering. There was a time when all she had to do was show her badge and that was enough. That was, of course, before 9/11.

The one big advantage of the Glock over her Sig was the extra two rounds in the clip. At this point, though, she'd spent so much time shooting her P226 that she automatically stopped squeezing the trigger after she counted out thirteen shots. Then she'd remember the other two and work through them quickly. The extra bursts made her smile.

"You're good." Reeva yelled the words because she'd left her ear protection over her ears at the end of the last round. Jude pulled them off and let them drop around Reeva's neck.

"Thanks." She stepped to the side to let Reeva move into position, then dropped her magazine out and set the pistol on the low shelf beneath the top counter. She didn't want Reeva grabbing the wrong gun by mistake because the kid was a shaking mess. Whereas Jude found the muffled gun blasts almost soothing, Reeva found them completely disturbing.

"I still don't understand why we're doing this."

Jude didn't really get it either, since the gun range was part of basic training and had nothing to do with terrorist-specific training. But it took up only a couple of hours at the end of the day, just like the insane course Hollis had made them run the previous week. Maybe those exercises were meant to give the students a chance to clear their thoughts and return to normal.

And that might have worked for her if it wasn't for the damn balls inside her. They shifted and slid every time she pulled the trigger. And of course she'd clench to keep them in place. The internal pressure against the motion of the balls had been building inside her all day. The shooting range was the evil, erotic cherry on top.

Hollis stared at her from across the range, a small, knowing grin on her face. She gave Jude the barest of nods, then turned her attention to a student closer to her. She knew how close Jude was to rubbing up against the nearest warm body until she came. The thought was mortifying because, how in the hell would she explain that to Reeva, the nearest warm body? Not to mention that if she gave in to the impulse, Hollis would punish her mercilessly later. Although that might make it worth it.

"Seriously, what does this have to do with terrorists?" Reeva continued her complaint as she snapped her ammo clip into place.

"No idea." Jude squeezed her thighs together and almost fell over. Maybe when the next round started and everyone else was distracted, she could do that a few more times and let herself come finally.

"Everything okay over here?" Hollis spoke from behind her, her mouth closer to Jude's ear than she ever got to any of her classmates, but still far enough away to not raise suspicion. It no longer surprised her when Hollis did that, came out of nowhere and spoke directly into her ear from behind. But it still set her heart to racing in anticipation of what was to come.

"Everything is fine." Jude tried like hell to keep her voice level, and it worked for the most part. Hollis knew her well enough to sense the slight tremble, but it wasn't pronounced enough that Reeva would have noticed.

"Really?" Hollis lowered her voice half a register, and Jude's body responded immediately. Just like that, she was ready to leave and let Hollis take care of the need that had been building inside her with every shift of those damn, wonderful, awful balls. She already knew how to shoot. She didn't need any more range time.

"How much longer?" She lowered her voice to match Hollis. Normally, she worked hard to remain indifferent during class, but normally she didn't have steel balls inside her cunt. It tended to make a girl a little bold.

"Why? Are you eager to get out of here?" Hollis's voice was deadly serious, her face deadpan. Still, Jude was pretty sure she was being teased.

"God, yes." She breathed her response. If Hollis didn't like the extra attention during class, she shouldn't shove Jude's cunt full of sex toys at the beginning of the day.

The light came on to signal the next round was about to begin. She could see people around her dropping their ear protection into place, but she waited. She wanted to hear what Hollis had to say.

"I want to take you to my house today. Is that okay?" Hollis asked the question, then took Jude's earmuffs in her hands and settled them over her ears. Then she did the same with her own. Apparently Jude's opinion didn't matter.

She nodded, pretty sure her mouth was hanging open. Hollis smiled and walked away.

Jude watched her go and checked the clock. Fifteen more minutes, and it couldn't pass quick enough.

Chapter Five

Reeva entered their room before Jude and turned to watch her enter. She stood with her arms crossed and foot tapping. She would make an excellent mom one day.

"When are you going to tell me?" Reeva asked.

That question could have meant any one of a million things, and Jude wasn't about to volunteer anything.

"What do you mean?"

"You and Special Agent Hollis." Reeva raised an eyebrow and tapped a little faster.

Jude dropped her book bag on her desk chair and debated changing clothes. They hadn't worked out at all that day and, other than the light scent of gunpowder, she smelled clean. Still, a shower was in order. She picked out a clean change of clothes, cargo shorts, a tight tank top, and her favorite belt. It wasn't particularly sexy, but it was clean and one of the few personal outfits she'd brought with her. And anything was better than the standard-issue FBI clothing she'd been forced to wear while at this damn training seminar.

"I don't know what you're talking about." Jude took her clothes into the bathroom and set them on the counter. She debated stripping with the door open, as that would surely convince Reeva their conversation was over, but given the state of her underwear and the fact that she had Ben Wa balls inside her, she decided not to. The thought of losing track of one and it slipping out and rolling across the floor with Reeva watching mortified her. Instead, she stood in the open door and propped one shoulder against the frame.

"Oh, come on. She was totally flirting with you today."

"I don't know what you're talking about." Of course Jude knew exactly what Reeva referenced, but she really, really wanted to enjoy the evening with Hollis. She was pretty sure that confessing to their illicit affair to Reeva ran counter-intuitive to her goal for the night.

Reeva threw up her hands. "I was standing right there! I could hear you guys."

Jude did her best to look nonplussed. "And? It doesn't mean anything, Reeva. If you're asking if I like flirting with her, the answer is yes. Who wouldn't? She's hot. Don't turn it into something it's not."

Reeva looked almost convinced. "That makes sense, but what about her? Is she supposed to flirt with her students?"

"Jesus, I'm not a child. I'm in my forties. Trust me, she's not going to take advantage of me or exert undue influence over my life. Fuck."

"Maybe you're right."

"Maybe? Reeva, you need to stop. The things you're saying could have a serious impact on her career, and for what? We're leaving in a week. What difference does it?"

"I don't want to hurt her. I just want to know what's going on." Reeva looked like Jude had hurt her feelings, something Jude couldn't wrap her head around. It wasn't like they were besties who shared everything. She'd known Reeva for two weeks.

"Nothing's going on. I already told you that." Jude struggled with her temper. This whole scenario was ridiculous. She should be able to fuck whoever she wanted. Still, pissing Reeva off wouldn't help the situation. "I'm sorry if I upset you earlier. I promise not to flirt with anyone else for the next week, okay?"

"Yeah, okay. I guess." Reeva scuffed her toe on the carpet, and it took every ounce of Jude's willpower not to laugh at the display. She was like a scolded child.

"I'm going to take a shower. Are we good?"

"Yeah." Reeva nodded sullenly and pulled out a textbook. She sat on her bed and started reading. Jude was dismissed.

Thank fuck. Jude didn't have time to keep hashing this over. She had more pleasant things to think about than Reeva's hurt feeling. As it was, she'd have to rush through the shower if she didn't want to keep Hollis waiting.

❖

Jude scanned the street for Hollis's car, then realized she didn't know what Hollis drove. She descended the steps, resolved to wait. Standing there wasn't particularly subtle, but she didn't know what else to do. Wait until Hollis showed up was her only option.

Hollis pulled to a smooth stop in front of her as Jude hit the last step. She climbed into the dark sedan, thankful for the dark-tinted windows. Hollis seemed pretty casual about taking her off-site, but after her conversation with Reeva, Jude was a little uncertain.

"Hey there." Hollis sounded disturbingly normal when she wasn't playing the role of instructor. Or Dom. Jude would freak completely out if Hollis held her hand like this was some sort of date.

"Hi." She answered because it was polite. But it still felt weird as fuck. She didn't spend a lot of time talking to Hollis casually. She followed orders. And tried not to scream when she came.

"How are you?" Hollis stared straight ahead, but the expression on her face indicated that this was all perfectly normal for her.

"Uncomfortable. It's hard to shower with Ben Wa balls inside your cunt."

Hollis smiled, lopsided and sexy, and said, "Language."

Jude felt the impact as if it were a paddle connecting with her butt cheeks. She stiffened and sat up straighter. "Sorry, ma'am."

"It's okay. I was teasing. Relax."

Jude tried to ease back into the seat, but her body simply wouldn't relax fully. She had no doubt Hollis would make her pay for her loose words when they reached her house. She squirmed and the balls inside her shifted.

"Talk to me. Tell me about your day." This time Hollis sounded as rigidly formal as Jude felt.

"Is this okay? Our relationship? Like you wouldn't get fired if anyone found out about it, right?" She spoke because Hollis told her to, but she should have considered her words a little more carefully beforehand.

"What is this about?"

"My roommate was asking about you."

"Reeva? That girl is very smart. She'll make a good agent someday. Not in counterterrorism. Maybe as a profiler." Hollis focused too closely on the details about Reeva, and not enough on the question Jude asked. It was irritating.

"But would it be a problem?"

"Depends. If she found out we're...seeing each other? That would be okay. If she found out *how* we're seeing one another? That would be awkward."

"You wouldn't lose your job."

"No, of course not. If you were a twenty-something, fresh out of college, that might raise a few more eyebrows, but even that would be overlooked."

That news was good enough that Jude was able to relax into the seat as previously directed. Until she thought about it. Then she was tense all over again.

"How often do you do this?"

"This?" Hollis asked distractedly as she turned onto the freeway on ramp.

"This, have an affair with a student." Jude knew she wasn't special enough to be the only one, and she *hated* the way she sounded all controlling and needy. Still she asked the question and cringed because of it.

Hollis chuckled. "Are you jealous?"

Whether she was or not, she certainly sounded the part. Jude considered her emotions and then answered honestly. "I think I might be, but I'm not sure why."

"How interesting."

Jude felt a little like a bug under glass, there for Hollis to examine and inspect. Of course she had to explain.

"I don't think this is some great romance. And I don't think I have any particular claim to you. But I like what we share enough to want it to be special."

"I see." Hollis nodded. "I think it is. I've had affairs before, just as you have, but nothing quite like this. We fit together effortlessly. I'll be sad when you leave."

"Me, too."

"Let's not talk about it then."

And then Hollis did the unthinkable. She picked up Jude's hand, laced their fingers together, then dropped it into her own lap, all without fanfare. Even more disturbing to Jude was the fact that she quite liked it. Given a choice, she'd choose the bite of leather cuffs digging into her wrists, but it was also nice to drive down the road and simply touch one another in an unassuming, completely vanilla way. It was comforting.

She tightened her grip on Hollis's hand and rested her head against the headrest. She closed her eyes for the remainder of the ride to Hollis's house and tried not to think about what it all meant. She didn't open them again until Hollis pulled to a stop and said, "We're here."

❖

As soon as they crossed the threshold, Hollis's demeanor changed completely. It wasn't anything noticeable, just a subtle shift in the way she stood. Yet it made all the difference in the world. The woman before her was firm, commanding, and so in charge Jude got wet just looking at her. She clenched and the balls inside her pushed against her inner walls, making her tremble.

"My bedroom is down the hall. Only door on the left. Wait for me there."

Jude nodded and kept her gaze averted. Yes, Hollis liked to be watched, but this was different. Right now she wanted to be obeyed properly, and that meant Jude's head needed to be bowed, her eyes focused on the floor. Her throat ached to voice her approval, but for now that wasn't allowed either.

She found Hollis's room easily. The lights were on a dimmer, so she set them to a low output and shut the door behind her. There was a large, four-poster bed in the middle of the far wall. No canopy. A matching trunk butted against the end of the bed. A tall chest of drawers sat on the wall opposite, close to the door. Several objects, toys Hollis hopefully planned to use that evening: nipple clamps, a pair of leather cuffs, a strap-on with a moderately sized blue dildo. Jude was pleasantly surprised because she'd expected something obscenely oversized and impossible to accommodate without risk of injury.

Jude had no doubt how Hollis wanted her. The message communicated through her tone and the few sparse words made her wishes clear. Jude stripped quickly, folding her clothes and stacking them neatly on the low settee by the closet. She set her shoes, laces tucked inside, beneath it. Then she kneeled by the door with her hands resting, palms down, atop her thighs. And she waited.

She focused on the weave of carpet directly in front of her. She'd already indulged too freely by looking around when she arrived. Any more would be a clear violation of the trust Hollis extended by bringing her into her home.

She didn't wait long. Hollis entered the room, her movements nearly silent. She sat on the trunk and said, "Come here."

She didn't specify how, and Jude wasn't willing to take any chances. She crawled over and knelt at Hollis's feet.

"Hands behind your back, please."

Of course, how could she have forgotten something so simple? Hollis liked her shoulders back, breasts jutting forward. She complied immediately and hoped she was graceful enough to earn forgiveness for her transgression.

"Thank you." Hollis stroked her hair, playing with the ends. "Are you hungry?"

She really was, but that didn't mean it was a good idea to eat now. She didn't know if she was allowed to ask, but wasn't sure how to do so.

"You may speak." And that was why she appreciated Hollis so much. She was the perfect Dom, paying close attention and anticipating her needs.

Jude raised her eyes and chose her words carefully. Hollis had prepared a plate of fruit, crackers, and cheese, easy-to-eat finger foods that were also filling. Jude didn't want to insult her efforts.

"I am hungry, but I don't know if it would be best to eat now or wait until later."

"Mmm, good point." Hollis selected a slice of strawberry and painted Jude's lips with it, then pushed it into her mouth. "You're probably right. We should wait."

Hollis picked up the plate and carried it somewhere out of Jude's line of sight, probably the chest of drawers. She heard the plate being set down and the sound of something else, something small and metallic, being picked up. Her skin pricked with awareness.

"Please stand." The command came cool and smooth and directly behind her. Hollis certainly liked to sneak up on her.

Kneeling with the balls inside her hadn't been too much of an issue. She'd been able to use her hands for support, and Hollis hadn't been there to witness her struggle. Getting up was another story entirely. Being graceful wasn't an option; it was required.

She clenched tight in her core to hold the balls in place and to give her balance, and it took every ounce of her control not to grimace with the shifting pressure inside her. The balls had been there too long, and she'd worked hard to ignore them while simultaneously being hyper aware of their positioning. It was a fine balance, and the longer she went, the wetter she got. They became harder and harder to hold in place.

After a deep breath, she rose without faltering. It wasn't as smooth as she would have liked, but given the circumstances, she was pleased.

Hollis trailed a fingertip over her shoulders as she walked into view. She stopped directly in front of Jude with one hand draped over her shoulder. She bounced the nipple clamps in clear view, and Jude was fixated. They were the adjustable kind with a weighted chain that dangled between the two. Very effective.

"I'd like to put these on you. Would that be okay?" Hollis asked the question formally and her words made Jude shiver.

Jude met Hollis's gaze and nodded steadily. She was being given so much control, and it left her confused and excited.

"Thank you."

Hollis dipped her head and kissed Jude's breasts, first one then the other. She licked and sucked them to hard peaks, then drew back to inspect her work. She drew one finger carefully over her lips. "You really didn't need that, but I certainly enjoyed it."

She held one clamp delicately between her thumb and forefinger, twisting it to catch the light, hypnotizing Jude with the reflection. As Hollis kissed her, Jude's eyes slipped shut and she lost track of the clamp until Hollis gripped her nipple, pulling it taut and then slipping the clamp into place. Fire burst through her breast and down to her overstimulated cunt. She moaned into Hollis's mouth. She wouldn't last long tonight.

Before she could open her eyes, before she could gasp, before she could fully appreciate one, Hollis slipped the other clamp into place, and Jude had to hold herself painfully still to keep from falling to the floor in a sopping-wet, delirious mess.

"Okay?" Hollis's question barely penetrated the fog in her brain. She was so focused on staying upright, so lost in the sharp crashing waves of pleasure and pain originating in her nipples and radiating down, her senses were muddied beyond the immediate.

Hollis was a good lover, an attentive Dom, and she deserved an answer. If she didn't get one, she would demand it. Jude nodded frantically, afraid to speak. If she let loose even the smallest sound, the strangled scream in her throat would escape and she didn't think she'd be able to stop.

"Good." Hollis teased the exposed tip of her nipple with the edge of her fingernail. It was exquisite and Jude squirmed under her touch. Hollis stopped immediately. A sharp, quick blow landed on Jude's ass, and Hollis issued a command. "Stay still."

She nodded again and hoped Hollis wouldn't force her to speak. Hollis smoothed her palm over the hot skin where she'd just slapped.

"Open your eyes."

Jude struggled to obey. It was such a simple request, but she hadn't settled into the constant, screaming sensation in her nipples. She needed better control before adding more stimulation. She finally opened them, far too slowly, judging by the frown on Hollis's face.

"Keep your eyes on me." Hollis unbuttoned her shirt and slipped it off. She wore a simple, utilitarian white sports bra. It suited her. It came off next. Her nipples were hard and elongated, as if in sympathy with Jude's.

Jude stared, fixated. Hollis popped the snap on her pants, then lowered the zipper slowly. She'd already removed her shoes, perhaps before she came into the bedroom. When she pushed her pants off, she took off her underwear at the same time. She stepped out of her slacks and stood gloriously naked for Jude to take in.

"Get the strap-on from the dresser and put it on me." She stood with her arms at her sides, completely comfortable with her nudity, which was making Jude pant.

She nodded and followed Hollis's command, quicker to respond this time. It wasn't her first time with a leather harness, but still her hands trembled slightly with anticipation. She didn't know where Hollis planned to fuck her with it, and the possibilities excited her.

Jude loosened the straps and held the harness open. Hollis stepped in easily, then stood impassively as Jude adjusted and tightened the straps and secured the cock in the *O* ring.

"That's good, thank you."

Jude stepped back, a full arm's length away. Any closer and she'd give in to the urge to touch Hollis more completely.

"You look beautiful." Hollis stepped behind her, moving easily with the cock bobbing between her legs. She looked completely comfortable.

She stopped behind Jude, her breath hot against Jude's skin.

"Let's have some fun." Her words made the hairs on the back of Jude's neck prick, and a shiver ran the length of her spine.

She was really going to miss Hollis and her particular brand of fun.

CHAPTER SIX

Jude waited, her mouth open slightly in anticipation. Hollis had stepped away from her several minutes ago, and Jude fought the urge to seek her out. The need frustrated her. The damn balls rolling around in her cunt had shredded her self-control, and if Hollis didn't remove them soon, Jude was going to fall apart completely.

The air behind Jude charged with tension, followed immediately by Hollis's hot breath on Jude's neck. Bumps rolled over her shoulders and down her back. Hollis pressed a tiny kiss to Jude's ear, then took hold of her wrist. Soft fur with the bite of hard leather at the edges slid around her, and she felt Hollis buckle the cuff securely in place. Then she did the same to the other and fastened the two together.

"Like this." Hollis guided her hands until they were flat against her own ass. The position strained her shoulders and made her chest jut out. Hollis's hands eased around her to stroke her breasts, fingering gently across her nipples. "Can you stay like this?"

It wasn't the most comfortable she'd ever been, but she understood the appeal from Hollis's point of view. Hollis's cock pressed against the backs of her hands. "Yes."

"Good." Hollis spoke directly into her ear, then kissed the sensitive spot right behind it. She kept one hand on Jude's breast, her fingers dusting over the clamped nipple and shooting fire through her body, as she worked the other hand lower, gliding over the taut skin of her stomach until her fingers slid into the V at the top of her thighs.

Hollis bumped into her hood and the touch resonated into her clit. She gasped.

"Spread your legs for me."

God, with the balls threatening to slip from her cunt at any moment, widening her stance was an impossible request. She struggled to edge her feet apart, moving slowly to gauge her body's response. When she hit about shoulder length, Hollis squeezed with both hands, distracting her from…everything. Movement would have to wait.

"That's good." Hollis slid her hand lower, opening her folds and teasing just inside her cunt. "I can play right here."

Hollis swirled her fingers, then drew them to her clit. Jude was already painfully hard and desperate for a little release. She moved her hips against Hollis, humping against the fleeting fingers.

"Stay still." Hollis slapped her hard and quick, and her clit threatened to explode. She sucked air through her teeth and focused on breathing until the intensity faded incrementally.

The black pressure at the edges of her vision receded, and Jude realized that Hollis had stopped moving as well. She was waiting for Jude to be ready.

"I'm sorry. I won't move again."

"Good." Hollis resumed her careful touch, circling the barest tips of her fingers over Jude's clit. "I'm going to take care of you."

All she could manage in response was a plaintive whimper. It was pathetic, and she didn't even have the wherewithal to care.

"Do you want to come?" Hollis asked lazily, her voice moving with the same lack of urgency as her fingers. Still the words, the hope for release, pushed the fire through her body at an increasingly rapid pace. If Hollis denied her after bringing her this high, Jude would break down and cry.

"Yes, please."

"You can. Whenever you're ready."

"Oh, thank God." Jude stopped holding back and let her body go. The thick band of excitement traveling from her nipples to her cunt pushed the heat rolling in her cunt deeper. She released with a shout, her body clenching tight then relaxing. The balls rolled out of her, slick with arousal, and Hollis caught them easily.

Hollis supported her until she was able to stand on her own; then she released her and stepped away. The bells inside the balls tinkled when Hollis set them down.

Hollis stepped back into Jude's field of vision. She stood with her hands on her hips and an impossibly smug smile on her face. Jude returned her smile weakly.

"How are you doing?" Hollis evaluated her closely as Jude nodded. She wasn't up for talking quite yet, after the relief and disappointment of removing the balls. If she spoke, she'd beg Hollis to put them back in. Hollis dipped her head and licked over one protruding nipple, then the next. "How about these? Do you need me to remove them?"

If Hollis spent just a few more minutes concentrating on her breasts, licking over her nipples, she would orgasm again. She definitely didn't want to remove the clamps just yet. That was worth risking speech. "They're okay."

Hollis nodded. "I want to fuck your mouth. Please kneel."

Jesus, any calm her body claimed with her orgasm fled, and she was flooded with renewed arousal. The sticky wetness between her legs grew slick and desperate. She dropped to her knees easily, even with the cuffs restricting her motion. Without the balls, her whole body felt lighter, easier to control.

"Good. Open your mouth, please."

Jude gripped her own ass tight, squeezing just to satisfy the need to hold on as Hollis rested one hand on top of her head, her fingers playing loosely in her hair. She licked her lips, then held her mouth open and waited.

"Don't move." Hollis gripped her cock in her right hand and eased her body closer to Jude. She brushed the tip against Jude's lip and withdrew, her hips rocking with the motion.

This was why Hollis had restrained her hands, she was sure. The desire to wrap her arms around Hollis's thighs and pull her in deeper was overwhelming. She dug uselessly at the flesh of her ass, her stomach drawing tight with excitement.

Hollis pushed the cock into her mouth, resting it on her tongue and pushing forward until she hit the back of Jude's throat. Jude forced herself to relax, to ease her gag reflex to allow the touch. After a moment, she swallowed, taking it in farther. Hollis pulled back immediately and tightened her hold on Jude's hair. The message was clear. She didn't want Jude to help at all.

Jude whimpered and forced herself to relax. Hollis had a plan, and she needed to trust her to take care of both of them.

The texture of the dildo against Jude's tongue, sliding between her lips, was foreign and not entirely pleasant. She'd much rather suck Hollis's clit into her mouth and lave it with her tongue. She craved the salty desire she knew coated Hollis's pussy and thighs.

But the twist of Hollis's fingers tightening in her hair had Jude riding the line between pain and the haze of endorphin-released pleasure. Hollis pushed in again, the same depth as before, right on the edge of breaching her throat, but not quite. She released the hold on Jude's hair and stroked her face, tracing over the high point of her cheeks.

Jude met Hollis's intense, demanding stare and held it as Hollis retracted, then thrust forward again. As always, she was lost in Hollis, caught up in her gaze. This time, rather than her regular placid look and impenetrable expression, Jude found deep longing. Hollis fucked her mouth gently, in and out, with more care than Jude ever expected while on her knees with a cock in her mouth. She stroked in and out at a calm, metered pace, her legs moving through the motions easily.

Hollis stopped with the cock at the back of Jude's throat, her eyes still focused intently on Jude's. She stood perfectly still, one hand on Jude's cheek, the other threaded loosely into her hair. "I need more." She spoke in a choked whisper.

Jude opened her throat, prepared to take the cock deeper, but Hollis pulled out completely and dropped to her knees in front of Jude. Hollis moved slowly, with careful deliberation, tracing the curve of Jude's body with her hands. She followed the natural path down to her hips, her touch so gentle Jude trembled with wanting more.

She brought one hand up to cup the back of Jude's neck and held her that way for several moments, one hand on her hip, her thumb moving rhythmically over her skin, and the other wrapped loosely around her neck, her fingers playing with the sensitive skin at the base of her neck. Jude felt more deeply penetrated by the intimacy of the moment, by the raw pleading in Hollis's eyes, than she had during any of their other encounters. Hollis had fucked her in creative and varied ways, but she'd never touched her like this.

She couldn't take the beseeching look any longer. Jude closed her eyes and let her head fall against Hollis's. She didn't know what Hollis was searching for and was lost in trying to give her the unknown. She stayed like that, with Hollis's hot breath puffing against her face, rushing down her body, and bringing bumps to the surface of her skin.

With her grip light and gentle, not the forceful ownership Jude accepted and submitted to, Hollis kissed her. Her mouth open, her lips lingered and tasted, but made no demands. Hollis left her breathless and panting, and she wasn't even really touching her. Not like she was used to, with force great enough to shake her from her feet and steamroll orgasms from her body.

Hollis inched forward, her grip still careful on Jude's body, her fingers not pressing tight enough to leave even the slightest red blotch upon Jude's skin. The cock pressed against her, sandwiched between their bellies and wet with Jude's saliva.

"Please." She didn't know what more Hollis wanted, but she would lay herself prostrate, flay herself open to give her what she needed. It was a futile, useless word, but the only one Jude could utter. "Please." She pressed the word against Hollis's lips in a whisper and imagined her plea sliding down Hollis's throat and making its way into her very soul, rooting them together in this moment.

"Yes." Hollis kissed her lips, flicking her tongue into her mouth with a slick reminder of how easily she could own every part of Jude. Then she moved south, her mouth sucking and licking down her throat to her chest. Her body rubbed against Jude's, pulling against her distressed nipples. The teeth of the nipple clamps dug in and held tighter, flaring her chest and cunt to life with ripping pain.

Jude tensed and arched, forcing her chest into Hollis, but Hollis maintained that maddeningly easy pace. Her mouth moved slow and gentle, sucking lightly as she murmured against Jude's skin— meaningless words of desire that slid into Jude, promising gentle release in complete opposition to the clamps wrenching her desire higher by force.

Jude fought against her cuffs. She twisted her wrists, willing them smaller. She wanted to touch Hollis. She needed the feel of skin against her palms to tether her. She felt as though she might float away at any moment.

She was about to beg, to plead with Hollis to release her, when Hollis reached behind her with an urgent moan. She kissed Jude again, this time easing her tongue between her lips. The slick slide of Hollis's tongue inside her mouth made Jude moan out in pleasure. She was shamelessly loud in a way she hadn't been in years, all her training forgotten.

Then, by miraculous intervention, her hands were free. She placed them both on Hollis's hips, uncertain where she was allowed to touch and where was off-limits. This was a new and rare pleasure. After her boldness during their previous encounter, Hollis had strictly enforced her no-touching policy. She preferred Jude restrained and helpless.

Hollis's skin was hot beneath her touch. She trembled, but otherwise remained still as Jude explored. She traced the leather edges of the harness, holding back and forcing herself to go slow, to touch gently. This was so different from their other times together, Jude wasn't sure of the boundaries.

She eased her hands upward until she was cupping Hollis's breasts in her hands. She squeezed gently, testing the weight. She met Hollis's gaze as she swiped her thumbs over her nipples. It was such a gentle touch that, given their history together, shouldn't have earned any response at all, yet Hollis stiffened and gasped.

Jude lowered her head until she was poised to take one turgid nipple into her mouth. "Is this okay?" She waited with her lips millimeters away.

Hollis nodded, her movements jerky and vulnerable, and drew Jude in with her hands on the back of her head. "Yes."

Jude licked over the nipple, flattening her tongue and simply getting to know the contours. Then she flicked her tongue, once, twice, and a third time, lapping at the stiff peak. Hollis's grip in her hair tightened and she pulled Jude in securely. She arched her back, forcing herself into Jude's mouth. Jude sucked her in, opening her mouth to take as much as possible, then pulling back while keeping the suction tight and hard.

Hollis gasped again, so quietly Jude wasn't sure it'd really happened. She repeated the motion and twisted the tip with her teeth before releasing her completely.

"Yes." Hollis hissed her approval loud enough that there was no mistaking it.

Hollis eased her onto her back before she was done exploring her new-found freedom. She wanted to trace every line, flatten her hands against every expanse of skin, and lick every drop of moisture from her body. But when Hollis positioned the tip of the cock at her opening and moaned, "I want to fuck you so bad," Jude forgot every objection to their change in position.

"Please." Hollis held her hips still, the dildo nestled just inside Jude without truly penetrating. "Please let me fuck you."

Jude spread herself wide and arched into Hollis, and the cock slipped in a little farther. "Yes." She wrapped one leg around Hollis and urged her to take her.

Hollis sank into her slowly, letting the cock slide in easily and completely. When she was fully inside, she thrust forward quick and hard, and Jude felt more fully penetrated than she ever remembered being.

Hollis held herself over Jude and lowered her head to her chest. She licked Jude's sensitive nipples, just slipping lightly over the flesh and avoiding the stainless-steel clamps. The pressure sliced through Jude hot and hard, ripping open the wave of pleasure the clamps always brought her. Then, before Jude could relax into the extreme stimulation, Hollis removed the clamp from one side, then the next.

Blood raced into the deprived areas and Jude felt like she was on fire. She gasped and squirmed, unprepared for the sudden rush. Hollis gripped both breasts and flattened her body against Jude's, her hands sandwiched between them. The pressure helped mute the experience, but didn't come close to quieting it completely.

"You can come if you need to." Hollis thrust again, pressing the cock deep inside.

Jude moaned and gripped Hollis by the shoulders, holding her tight against her. She let herself feel the bands of heat flowing within her, ready to unfurl and explode. It would take so little. "Close."

Hollis eased her hips back while maintaining full contact with the rest of her body, and just as carefully thrust forward. A few more controlled thrusts and Jude's orgasm swept over her, slow and easy, like a heated drink overflowing the cup. She rode it until the heat and tide receded, but instead of feeling empty and wanting, her body clenched around Hollis's cock deep inside her. She started the steep rise toward orgasm again.

"So good." She arched into Hollis, urging her to stop holding back and fuck her for real.

Hollis kissed her languidly, her lips and tongue owning every part of Jude. She ended the kiss with a tight tug at Jude's bottom lip, catching it between her teeth. She held it and sucked, then released it slowly. "Are you ready?"

"Ready?"

"I want to fuck you now. Just us." She thrust into Jude to punctuate her point.

There was a time in her life, years ago, when the statement would have seemed absurd. Hollis was penetrating her with a fake cock. She was stretched and filled and so wet for more. She wanted to be pounded through the floor, and the look in Hollis's eyes promised that she'd deliver. But with the cock between them, it was so much more than *just us*.

Jude understood what she meant, though, and was touched by the sentiment. No cuffs, no clamps, no commands, and no safe word. Just the two of them feeling each other, making each other feel without the formality and rules. She stared into Hollis's eyes and lifted the other leg up until they were both wrapped tight around Hollis's waist. She nodded and tightened her hold on Hollis's shoulders.

She was there, beneath Hollis, open and offering herself in the most pure way she knew. Hollis kissed her again and shifted her grip, moving her hands from between them and back to the floor at Jude's shoulders. She pushed up, angling her body for better, deeper penetration.

Jude hadn't thought it was possible, in that position, for Hollis to touch her any deeper. She had been wrong. Just the subtle shift in body position forced her deeper into Jude, forcing a strangled gasp from her lips.

"Hold on."

Hollis fucked her slowly and thoroughly, pushing into her with careful, deep strokes. The firestorm brewed within her, swirling low in her cunt and curling out and traveling through her belly and up into her chest.

Jude rose hard and fast, in counterpoint to Hollis's slow, controlled movements. She reached the brink of falling shamefully fast and didn't care. Hollis fucked her so good, and all she wanted was to find the orgasm her body was chasing.

Hollis thrust once more, sharp and hard, and Jude fell, flew, shattered. Her body slumped into a puddled, weak mass, too spent to hold herself together. Her legs fell away from Hollis, her hands slipped to the floor. She was a quivering, happy mess.

"Not yet." Hollis's command barely penetrated her fog, but she knew, as Hollis gripped her ankles and urged her legs up to her chest, that the command wasn't about Jude's orgasm, but more about her own desire to continue.

With Jude's body folded open, her cunt angled up to meet Hollis's cock, Hollis began to fuck her hard and fast. She slammed into Jude with so much force her body inched back across the floor with each thrust. Hollis pushed her forward, crawling forward to push into her over and over and over.

When Jude's head touched the chest at the foot of the bed, Hollis released the hold on her ankles. She gripped Jude's hips, letting her feet rest against her shoulders. She jerked Jude's body onto her cock with each punishing thrust until they were both covered with a thick sheen of sweat.

Jude let herself be manhandled, her hands grabbing at the floor uselessly with each forward thrust of Hollis's hips. Her cunt was oversensitized and buzzing with each stroke. Just a little more, a little harder, and she'd come again.

"Harder," she pleaded. She wanted Hollis to abuse her body, to pound through her cunt until she exploded.

Hollis jerked Jude's hips up higher and arched back, changing the angle and the depth of her stroke slightly. Her back and legs trembled as she thrust, pushing forward with the full power of her body in each stroke.

"I'm close." Hollis gritted the words out, but they didn't matter.

Jude came on the next stroke, when the cock pressed against her back wall and her exposed, raw clit rubbed hard against Hollis. She shuddered and orgasmed in sloppy, wet completion.

As she trembled through her orgasm, Hollis jerked and stiffened. She came with her cock deep inside Jude, then collapsed on top of her. Her back and legs twitched helplessly as she rode out the power of her release.

"Stay with me." Hollis whispered the words.

"Yes." Jude wasn't sure if Hollis was talking about the night or if she meant something longer. She didn't question it as Hollis led her to her bed and held her close until they both fell asleep.

CHAPTER SEVEN

"Oh, you're in here." Reeva stopped in the doorway, her arms full of books. Several people stood behind her waiting to enter.

Jude raised her text. "Studying."

"We'll just go to the common room." Reeva started to back out of the room.

"That's not necessary." Given a choice, Jude would rather study in silence, but in fairness, it was Reeva's room, too. She could hardly deny her access just because she liked the quiet.

"Are you sure?" Reeva looked as skeptical as Jude felt.

They hadn't talked much since Reeva's third degree about her relationship with Hollis. Ironically, Hollis had avoided her for the last week as well.

"Sure." Jude went against her instincts. "Why not?"

Reeva looked at her like she didn't quite believe what she was hearing, but she came in anyway. Four of their classmates followed her.

"We're hitting the books before the final tomorrow."

Jude doubted Reeva needed the book time at all. Girl wasn't kidding when she said she remembered everything.

Reeva and Tim sat on her bed, and the other three looked at Jude's bed, then sat on the floor. Apparently she was disrupting their usual seating arrangement. That explained why her bed was crumpled when she got back to her room on most nights.

"What's going on with you and Hollis? Did you break up or something?" Tim asked with an open smirk. Jude couldn't for the life of her understand what Reeva saw in him.

"Is this how you spend your study time? Gossiping about things that are none of your business?"

Tim was unperturbed. "All I know is, she was in a lot better mood the past two weeks. Then suddenly on Tuesday, she's turns into a total bitch."

"Nah, she's always been a bitch. It's just worse now." Their classmate didn't even look up from his book when he spoke.

"Right," continued Tim, "can't you do the rest of us a favor and make up with her before the test tomorrow?"

"Fuck off." It wasn't the most eloquent response, but Jude enjoyed saying it nonetheless.

"I'll take that as a no."

"I'm sorry, Jude. We shouldn't pry, but I'm worried about you." The look on Reeva's face convinced Jude that might actually be true.

"You might be, but the only thing he cares about is his grade."

"Damn right. This test will influence placement. I want behavioral sciences." Tim was ambitious.

A gentle knock sounded and then door opened. Hollis poked her head in. "Excuse me, I don't mean to interrupt." She nodded to the full room, then met Jude's watchful gaze. "Can I have a word?"

"Sure." Jude left her book in the middle of her bed and open to the page she was studying. It was a test to see who was brave enough to close it and move to her vacated seat.

"Thank fuck." Tim's voice carried through the closed door.

"Can we go for a ride?" Hollis looked more uncertain than Jude had seen her during the entire past three weeks. Her eyes were red rimmed and vulnerable.

"I have a test tomorrow, I really should study." Jude wanted to be sympathetic, but she was too pissed for that. Hollis had touched her in a way she'd never been touched before, and then completely ignored her afterward. Jude hadn't asked for the change in their relationship, but it'd happened nonetheless. She wasn't the one running from it, or punishing the other person because of it.

"Please? We need to talk."

As much as she should be studying, Jude had to admit that Hollis was right. They had to talk and this might be their last chance to do so.

"Okay." She debated taking Hollis's hand as they walked toward her car. Jude wasn't a fan of handholding, so the impulse caught her off guard. How would Hollis respond? Would she allow it? Would Jude be able to stand the simple niceness of it? She doubted it.

Hollis opened the door for Jude and held it until she was safely inside with her seatbelt on. Then she circled the car, her steps slow and deliberate. Her lips moved as though she was rehearsing a speech.

She didn't speak until they'd been driving for over ten minutes. "I don't know exactly what to say."

"Figure it out," Jude said. This is why she liked the rules of BDSM. She didn't have to wait for her partner to sort out her emotional shit. She had enough baggage of her own, but it didn't keep her from voicing her thoughts. All the wishy-washy bullshit made her crazy.

"I like you." Hollis's simple admission was more than Jude expected. It surprised her, but it didn't exactly get them anywhere.

"I like you, too."

Hollis took her hand in hers as she had on the drive to her house Tuesday night. "A lot. I like you a lot. More than I was prepared for and I'm not sure what to do about it."

"There's not a lot to do about it. I'm headed back to Portland on Saturday morning."

"I know, but I'm not ready to let you go."

"I don't have a choice." Jude's whole life was in Portland. Her family, her friends, her job. Everything.

"I could come with you." Hollis spoke quietly, but very clearly. There was no mistaking the words, or the emotion behind them.

Jude tightened her grip on Hollis's hand.

"Is that an option?"

"There are openings in the Portland Field Office. I checked."

"So you put in for a transfer? Then what?" Jude didn't care about the semantics of FBI protocol, she just didn't understand what this all meant for their relationship.

"Then we could try. It might not work, but it just might. I want to find out."

"How would it work? Do you want to move in together and play house?"

Hollis scrunched up her face in a thoughtful frown. "I don't think I could live with anyone, not even you."

"Okay, then what?"

"I figured I'd get an apartment."

"An apartment?" This was all just a little too cookie dough and pearls normal for Jude. She liked Hollis with reflector glasses over her emotions and a riding crop in her hand.

"Yes, one with sound proofing and eyebolts in the ceiling." And there was the Hollis that Jude loved.

"You know, my house has a basement. With a playroom."

Hollis flipped around in the middle of the street and the car behind them honked. Jude gripped the door to keep from toppling into Hollis.

"Where are we going?"

"My place. You don't really need to study do you?"

"No, I'm good." In truth, Jude hadn't needed the review at all. Unlike her classmates who were actual FBI, she wasn't being graded. She just needed to do something with her time to keep from going crazy over the distance Hollis had placed between them.

"Good, then you'll spend the night with me."

Jude didn't answer because it wasn't actually a question. She reclaimed Hollis's hand. It seemed the more she held it, the more she liked holding it.

As they drove toward Hollis's house, Jude reflected on the past few weeks. She'd arrived feeling spent, worn out from the demands the homicide department placed on her, but couldn't wait to get back home. She had a stack of open cases that needed to be closed. She had victims who needed a voice and families who deserved closure.

She'd come only because her captain insisted. She didn't expect to learn anything new, and she certainly hadn't expected to find her future on that first day.

Hollis squeezed her hand, then released her hold to press the garage-door open button as she pulled into her driveway. Coming home together was such a simple act. So *normal*. She'd never expected to want something like that in her life, but it'd found her anyway. She wasn't sure how all of this would work out, but Hollis made her want to try.

About the Author

Jove Belle was born and raised against a backdrop of orchards and potato fields. The youngest of four children, she was raised in a conservative, Christian home and began asking why at a very young age, much to the consternation of her mother and grandmother. At the customary age of eighteen, she fled southern Idaho in pursuit of broader minds and fewer traffic jams involving the local livestock. The road didn't end in Portland, Oregon, but there were many confusing freeway interchanges that a girl from the sticks was ill prepared to deal with. As a result, she has lived in the Portland metro area for over fifteen years and still can't figure out how she manages to spend so much time in traffic when there's not a stray sheep or cow in sight.

She lives with her partner of twelve years. Between them, they share three children, two dogs, two cats, two mortgage payments, one sedan, and one requisite dyke pickup truck. One day she hopes to live in a house that doesn't generate a never ending honey-do list.

Incidentally, she never stopped asking why, but did expand her arsenal of questions to include who, what, when, where, and, most important of all, how. In those questions, a story is born.

Books Available from Bold Strokes Books

The Quickening: A Sisters of Spirits Novel byYvonne Heidt. Ghosts, visions, and demons are all in a day's work for Tiffany. But when Kat asks for help on a serial killer case, life takes on another dimension altogether. (978-1-60282-975-6)

Windigo Thrall by Cate Culpepper. Six women trapped in a mountain cabin by a blizzard, stalked by an ancient cannibal demon bent on stealing their sanity—and their lives. (978-1-60282-950-3)

Smoke and Fire by Julie Cannon. Oil and water, passion and desire, a combustible combination. Can two women fight the fire that draws them together and threatens to keep them apart? (978-1-60282-977-0)

Asher's Fault by Elizabeth Wheeler. Fourteen-year-old Asher Price sees the world in black and white, much like the photos he takes, but when his little brother drowns at the same moment Asher experiences his first same-sex kiss, he can no longer hide behind the lens of his camera and eventually discovers he isn't the only one with a secret. (978-1-60282-982-4)

Love and Devotion by Jove Belle. KC Hall trips her way through life, stumbling into an affair with a married bombshell twice her age. Thankfully, her best friend, Emma Reynolds, is there to show her the true meaning of Love and Devotion. (978-1-60282-965-7)

Rush by Carsen Taite. Murder, secrets, and romance combine to create the ultimate rush. (978-1-60282-966-4)

The Shoal of Time by J.M. Redmann. It sounded too easy. Micky Knight is reluctant to take the case because the easy ones often turn into the hard ones, and the hard ones turn into the dangerous ones. In this one, easy turns hard without warning. (978-1-60282-967-1)

In Between by Jane Hoppen. At the age of 14, Sophie Schmidt discovers that she was born an intersexual baby and sets off on a journey to find her place in a world that denies her true existence. (978-1-60282-968-8)

Secret Lies by Amy Dunne. While fleeing from her abuser, Nicola Jackson bumps into Jenny O'Connor, and their unlikely friendship quickly develops into a blossoming romance—but when it comes down to a matter of life or death, are they both willing to face their fears? (978-1-60282-970-1)

Under Her Spell by Maggie Morton. The magic of love brought Terra and Athene together, but now a magical quest stands between them—a quest for Athene's hand in marriage. Will their passion keep them together, or will stronger magic tear them apart? (978-1-60282-973-2)

Homestead by Radclyffe. R. Clayton Sutter figures getting NorthAm Fuel's newest refinery operational on a rolling tract of land in Upstate New York should take a month or two, but then, she hadn't counted on local resistance in the form of vandalism, petitions, and one furious farmer named Tess Rogers. (978-1-60282-956-5)

Battle of Forces: Sera Toujours by Ali Vali. Kendal and Piper return to New Orleans to start the rest of eternity together, but the return of an old enemy makes their peaceful reunion short-lived, especially when they join forces with the new queen of the vampires. (978-1-60282-957-2)

How Sweet It Is by Melissa Brayden. Some things are better than chocolate. Molly O'Brien enjoys her quiet life running the bakeshop in a small town. When the beautiful Jordan Tuscana returns home, Molly can't deny the attraction—or the stirrings of something more. (978-1-60282-958-9)

The Missing Juliet: A Fisher Key Adventure by Sam Cameron. A teenage detective and her friends search for a kidnapped Hollywood star in the Florida Keys. (978-1-60282-959-6)

Amor and More: Love Everafter edited by Radclyffe and Stacia Seaman. Rediscover favorite couples as Bold Strokes Books authors reveal glimpses of life and love beyond the honeymoon in short stories featuring main characters from favorite BSB novels. (978-1-60282-963-3)

First Love by CJ Harte. Finding true love is hard enough, but for Jordan Thompson, daughter of a conservative president, it's challenging, especially when that love is a female rodeo cowgirl. (978-1-60282-949-7)

Pale Wings Protecting by Lesley Davis. Posing as a couple to investigate the abduction of infants, Special Agent Blythe Kent and Detective Daryl Chandler find themselves drawn into a battle over the innocents, with demons on one side and the unlikeliest of protectors on the other. (978-1-60282-964-0)

Mounting Danger by Karis Walsh. Sergeant Rachel Bryce, an outcast on the police force, is put in charge of the department's newly formed mounted division. Can she and polo champion Callan Lanford resist their growing attraction as they struggle to safeguard the disaster-prone unit? (978-1-60282-951-0)

Meeting Chance by Jennifer Lavoie. When man's best friend turns on Aaron Cassidy, the teen keeps his distance until fate puts Chance in his hands. (978-1-60282-952-7)

At Her Feet by Rebekah Weatherspoon. Digital marketing producer Suzanne Kim knows she has found the perfect love in her new mistress Pilar, but before they can make the ultimate commitment, Suzanne's professional life threatens to disrupt their perfectly balanced bliss. (978-1-60282-948-0)

Show of Force by AJ Quinn. A chance meeting between navy pilot Evan Kane and correspondent Tate McKenna takes them on a roller-coaster ride where the stakes are high, but the reward is higher: a chance at love. (978-1-60282-942-8)

Clean Slate by Andrea Bramhall. Can Erin and Morgan work through their individual demons to rediscover their love for each other, or are the unexplainable wounds too deep to heal? (978-1-60282-943-5)

Hold Me Forever by D. Jackson Leigh. An investigation into illegal cloning in the quarter horse racing industry threatens to destroy the growing attraction between Georgia debutante Mae St. John and Louisiana horse trainer Whit Casey. (978-1-60282-944-2)

Trusting Tomorrow by PJ Trebelhorn. Funeral director Logan Swift thinks she's perfectly happy with her solitary life devoted to helping others cope with loss until Brooke Collier moves in next door to care for her elderly grandparents. (978-1-60282-891-9)

Forsaking All Others by Kathleen Knowles. What if what you think you want is the opposite of what makes you happy? (978-1-60282-892-6)

Exit Wounds by VK Powell. When Officer Loane Landry falls in love with ATF informant Abigail Mancuso, she realizes that nothing is as it seems—not the case, not her lover, not even the dead. (978-1-60282-893-3)

Dirty Power by Ashley Bartlett. Cooper's been through hell and back, and she's still broke and on the run. But at least she found the twins. They'll keep her alive. Right? (978-1-60282-896-4)

The Rarest Rose by I. Beacham. After a decade of living in her beloved house, Ele disturbs its past and finds her life being haunted by the presence of a ghost who will show her that true love never dies. (978-1-60282-884-1)

Code of Honor by Radclyffe. The face of terror is hard to recognize—especially when it's homegrown. The next book in the Honor series. (978-1-60282-885-8)

Does She Love You? by Rachel Spangler. When Annabelle and Davis find out they are both in a relationship with the same woman, it leaves them facing life-altering questions about trust, redemption, and the possibility of finding love in the wake of betrayal. (978-1-60282-886-5)

The Road to Her by KE Payne. Sparks fly when actress Holly Croft, star of UK soap Portobello Road, meets her new on-screen love interest, the enigmatic and sexy Elise Manford. (978-1-60282-887-2)

Shadows of Something Real by Sophia Kell Hagin. Trying to escape flashbacks and nightmares, ex-POW Jamie Gwynmorgan stumbles into the heart of former Red Cross worker Adele Sabellius and uncovers a deadly conspiracy against everything and everyone she loves. (978-1-60282-889-6)

Date with Destiny by Mason Dixon. When sophisticated bank executive Rashida Ivey meets unemployed blue collar worker Destiny Jackson, will her life ever be the same? (978-1-60282-878-0)

The Devil's Orchard by Ali Vali. Cain and Emma plan a wedding before the birth of their third child while Juan Luis is still lurking, and as Cain plans for his death, an unexpected visitor arrives and challenges her belief in her father, Dalton Casey. (978-1-60282-879-7)

Secrets and Shadows by L.T. Marie. A bodyguard and the woman she protects run from a madman and into each other's arms. (978-1-60282-880-3)

Change Horizons: Three Novellas by Gun Brooke. Three stories of courageous women who dare to love as they fight to claim a future in a hostile universe. (978-1-60282-881-0)

Scarlet Thirst by Crin Claxton. When hot, feisty Rani meets cool, vampire Rob, one lifetime isn't enough, and the road from human to vampire is shorter than you think… (978-1-60282-856-8)

Battle Axe by Carsen Taite. How close is too close? Bounty hunter Luca Bennett will soon find out. (978-1-60282-871-1)